Also by Martha Kemm Landes

Pity the Movie Lover

PITY THE
GARAGE SALE ADDICT

Martha Kemm Landes

Elemar Publishing

Print ISBN: 978-1-956912-03-6
eBook ISBN: 978-1-956912-04-3
Audiobook ISBN: 978-1-956912-05-0

Cover design by Samantha Galasso

First Edition

www.marthalandes.com

Dedication

To all the people who sell enticing items at garage sales,
you inspired me to write this book.
Special thanks to my husband,
who puts up with my crazy purchases.

PROLOGUE

1997

She unfolded the paper, dreading the words that might come. Though obviously written by him, the handwriting seemed angrier than the last note.

With each word she read, her heart sank further. Could he really do something like that? Would he?

She felt sick to her stomach knowing it was too late to stop him. Tears stained her face as she bundled the newest note along with the others and hid them in the back of the desk.

Laying her head on her arms, she sobbed, wishing there was some way to get out of this horrible mess.

Garage Sale Tip #1
Bargaining is half the fun

PRESENT-DAY

"Can you drive any slower?" I grumbled while following a white-haired woman who peeked over the steering wheel of a faded green Bonneville. I wouldn't have known the type of car, but driving at a snail's pace, there was plenty of time to read the make and model, plus two bumper stickers that read, 'Don't honk. I can't hear you anyway,' and 'I brake for yarn shops.'

Based on her bumper stickers, the old lady seemed like someone I would like to know, but at this rate, I would be late for my first stop. It was 6:55 on Saturday morning, and I wanted to get there.

My left hand clutched the list I'd compiled from Craigslist and Facebook Marketplace. I'll admit it. I'm a garage sale addict and not a very patient one at that.

The nonagenarian opted to make a left turn, which should have been easy with the obvious lack of oncoming traffic. But nope, she stopped full out and spent 20 seconds staring at the empty street. When she finally began the slow turn onto Elm Avenue, I skirted past her and gave her a smile and wave, chanting my new Saturday morning mantra aloud: "Don't get a ticket, Pity. Use your blinkers, Pity. Don't have another wreck, Pity."

My heart raced as I saw the first neon pink sign. I was getting close. Turn right. Turn left. Turn left again. There it was! Shoot!

People were already milling about. Luckily, parking rules don't apply to garage sales, so I drove halfway into the driveway of a red brick house, coming dangerously close to hitting a box marked "Free."

As I opened my door, two boys punched each other. That happens a lot when I arrive at places; not because I personally invoke violence, but because my car is a slug bug. It doesn't seem to matter that Liesel, my beetle is a newer model, people still play the game.

There was no need to turn the car off since I'd only be a moment with more sales to attend. I hopped out with my wallet in hand, pumped and hopeful on this cool crisp morning. I scooted past the "free" box, beyond a rack of used clothing, and onto the boxes and tables. I scoured the items for could-be treasures.

Why would someone even think to try to sell a half-empty bottle of baby shampoo? And yet, the lady standing next to me snatched it up like it was a prize. I glanced at her, surprised to see an attractive lady in her fifties dressed way better than I was. People are so strange.

I picked up an old pot lid marked 25 cents and smiled. Holding it up by the handle, I pinged the metal lid with my fingernail, nodded, and said, "Perfect." The woman with the used baby shampoo crinkled her nose at me. What was she staring at?

"Are you looking for anything in particular?" the homeowner asked, as I passed her rickety card table.

"Nope. Just looking for that treasure I don't know I need."

On the next table, I picked up an unopened box of water filters marked $3 and asked, "Would you take $2?"

"Sure." She looked happy to make a sale.

Some people may think it's rude to dicker, but it's what you do, or at least what I do at garage sales. Half the fun is finding a prize and the other half is getting it at a bargain. Would I have bought the filters for $3? We shall never know because she said yes to $2.

I paid and thanked the woman before rushing off to my car. There were many more sales to hit, and if I wasn't early, I'd miss the best stuff. To add to my urgency, it was nearing the end of garage sale season in the area, so I wanted to take advantage of all I could. The next three sales weren't even worth a call to Kay, my sister in L.A. who also loves garage sales. But the next one was in an adorable neighborhood lined with houses from the 1940s. The driveway had so many tables and boxes that I hoped for some interesting finds.

I skipped up the driveway of the darling brick house surrounded by flowering mums and pumpkins, a usual sight this time of year. I was quickly deflated when most of the items were baby clothes, Christmas decorations, and toys.

When a man asked, "What's in that box?" I stopped short to listen to the answer.

The male owner answered with an Okie twang, "Concrete tile molds for making garden steps."

I whipped around in time to see a heavyset shopper bend over, displaying a hefty-sized butt crack. I cringed at that, but then out of the box, he pulled plastic molds: one was a square shape and one was shaped like a triangle. Oh My Gosh! What I could do with those! I considered tackling the guy, but he was pretty big. So, instead, I walked over and asked casually, "Are you interested in making stepping stones?"

"Not really." He turned to the owner and asked, "How much?"

Now, why did he need the price if he didn't want to use them? He probably wanted to resell them online. Humph.

The owner answered, "How about $10 for the box?"

I silently gasped at the low price, but because of the unwritten garage sale rule, I had to stay calm and wait to see if he would leave the box before grabbing it myself.

I nonchalantly looked at Christmas decorations while keeping an eye on the guy. I had just picked up a package of Simpsons ornaments when a VW bug the same color as mine zipped down the street. How fun to see what Liesel must look like when I drive her. Cute!

I studied the plastic Bart and Homer, wondering if my youngest daughter, Ree, needed them for our Christmas tree. My heart leaped when I saw the man stand up and walk to another table without the box of tile molds.

I hurled myself toward the box, kneeled on the cold concrete, and dug through the molds. I blew the dust out of one but must have sucked some in because I had a coughing fit. I chose not to clean any of the others. There were at least 20 different shapes and sizes. Lucky me! The box even had concrete colorant. This was the treasure I needed. Now I could create my very own mosaic walkway! I managed to pull myself up to standing while heaving the box, a task much more difficult ever since turning 40. I carried the box to the checkout table.

The pasty-looking man protested, "Hey, I was still thinking about getting that."

A bit worried, I asked, "Oh, did you tell them you wanted it?" I nodded toward the owners having the sale.

"No, but I was going to look at it again." His brow furrowed.

Trying to sound nice, I shrugged, "I'm sorry, Sir, but you left it, so it's fair game." I set the box on the table and added, "I learned garage sale etiquette the hard way myself when someone snatched up a bicycle I wanted. I had left it for just a second and then it was up for grabs."

The man looked like he was going to reply, but the homeowner said, "I have to agree with her."

I quickly paid the full $10, not wanting to bargain after my lecture. Almost giddy, I carried the awesome prize to my awaiting car, but there was no car waiting. Seriously, my car was gone! I searched the driveway, but Liesel was nowhere to be seen. I tossed the box on the damp grass and ran behind a big red truck to see if she was hiding there but there was only a black Camry. I searched up and down the street to no avail. I patted my jeans' pockets - no keys. My stomach lurched. Someone had stolen my car? Stupid, stupid me. Who leaves keys in a car anyway?

I ran back to the driveway and shouted to the shoppers, "Did anyone see somebody drive away in my silver VW bug?"

A few people shook their heads. A woman holding up a string of Christmas lights said apologetically, "I saw a teenage boy get in a Beetle, but I just thought it was his."

Oh My Gosh! The car that looked like Liesel was her. My stomach lurched when I realized she was gone. I reached for my phone to call the police and file a report but remembered my phone was in the car. My eyes began to fill.

The woman running the sale said, "Oh, it must have been Georgie, our neighbor." She pointed across the street. "He's always doing odd things. I'll call his mom." Her husband handed her a cordless house phone, and she dialed.

My heart pounded as the woman explained the situation into the mouthpiece. She nodded, hung up, and turned to me. "She's calling Georgie and making him come back. He's a loveable kid, but a little different. Maybe Asperger's?" she shrugged.

I wiped my eyes and stepped forward to look around the pecan tree next door and watch down the street. With my cold hands on my hot face, I willed the boy to return my baby in one piece. I felt heartbroken as if I'd actually lost a child. What a bad, bad car mom.

A few other shoppers joined me in eyeing both ends of the street as if we were watching a slow ping pong game. After what seemed like an eternity, I couldn't stand it any longer and turned to a girl holding a baby next to me. "Excuse me. Could I borrow your pho…"

Before I could finish my sentence, there turning the corner, was my little German VW. She raced towards us and pulled into the driveway across the street where a woman of about my age stood with hands on her hips, shaking her head. I ran across the street just as the car door opened. Out stepped a lanky boy wearing a big smile. His long brown bangs partially covered his eyes. When he saw his mother's stance, he hung his head and readied himself to be reprimanded. I wanted to wring the kid's neck but managed to hold back.

His mother spoke very slowly and calmly, "Georgie, I know you just got your permit to drive, but remember you always have to drive with an adult. And even though the keys were in the car, it is not our car. It belongs to this lady." She pointed at me. "Do you see how upset she is? She was very worried."

The boy looked my way without making eye contact and said nothing.

"You need to tell her you are sorry, and give her the keys, please."

The teen kept his face down and said in a robotic tone, "I like the slug bug. It's my favorite German vehicle. It has Farfegnugen. That means driving pleasure. I wanted to try it."

I felt a rush of compassion for the boy and his mother. She certainly had her hands full with a special needs son.

Having taught music to many students with Asperger's and autism over the years, I've grown to appreciate their honesty and unique outlook on life. I also know how sweet most of the kids are, so I took a deep breath and exhaled before speaking.

"I'm glad you brought my car back, Georgie. Her name is Liesel. She's fun to drive, isn't she?"

He lifted the corner of his mouth but didn't look me in the eye.

In a more serious tone, I said, "I forgive you for borrowing my car, but promise your mother that you'll never do it again."

Georgie handed me the keys with his eyes still on the ground, then turned toward his mom and said in a monotone voice, "I promise I won't take that lady's car ever again." His mother threw back her head and laughed. She took him by the hand and led him inside the house - probably to explain that he shouldn't take anybody's car.

My heartbeat finally slowed to a manageable tempo and I turned back toward the sale. The shoppers went back to shopping or entered their cars with keys in hand, go figure. The man who wanted my molds walked across the street carrying my box.

I felt like Georgie, not wanting to look this guy in the eye. I mustered a slight smile and said, "Thank you."

As he put the box in Liesel, he joked, "Might I suggest you learn the rules of driving and not leave your keys in the car?"

Completely humiliated, I nodded. "Yes Sir. Lesson learned."

Back in my car, I thought there must be something wrong with me. I was given a brain. Why not use it? I know I have ADD, but seriously?

I frowned as I recalled a few previous bargain shopping mishaps; I'd gotten speeding tickets, had run over a mailbox, been lost, and I totaled my van by turning too quickly into a thrift store parking lot last year. And today I almost lost the van's replacement!

When I caught a glimpse of my cool treasures in the back seat, I smiled and decided to keep shopping, but vowed to be more careful.

At the next sale, I parked in a legal spot on the street - not in front of a driveway or even a mailbox. I felt like a responsible adult as I turned off the car, locked it, pocketed the keys, and even looked both ways before walking calmly across the street.

A little girl sat at a table selling donuts. What a perfect storm: A small child selling something and a sickeningly sweet donut, both impossible to resist. The scene brought back memories of me as a child, sitting with my wagon in our driveway selling Kool-Aid to passersby, just the first of my many entrepreneurial attempts. Unfortunately, none have made me rich, but I keep trying.

The little curly-haired blonde wearing a lavender tutu pointed to her crayon-written sign that read, Do-Nuts $75. I thought the price was pretty steep, but when I saw that she had a little cup holding coins, I assumed she was actually selling donuts at the fair market price. I handed her three quarters and she put them in her cup. She grabbed a donut with her grubby little fingers and handed me the chocolate glazed treat with no napkin. Did I eat it? Of course, I did. After teaching elementary school for 15 years, I'm immune to most everything. Besides, who was I to judge? After all, my fingers were still dusty from digging through the box of molds.

While looking through a rack of clothes, I overheard a man ask the homeowner, "Do you have change for a hundred?"

She laughed and said, "If I had change for a hundred, I wouldn't be having a sale."

I chuckled at her response as I glanced at the clothing sizes in vain. Why are all garage sale clothes either tiny or huge? I actually found a pair of jeans in my waist size, but they only came up to my calves. I guess I should be happy to be tall and slender, but it does make bargain shopping for clothes difficult.

Instead of jeans, I bought six blue Mexican wine glasses ($4 for all) and a red wig (50 cents) from the little girl's mother.

Arriving at the next sale, my heart pounded so loud I couldn't hear my radio. The driveway, garage, and yard were completely covered in furniture, assorted boxes, and other goodies. I could hardly contain myself and flitted up to check it out.

When I passed a lemonade stand run by two little boys, I said, "Hey guys, how are sales?" They shook their heads slowly as if their beloved goldfish had just died. I handed them two quarters, and their faces brightened. Coming to life, one sloshed lemonade into a tiny cup, and the other put my quarters into an empty box. I hoped more people would pretend to like their warm drink. But despite the unrefreshing temperature, it did help wash down the donut.

A glass shower door marked $1 caught my eye, but I decided against it; partly because I didn't really need another and also because I was pretty sure it wouldn't fit in my Beetle.

I started collecting other treasures immediately:

- Juice glasses for my mom
- A set of Campbell's soup salt and pepper shakers for my dad.
- 4 packets of Henna to give my hair a healthy shine
- Concrete sealer for my new stepping stones
- And a small purple desk to put in my bedroom for $7!

The tall, thin homeowner rubbed his wimpy mustache as he stared at me. I licked my lips to see if I still had chocolate on them. Not noticing any leftover icing, I pointed to my finds. "Would you sell all of this for $20?"

He croaked in a raspy voice, "Hell, I'd let you have it for free, but my wife will kill me if I don't make some cash." He laughed a creepy laugh.

I gave him a stilted smile along with a twenty.

A lady saw me struggle to hoist the desk into the car and helped me. We were both surprised at the amount of room in my bug.

I waved to the boys and put Liesel in drive. Immediately, my obnoxious Bluetooth phone rang through my speakers, startling me so much I almost ran over a curb. I pushed the phone button and said, "Hello?"

"Are you already rummaging?"

There, through my loudspeakers, was the voice of Lin, my best friend. She was raised in Minnesota, and her northern accent and expressions crack me up. Nobody in Oklahoma calls a garage sale a rummage sale. I answered, "Duh. I've been out for hours. What do you think I am, a slacker?"

"I swear, nothing can get you out of bed but a rummage sale."

"Hey, I make it to work every day, don't I?"

"Yes, but are you on time?"

She had a point, but I came back in defense. "I get there before the kids arrive. So there. What's up?" I looked at the next address on my list while trying to navigate the road.

"I just wanted to know what you're wearing tonight."

"Oh yeah. I almost forgot. Umm....jeans and that new striped top? I sure hope these guys don't end up being a couple of Kennys." I groaned, thinking of the annoying guy I just couldn't ditch.

"Oh? You don't want another stalker in your life?" she asked.

"I don't know how to get rid of him. He sent red roses yesterday!"

"Kenny moved up from daisies to roses? Ooh, la, la. Red roses mean love. You must have bewitched him back in February. Are you sure you're not encouraging him?"

"Yes, I'm sure." I stopped at a stop sign and rolled my eyes. "I rarely answer his calls and last week I told him I was dating someone else, but he refuses to get the hint."

"You lied to poor Kenny?"

"I'll do anything to get rid of him. He's called weekly for eight months. And stop calling him poor. We all know how rich he is."

"OK. Well, we'll hope for better blind dates tonight. Since we're riding together, we can ditch the guys if they're weirdos."

"Definitely. See you at 6:00."

I slowed down but didn't stop at the next sale because it only had one card table loaded with baby clothes. I pulled over to the curb to get the next address and marveled at the beautiful mums in the garden to my right. Why can't I grow anything?

It seemed silly to go to another sale with only $2 in cash left, but it was a moving sale, and was on my way home so why not check it out? I typed the address into my GPS and made my way there. After a few turns, I heard, "Your destination is on the left."

I pulled up partly in the driveway, already forgetting my new parking rules, and checked the last few sales off my list, congratulating myself on a great haul.

When I looked up, I realized my mistake. I had arrived at the new house of my ex-husband, Todd.

Garage Sale Tip #2
Check inside everything you buy

Seriously? I was at Todd's house? I considered driving away, but the man I was married to for 13 years was already sauntering down the driveway scuffing his cowboy boots as he walked.

I figured I should acknowledge him, so I rolled down Liesel's window and put her in park. He leaned in to the window's opening and said in his smarmy drawl that he thinks sounds like Matthew McConaughey, "You know, I figured you would show up today - just can't resist a bargain. Aren't you going to come see what I have for sale?" He pointed to the driveway, and I instantly recognized most of the contents.

"No, I'm good. It's probably just the stuff you wouldn't give me in the divorce." I sighed and finally looked at him. Although his face was shaded by his cowboy hat, I noticed he had acquired more lines, and the dark brown eyes that had once captivated me looked dull.

He smirked. "Only a few things, but you can sure buy them back. Let's take a look-see..." He pointed. "Why, there's your grandmother's red bowl. It's marked $2, but YOU can have it for $20," he chuckled and bit off a piece of black licorice that appeared from nowhere.

"Jeez! Let me go, Todd."

He peered at my haul and made a face. "All right, get goin'. Ya don't want to miss out on any more junk. Sure am glad my Shelly doesn't like secondhand crap."

At that, I shut the window, almost catching his fingers, and sped off as fast as Liesel could go. I felt proud that I even burned a little rubber in his driveway. Todd is a thorn in my side. As I continued down the street, I imagined for the umpteenth time taking the girls and moving far away to be rid of him. But alas, our lives were here in Oklahoma.

Shelly, or Smelly Shelly, as my daughters call her because of the acrid perfume she wears, is Todd's girlfriend. I used to be sad he found someone so fast. Now I smile when I picture her batting her fake eyelashes at Todd, begging him to buy her more and more from the fancy shops at Utica Square. Shelly thinks she's a celebrity because she's featured in commercials for her dad's 'Big Jack's Cadillacs' dealership. The TV spots are lame and she's more of a local joke than a star.

I've practically raised my daughters alone for the past several years, especially since Shelly doesn't want them around much. Single parenting on a teacher's salary is one reason I bargain shop. The upside of being divorced is that I've become very independent. I can mow the lawn, pay bills, and even put together a bed frame. Yep, a real superwoman.

Once my temper calmed from seeing my ex-jerk, I called Lin. "Doesn't that neighbor of yours, Mark or Mike, have a pick-up truck? Do you think he would do a big favor for me today?"

"Mike? Yeah, he has a truck. Why?"

"Can you beg him to go to Todd's moving sale and buy my grandma's red bowl, the accordion, and the kayak and then bring them to me. That is if he wouldn't mind."

"Pity, what in heaven's name are you going to do with a kayak?"

"It was the kayak we used at our cabin. He just had to have it in the divorce and Shelly's probably making him sell it, and he wants to charge me double. Since Mike doesn't know Todd, maybe he can get a good price? I'll pay him back with interest for his trouble."

"OK, I'll call and see if he is free. You need an accordion too?" she asked.

"Hello…I am a music teacher." I had taught Lin's three kids, so she should know I need an accordion.

"Well, that's true," she admitted. "Did you get to see Shelly?"

"Get to? Thank God, no. I'm going home now to unload my treasures. See you tonight, and thanks for calling Mike. Oh, are you driving top down or top up?"

"It looks like a nice evening, so I vote top down."

"Oh, goodie!" I gave her Todd's new address and pulled into my garage, scanning the area. I hoped to find space for my new purchases. There was a huge costume closet to the right, tubs to the left, tools in front, and a ladder hanging overhead. I gave up and carried the items one by one into the kitchen, working quietly to avoid waking the girls since it was Saturday morning and their only day to sleep in.

With nothing pressing to do, I decided to apply a pack of henna to my hair. Why not have a fresh look for the blind date? I'd had blond highlights in my brown hair forever and it was time to do something different. After following directions, I wrapped my head in plastic.

I had an hour to wait for the henna to take effect and checked out the purple desk I had parked in the kitchen. On closer inspection, the exterior had been painted sloppily. No problem. I could easily sand it and repaint the desk in a more attractive color than grape. The design was simple and looked vintage.

One important thing I've learned to do with used items is to always check inside. Once, after buying a purse at a flea market, I found a $10 bill inside; twice as much as I'd paid for the purse. I kept the money because the guy who sold it to me was very rude. Another time, I bought a suitcase that had a little zipper pocket holding a gold ring. Luckily, I remembered where I had bought the suitcase and returned the ring, much to the relief of the old woman who sold it.

I opened the wide purple drawer and was surprised to see the inside was painted gunmetal green. The drawer was empty so I pushed it shut, but something kept it from closing. After taking the drawer out completely, I saw the culprit. It was a paperback book jammed in the back. I pulled it out and was thrilled to see it was a Mad Libs that hadn't been filled out. Nice bonus!

Glancing through the opening, I saw something else in the back. I reached in and pulled out a bundle of faded papers, held together with a brittle rubber band.

I stood at the kitchen counter excited to read what I assumed to be a stack of love letters. The rubber band broke as soon as I pulled out the first note. I carefully unfolded the top note and read, *No more Jones. We can start thinking of the future now. Just act surprised and upset if anyone asks you about it. Don't give anything away.*

Well, this was not the love note I expected. No More Jones? What did that mean?

I read another. The second note in the pile had the same handwriting on the same type of paper torn from a small thin-lined spiral notebook and folded in half.

Tonight's the night. I'll make an excuse to be late and make sure it gets done. I'll stop by Ken's, then home to eat. I love you so much.

Get it done? Was this written before or after the last one? My heart started pounding...did it mean what it sounded like? Getting rid of someone? Come on, Pity. Don't jump to conclusions.

The doorbell rang, so I stashed the notes in my purse. I shouldn't get excited until I had a chance to read more. I opened the door, wearing my old stained t-shirt and garage sale jeans spotted with donut icing. Standing on my front porch, blocking out the sun was a tall man, whom I could only assume was Lin's neighbor, Mike.

I had met the guy briefly once before across the fence in Lin's backyard. I said, "Hi, Mike! Were you able to get the stuff?"

He pulled my red bowl from behind his back and handed it to me. "Yep, and he never knew what hit him."

That sounded a lot like mafia jargon and I mimicked a Chicago mobster, "Oh yeah? A real shakedown. That's just what I like to hear." Then I realized he may not get the reference.

He surprised me and said with his mouth partly open, "That sap was an easy mark, a grifter, I tell ya."

I was in shock but laughed and stepped onto the porch so I could see the clever man without the sun glowing around him. His size was rather intimidating but I remembered Lin saying he was super nice. He looked somewhat familiar and very handsome.

He smiled at me and said, "Yeah. His bragging got under my skin, so I talked him down on all the stuff. A mere $40 for all of it!"

I gasped at the unbelievable price. I had the urge to kiss him, but of course, I didn't since I barely knew him. "Wow. You sure know how to bargain! I can't thank you enough, Mike. If I had gone there, he would have raised the price tenfold. You didn't happen to meet his lovely girlfriend, Shelly, did you?"

He shook his head.

"You're lucky." I continued with my typical babble as we walked to his truck and got the accordion. I put it on the porch and together we carried the kayak into the backyard and past my wall of mirrors. I explained, "We'll set it by the apple tree. I put the mirrors here to make the yard look bigger. Silly, huh?"

I bent down to pick up an apple that had fallen from the tree and caught a glimpse of my reflection in one of the mirrors. The giant baggie was still on my head! Drips of brown oozed down my cheeks and looked hideous. I stammered, "By the way, I don't normally look like this."

He nodded. "I know. I remember.'

He remembered me? Hmm. Harriet, our shaggy sheepdog, bounded over to meet Mike. In the multitude of mirrors, she looked like a giant white cotton ball had exploded. Reaching down to pet her, he said, "There you are - safe at home in your big backyard."

I thought that sounded weird. Why wouldn't she be safe? But when he glanced around the yard with a dazed look on his face, I forgot that odd statement and said, "Sometime, you should take the full tour of the yard. I'd show you now, but I need to wash this gunk out soon or my hair may fall out."

"OK, but are those shower doors?" He pointed to the row of upright panels carefully planted on the other side of the yard. I studied the design layout of the towering glass doors and thought I had made the right decision not to buy another glass door today.

"Um…. Hello? Don't you have shower doors in your backyard?"

"No, I do not. I've never seen any of these items in anyone's yard. I'm just curious enough to come back for that tour." He shook his head as we walked to the front of the house. I invited him into the foyer so I could pay him.

I wrote a check for the goods and added extra for gas. "Mike, what's your last name?" While waiting for him to answer I studied him. He was very tall, maybe 6' 4", with broad shoulders. I thought his eyes might be blue, but with the sunlight still behind him, I couldn't tell. His face was nice and friendly-looking, like a taller version of Matt Damon.

He ran his fingers through his wavy brown hair, which looked so soft I had to resist the urge to jump up and touch it. There was a little gray around the temples adding to the appeal.

He said, "Potter."

I brightened. "Oh, my youngest daughter, Marie, whom I call Ree, would love that. She's still obsessed with the Harry Potter series." I added his last name to the check, ripped it out, and handed it to Mike. "Thank you so much. I owe you big time. Now, don't forget to come back for the tour."

"I look forward to that," he said and then stopped and turned back to me looking at the check the whole time, "I thought Lin said your name was Pity – with a P."

"Well, Pity is my nickname. My real name is Kitty." I explained, "You see, when I was born, my sister was a toddler and called me 'Baby Pity'. I think she was trying to say how pretty I was, but my family says, 'No, she just couldn't say her K's and besides, you weren't that pretty.' So, I've been Pity ever since."

"Well, it's a cool name, and you are certainly pretty now," he said with an adorable smile. He winked, then walked to his bright red pickup truck and drove off.

My face flushed as I stood dumbfounded. What a cutie pie! Then, I realized Mike had totally been joking. After all, brown gunk was dripping down my face. Oh, well…

With five minutes left on my hair, I went back in the kitchen to the notes. There were no envelopes, dates, or names; just nicely handwritten notes in pen. Although I'm no handwriting analyst, it looked as though the writer pressed down pretty hard - so maybe it was a guy who wrote them. The next one said, *We can talk at the meet. Come sit by me. He's bound to break every record, so he won't notice us.*

I leaned against the kitchen counter, perplexed. It sure sounded suspicious. Maybe I should give the notes to the police, but there certainly wasn't a hurry. It must have happened long ago if anything actually happened.

Looking back at the second note, I wondered if the person meant he was stopping at a house owned by a guy named Ken? Or Ken's Pizza? If it was Ken's Pizza, that chain had changed to Mazzio's years ago, so I would have a time frame to think about. It was a darned shame because Ken's thin crust sausage and black olive pizza was to die for.

My mind reeled and my stomach churned. Although I love pizza, I am pretty sure the churning wasn't from hunger.

Just as I was ready to read another note, my tall, olive-skinned daughter, Ren, short for Lauren, walked into the kitchen rubbing her green eyes. She approached my new desk and yawned, "What is that?" Then, she looked at me with accusatory eyes. "Mom, did you go garage saling again today? We already have too much stuff."

"Yep, I'm going to put it in my bedroom after I paint it." I quickly hid the papers behind my back, but too late, for Lauren's gaze followed my hand."

My shorter, fairer daughter, Marie, appeared in the doorway carrying her staple sidekick, an open book. She looked at the desk and then at me with her blue eyes shimmering. I'm still amazed that both of my girls got their dad's light eyes and hair when mine are so dark.

Ree asked, "What's going on? Why do you have that bag on your head?"

"Mom's hiding something behind her back."

"No, I'm not," I stammered. Ren raised her eyebrows and I gave in. "OK. But it's a surprise. And I'm not ready to show you yet."

"Mmm, I like surprises. But what is on your head?" repeated Ree.

I winced. "I bought some henna at a garage sale today and I'm hoping it will give my hair a nice auburn sheen."

As expected, Ren cried, "Eew, Mom, do you even know if it's good anymore? What if it eats your hair and you go bald? Remember the rancid box of mac and cheese you bought for a dime?

If we'd eaten it, we might have died." Often, my dramatic 17-year-old played responsible mom better than I did.

"It's henna, Lauren. It's all-natural," I said, shaking my head confidently. "The worst thing it could do is not work at all." At least, I hoped that was the worst. I looked at my watch. "Oh man, it's past time to wash it out."

I left the kitchen with the bundle of notes in hand and hurried to my room. I locked the door since my girls have been known to sneak peeks at presents.

In the shower, I tried to figure out the meaning of the last note. 'Meet? So, Jones is a guy and an athlete. What kind of meet? Track? Cross Country? Swimming? I knew a lot about swim meets since Ren is captain of her high school girls' swim team.

I watched the reddish-brown dye pool in the white tub like blood and wondered if "Jones" had really been killed? If so, was it in a shower? That gruesome thought gave me the shivers, so I got out quickly. With my body wrapped safely in a robe and my hair in a towel, I sat on the bed and opened the next note in the stack. It was on a different kind of paper but in the same handwriting.

I'm glad you understand that this is the only way out. Everything will be all right.

Wait a minute...who writes notes anyway? It seemed weird someone would plan a murder and write notes about it and then what, hand them to someone? There was a loud banging at my bedroom door, causing me to jump.

"MO-OM, she won't let me have the remote. Remember last night, you said to take turns? She had it all night, and now she still won't let me have it."

I put the letters in my makeup drawer, opened the door, and called, "Ren, seriously can you let Ree have a turn?" I heard a grumble from the living room.

Satisfied, the 13-year-old walked into my room. "How does your hair look?"

"I don't know. I haven't seen it yet. Let's check it out."

I uncovered my damp hair. It looked dark, but I combed it and started the hairdryer while she watched me. I shouted above the loud appliance, "Looks pretty good, don't you think? It's shiny and feels nice to the touch."

I turned off the dryer and Ree said, "Um, Mom...?" She cocked her head sideways and scrunched up her nose. "You know your blonde highlights? Well...they look kind of green."

"No, they don't," I said, and peered closer in the mirror. Oh great. Parts of my hair did look grayish-green. "Marie, quick, get me that other box over there that says chestnut. I'll try that one."

"Can you do two in one day?" She raised an eyebrow as she handed me the box.

"Oh. Maybe not, but I can't go on a blind date with hair like this." How odd. I always thought henna gave a red tint if anything. Maybe the old packet didn't react correctly on my lightened streaks. Yikes.

I considered my options and realized I didn't have any. I figured the pub would be dark so maybe no one would notice tonight.

I decided to try it out on Lauren, who had stomped off to her room after relinquishing the TV control. "Hey, Sweetie," I said from her doorway. She was lying on her bed reading. "Whatcha doing?"

"Just reading a magazine while Ree gets her way – again."

"You don't need no stinkin' TV anyway. So, what do you think of this hair color?"

She looked up at me for the first time. "Well, it's pretty dark." She squinted at my hair, sat up, and stared. "But kind of a weird color.

Is it…green? I told you not to use that old garage sale stuff! Will you ever learn?" She laid back down in exasperation.

"Obviously not. You think anyone will notice tonight?"

"Lin will. That's for sure. So, who are these guys?" She rolled her eyes at me. "Did you find them on OKIEsingles.com again?"

"Yes, but this time it's a double date and it should be fine," I said with confidence.

"Why do you want to meet someone so bad?" she asked.

"I don't want to meet someone 'so bad,' but there might be a guy out there that I could hang out with. I'm not looking for anything serious, but I could stand a little male company now and then."

She sat up and gave me a serious look. "Whatever you do, don't settle for some moron. Make sure he's worthy of you."

I smiled at the familiar phrase. "Didn't I just tell you the same thing last month? Besides, you know how picky I am at a restaurant?"

She nodded.

"Well, I'm way choosier about men than food. Or haven't you noticed the most I've gone out with anyone was three dates?" This was true. Aside from their father, I hadn't had any long-term relationships ever. I still wonder how I fell for him.

Ree, who stood behind me listening, stuck her head in the door cautiously. She looked up at me with big clear eyes. "Why don't you give Kenny another chance. He must have a lot of money to send you so many flowers."

I pushed a strand of blond hair out of her eyes. "He may be the richest guy in town, Ree, but I have no interest in Kenny or his money. He's nice but so boring I wanted to pull my hair out. I'd like a guy who is clever and fun."

Mike's face popped into my head and I shook it away. I didn't have a chance with someone like that.

Ren added, "And you need someone who can keep up with you."

Garage Sale Tip #3
A garage sale by any other name is still a garage sale.

Ree pouted, "Can I have a snack while I watch my show?"

I smiled at my growing girl. "Sure, if you will go feed Iggy first."
She ran off to chop veggies for her four-foot-long, prehistoric-looking iguana that lives upstairs in a temperature-controlled aquarium. I swear Iggy eats better than we do with fresh lettuce, zucchini, tomatoes, and fruit. She chomps it all up like a Brontosaurus.

I turned back to Ren. "What are you doing tonight? Something with Jennifer?"

"Yeah, we'll probably go see a movie since Ree's having Caitlyn over to spend the night again." She frowned. "She's here all the time and is so annoying!"

"And Jennifer isn't a little annoying and here all the time, too?"

I walked down the hall to answer the door and nearly got run over by Ree. When she turned the doorknob, she emitted a deafening squeal, "Hi, Caitlyn and Grandpa Brian!"

The chubby red-headed girl stood in front of the older man. Grandpa Brian isn't Ree's grandfather, but she always calls him that.

The ruddy-complected man quipped, "Well if it isn't Goldilocks!"

Ree grinned as I stepped forward and patted Caitlyn's little freckled face. "Hey there, Caitlyn." She beamed at me, and I turned to her grandfather, "So, you are on chauffeur duty tonight?"

Brian said in his captivating Irish brogue. "Aye, Trish is getting ready for a gala affair and asked me to drop the little bug here." I smiled. "What else are grandpas for? I'm going out to dinner myself this evening, but the girls should be able to fix something to eat without getting into too much trouble." I glared at them in jest.

He said, "And they can call me if there is any problem." He gave them a warm smile. "Well, have a nice evening, ladies."

And with that, he headed towards his black luxury car.

I shut the door and the duo rushed down the hall already giggling. Once I got in the kitchen, I heard a creepy deep southern voice come from the living room, "What do you think you're doing?"

I didn't flinch at the man's voice or even at the seven high varying tones, that followed: "Beep, beep, beep, beep, beep, beep, beep" I filled my glass with ice and, just as I expected, the next sound was a young girl's voice saying, "Hi…What's going on? Oh really?"

Then it was back to the low, dirty old man's voice, "Wanna go for a walk?"

My African Grey parrot, Edgar, was going through his schizoid routine of imitating sounds. Besides beeps from the phones and microwave, his favorites seemed to be the voice of an old man who owned him before us and Ren's one-sided conversation on the phone from years ago. He has repeated the same things in the same order for ages. Funny thing is, Edgar never speaks while we're in the room – only when he thinks he's alone.

When I told one of my second-grade music classes that my bird could talk, they didn't believe me. So, I set up the video camera in the living room and pointed the lens at Edgar before leaving the room. I hoped I would catch him going through his repertoire to prove to the kids that he could speak. It worked, and I took the video to school.

After viewing it, a child asked, "But who is talking, Mrs. Kole?" I explained, "The bird is. He's imitating his old owner, my daughter, and other sounds he hears around the house".

Another kid sighed and rolled his eyes like I didn't understand the question and said, "But who is saying the words?"

I repeated, "The BIRD is doing the talking." After 10 minutes of complete confusion, I realized I was wasting class time and returned to the music lesson of the day.

This time, as usual, Edgar hushed the moment I re-entered the room. I walked over, reached my fingers through the bars of the huge cage, and petted his soft, gray feathered head. Even though his large beak is strong enough to break my fingers, I've never been afraid of him. Most people stay clear of Edgar, especially when he moves quickly towards them. It's usually just to be petted, but I guess it could be to draw blood.

The first time I heard Edgar imitate someone, I was amazed he could sound so spot on. It made me wonder; if a bird can do it, why couldn't I? So, I began my quest to do voices by imitating people I knew with unique dialect; Lin with her Northern accent, my next-door neighbor, Mrs. Garmin, with her New Jersey "twalk", and I had to throw in a classic Southern drawl.

Being a big multi-tasker, I practice in the shower or while driving. I don't show my imitations to anyone except my girls or students, and that's just to be silly.

One of Edgar's red feathers was lying on the floor so I picked it up and added it to a jar on the nearby piano. The most striking feature of my African Grey Parrot is his gorgeous red tail. Once, I googled how to keep Edgar from pulling out his gray wing feathers, and discovered people were selling the red tail feathers for $10 each! I never planned to sell plumage, but once I read that, I figured that jar of red feathers was our nest egg.

I looked the big guy in his yellow eye and attempted to speak in Grandpa Brian's Irish brogue, "Stop pluckin' out your feathers, Laddie, or you'll soon be goin' bald."

He cocked his head as if he was listening. I handed him a peanut through the bars and watched him grab it with his beak, stand on one foot, and hold the nut with his other foot. He cracked the shell, removed the nut, and ate it without taking his eyes off of me.

I said, "Good boy," and went back to my room.

At this late time, I had accepted the fact that I'd have greenish hair for the date and shut my door to contemplate the meaning of the hidden notes.

What kind of meet were they talking about? Who is (or was) Jones? I pulled out my iPhone and started a new notes category – probably my 50th topic – CLUES. I really love lists!

Clue #1 Ken's pizza?

Clue #2 A boy named Jones – dead top athlete?

Clue #3 Meet – track, cross country, swim, something else?

I thought about going online to look up a dead Jones, but with such a common name and no idea, if this murder even happened, I decided to wait and get Lin's opinion tonight. Heck, the notes could have been a writing assignment for a class, for all I knew. My imagination tends to run wild.

I glanced at my vintage alarm clock, hoping I had time to do everything before the date. I put the notes away and fixed lunch, ran to the grocery store, called Mom, and fed Edgar and Harriet.

Then, I walked next door to Mrs. Garmin's house. The tiny, 81-year-old called me again to adjust her thermostat. She forgets whether to move the lever up or down to make it warmer, despite my handy sticky notes of a snowflake and a sun I'd left beside the thermostat.

She said, "Stay and have some coafee?"

I looked into her lonely eyes and felt bad leaving. "I'm sorry, Ellen. I don't have time today."

As I turned to leave, Mrs. Garmin asked in her brash northeast accent, "Did you go to that tag sale on the next block today?"

I scrunched my face, wondering what a tag sale was, then I remembered it was what they called garage sales in New Jersey. "Oh, yes I did."

As if she could read my mind, she said, "My sister in Brooklyn calls them stoop sales."

"Really?" On my way home, I thought I should look up all the names for garage sales someday as my little research project.

Back in my room, I picked up another note to read before dressing for the evening. This one looked a little longer, so I hoped it would have more clues.

He didn't take the bribe I offered. I think he wanted more. I'm afraid we'll have to get rid of him. There is no other way. He's just no good. You believe me, don't you?

Jeez! Now I was sure it was murder. I wished I knew what year, school, sport, and what Jones? This was getting kind of scary.

A horn honked outside, startling me. Already? I quickly crammed the notes in my purse, ran to the front door, and hollered, "I'll be right out!" I hurried back in, threw my top, and glanced at my makeup. Not too bad. At least with my dark eyelashes, mascara wasn't always needed. I ran a brush through my hair, although I'm not sure why since I was about to ride in an open convertible. I grabbed my phone and purse, kissed my girls, and ran out of the house.

Lin sat behind the wheel of her dark blue Fiat Spider. Her face was flawless. Add to that, her honey-colored hair shone in the waning sun, made her look like a cover-girl model. I thought about how I looked in comparison; an average face topped with shoulder-length greenish-brown wavy hair. Unfortunately, my best feature was hidden because of the cool fall evening. I hate to brag, but even back in high school, some boys in my choir called me "legs."

"What in the world?" Lin stared at me as I approached. Dang, she already noticed my hair? She frowned. "No lipstick or earrings?"

My hand flew to my ear, "Oops? Hold on."

"Well, hurry, I'm starving."

Glad she hadn't noticed my hair, I ran back in to put on lipstick and grab earrings, then went back out and stuffed my long legs into her low car. I waited for the next realization.

"Better," she said as she started to back out of the driveway, then looked at me again. She slammed on the brakes hard enough to deploy airbags. Luckily the old car wasn't equipped with that feature, but with no headrest either, my neck got a jolt. "What is up with that hair?" She was the third person to squint at me today. "Is it... green? Pity!"

"Oh, just drive. I can't do anything about it now." I looked straight ahead, waiting for the car to move. She still didn't drive, so I slowly turned to her. Her head was tilted as she stared, mesmerized. I said, "What? Seriously, let's go." Lin continued to stare until finally, I'd had enough.

I explained my henna fiasco, then glanced in the side view mirror to look at it. It did look pretty darned bad in the dimming light of dusk, but what was done was done. "We won't be in direct light, right? Come on – let's go."

"Well, I've heard just about everything now. I sure hope your date is an open-minded kind of guy." She shook her head and put 'Old Navy' in reverse, backing out onto the street.

Relieved we were finally moving, I said, "Lin, I have so much to tell you."

"Yeah? Besides ruining your hair? Did you find some great treasures today?"

"Uh... actually yes." I wanted to tell her about the concrete tile molds, but the notes were more important. "But I have even bigger news."

Lin accelerated onto the expressway and I couldn't hear her next words for all the wind. "WHAT?" I yelled.

She shouted, "I SAID, SO WHAT IS THE BIG NEWS?"

"I HAVE TO FIND A MURDERER!" I returned.

"HA!" She laughed then hollered, "I THOUGHT YOU SAID YOU HAVE TO FIND A MURDERER".

"I DID – I DO!"

She turned her head toward me as her foot increased on the gas pedal, surging us forward faster than the little car had ever gone before. I looked ahead and stared in horror. "LIN, LOOK!"

She turned her head and saw the quickly approaching bumper of a semi ahead. I envisioned our heads being severed from our bodies as we slid beneath the vehicle, but Lin slammed on the brakes just in time, avoiding the catastrophe.

Recovering from the near-miss, I took a big breath and rolled up my window to cut down on the wind noise and let out a relieved sigh.

Once we exited the highway, I filled her in on the desk and the notes. She pelted me with questions as we drove past the beautiful downtown churches, art deco buildings, and Black Wall Street in downtown Tulsa.

Lin easily parallel parked the tiny car in front of McNellie's, my favorite burger and beer pub, and asked with wide eyes, "Are there more notes that you haven't read?"

"Yes. Just a few," I said, checking my messy green hair in the mirror. "I kept getting interrupted, but I brought them with me." I strained to climb out of the low Fiat.

"Uffda, I can't believe we have a mystery to solve!" Lin squealed.

"Well, don't mention any of it to these guys." I looked at my watch. "Great. Bad hair AND we're late."

"OK, let's do this," she said as she opened the big brass door of McNellie's

We walked in the noisy crowded entry of the popular pub and up to the hostess stand. Lin announced with a smile, "We're here to meet two guys – Jay and Scott."

The twentysomething hostess looked us over, made a little face, and shrugged. "Follow me." She turned to reveal a cute new McNellie's t-shirt. As we walked, I tried to read the silkscreened saying between swishes of her long ponytail; "BEER IS PROOF (swish) THAT GOD LOVES (swish) US AND WANTS US (swish) TO BE HAPPY" – Ben Franklin.

I surveyed the place, wondering which table would hold our blind dates. There were two older businessmen eating hamburgers on the left, and a table of giggling college girls having burgers to the right. Beyond them was a couple in their 30s with glasses of wine. Then there was a table with two rough-looking men drinking beer, one in a sweat-stained cowboy hat and faded plaid shirt. The other wore a farmer's style ball cap and a greasy work shirt. I looked ahead hoping there was another pair of single men, but nope – she stopped right there in front of the unsavory-looking guys. She lifted her eyebrows at us as if to ask, "Are you sure these are the guys?" I shrugged, and she walked back to the hostess stand.

The men, both holding bottles of PBR, slowly checked us out by looking us up and down. The ball cap guy lingered a little too long on my chest area – not because it's big and voluptuous, but probably because I'm way too small for his taste.

They didn't stand up, just nodded their heads and muttered..." Sup?" in unison.

I let out a sigh and said, "Hi, I'm Kitty, and this is Lin."

We waited for them to say their names or something, but they remained silent, so we just sat down in the empty chairs.

Lin asked, "So, which one of you is Jay?"

The guy in the cowboy hat raised his bottle with grubby fingers.

"Then you must be Scott?" I said to the one in the Valvoline hat.

"Yo," he said, just before he took a big gulp of his beer then burped aloud. I glanced at Lin, and she caught my eyes with a quick roll of her own. My instinct was to leave. In retrospect, we should have.

A cute server stopped and said, "Ya'll want another round?"

Scott answered, "Yup."

"You girls know what you wan?" she said in a thick Okie twang as she pointed to the beer menu.

I picked up the menu, covered my face with it, and asked Lin, "How many do you think they've had?" Not waiting for an answer, I looked up to the girl and asked, "What's your favorite beer?"

She responded, "Um...I'm too young to drank, but iveryone says the local Marshall is great if you don't mind it hoppy. The Red is 'posed to be smoother."

Her accent was captivating. I'll have to practice that dialect soon.

"Oh, I actually like IPAs, so I'll try a sample of that, but can I also try the red? And we'll have water with lots of ice and lemon, please." I noticed the guys look at each other.

"Of course," she said, ever so chipper.

Lin said, "I'll have a Bud Light on draft if you have it."

"Yes, ma'am." I loved the way the server stretched out both words, then bounced away.

I turned to Lin. "Why don't you ever try anything new, Lin? This pub has over 100 beers on tap and all you ever choose is Bud Light."

"Well, maybe I don't want to waste everyone's time trying to make up my mind like you do." Lin handed me the food menu and said, "Here, start studying it now, so you don't make that poor girl wait all night for your food order." She turned to the guys, pointed to me, and said, "She's just like Meg Ryan in *When Harry Met Sally*," if you know what I mean." The two guys just shrugged and finished off their beer.

I turned to Lin and said, "I don't think they are exactly the target audience for romantic comedies. And I'll have you know that I already decided on a burger: well done, and sweet potato fries because they're ama-ha-zing here!" I turned to our "dates." And asked, "What are you two going to have?"

Scott, who never took his eyes off my chest slurred, "Shicken fried steak." Was he already drunk? And to think I was worried about my hair color. He never looked high enough to see my head.

"I'm havin' a steak and baked 'tater. That's a real man's meal," said Jay. He leaned his chair back on its legs and stared at Lin with a smug expression beyond creepy.

The perky waitress brought me two sample beers. I chose the IPA and ordered a pint along with my meal, with no extreme substitutions except to ask for ketchup.

Lin nodded and said, "Good job, Pity." Then she ordered, followed by the guys.

When the server left, Scott chuckled. He looked like he just rode in on the back of a pick-up truck with his wrinkled and dirty work shirt. I'd have to watch them leave to find out if that's truly how he traveled. He said with a strong hick accent, "You called her Pity. Are you drunk?"

I took a breath, gave a "here we go again" sigh, and gave my stock answer of how I got my name. I ended with, "So it just stuck. I'm Pity to friends and family."

"That's stupit," Jay said through his teeth.

Lin retorted, "Maybe so, but we love her anyway."

The waitress returned with our drinks, and we sat quietly sipping our beer while the guys guzzled theirs with occasional burps.

I whispered to Lin, "Why are we with these yokels when we could be solving a murder?" Then, I turned and spoke loudly across the table, "So what do you two do for a living?"

Jay took a swig and said, "We work over at Hawkins Construction."

I said, "Oh, that's nice." Then, I answered what should have been their question, "Well, I'm an elementary music teacher and Lin stages homes so they sell faster."

The guys just stared in their beer mugs as if I wasn't even talking. Bet I would have gotten their attention if I'd said we were strippers.

Lin attempted to make conversation next with her lilty voice, "I have a daughter the same age as Pity's daughter. They're best friends and hang out together – just like us."

Scott wrinkled up his weathered face and said, "You have kids?" as if having children was a deal-breaker. Little did he know, the first belch out of his mouth broke any possible deal for me. I tried to catch Lin's eye to see if she was ready to leave, but I remembered she was super hungry and figured we could wait until after eating.

Our food arrived, and we ate in silence – except of course for the slurping across from us. When Scott speared his whole chicken fried steak and picked it up to take a bite, I made a face at Lin in disgust. Hadn't he heard of a knife? Jay did at least cut up his steak, but in such huge chunks that his mouth was forced wide open while he chewed, revealing a bunch of gold teeth.

We managed to finish our meal by keeping our eyes averted from the guys. It was a relief when the waitress brought the check. Lin and I got out our wallets, but surprisingly the guys took the ticket and paid.

I said, "Well, Lin, I guess we'd better go home. Thanks for dinner, Scott and Jay. Nice to meet you." I started to stand.

"Hey, we got you supper. The least you can do is have a beer next door at the pool hall." Scott slurred the words.

I looked at Lin, hoping she'd say no, but she just shrugged.

I sighed, "OK, but just one. My youngest is having a sleepover and I need to get back to make sure two 13-year-olds aren't jumping off the roof or painting the dog's toenails again."

"Well shit! How many rug rats do you have?" Jay grumbled.

"I have seven, and she has six," I lied. I wanted to add – 'and you guys will never ever meet any of them, made up or real.'

When we stood up, I found myself taller than Scott by a few inches, which is fairly normal. We walked behind the crude men, as they wove back and forth across the sidewalk to the "Billiards and Beer Hall" next door. I considered dragging Lin directly to the car to escape, but I figured there was no harm going along for a minute.

We were greeted at the door of the smoke-filled bar by two scantily clad Miller Lite girls handing out blinking bottle cap pins. I put mine on my striped top, thinking it was cute, and smiled as Lin stuck hers on her purse. Scott attached his to his Valvoline hat, which was an actual improvement as it covered up a grease spot. Jay did the unthinkable and promptly stuck his blinking button on his crotch!

Garage Sale Tip #4
You may kiss a lot of frogs before you find a great garage sale.

You would think having a date wear a blinking button on his crotch would be the worst thing ever. But nope – Lin's date went down a notch by gyrating around the bar to show off his blinker. I tried to stifle a laugh when her eyes bulged in horror, but I couldn't contain a snort.

The guys bought four bottles of beer, handed us each a Pabst, and grabbed the only empty pool table. Scott came uncomfortably close to me and with strong, foul breath he puffed, "Y'all gonna play, or just stand around?

I said with a half-smile, "No, that's OK. We want to watch you play." He shrugged, seemingly satisfied. Lin and I took our drinks to a tall sticky table in the corner as far away from the guys as we could get. I sat on a stool and pulled the papers from my purse.

Lin huffed," Can you believe those idiots?"

"Not really. They're pigs." I showed her the notes. "Here are the ones I already read." I handed the first four to her outstretched hands. "I think they are in order with most recent on top".

She read, shaking her head the whole time. "You found them in a desk from a garage sale? This is crazy. You're pretty sure the killer is a guy, right? Do you think he was writing to a girl or a boy?"

"Well, I don't know for sure, but I assume it's a girl, since he said, 'Do you still love me?' AND the desk they were in is purple."

"Sure, that makes sense. Plus, what guy would keep notes bundled in a desk? This is just awful." She shook her head. "Are you going to turn these into the police?" she asked, holding up the notes.

"Do you think I should? I wanted to find out if it's real before handing them over." I had cried wolf many times before and learned to make sure before causing alarm.

"Yeah, I can see that," she said and added with a laugh, "I mean, look what happened last time you called the police."

"Oh yeah." My face got hot as I recalled the time I was convinced Harriet had been dognapped.

"Alright. Back to this case; I just want to find the culprits and turn them in if they are even still around. Let's read the next one." The paper I picked up was on regular lined notebook paper folded in quarters. I unfolded it and read:

I'll threaten him and see if he's willing to give you up. Don't worry, we'll work it out. You deserve better than him. PS, you should have someone like me.

Lin sighed. "I wish someone loved me enough to kill for me."

"Lin, you're kidding!"

"Well, I wouldn't want anyone to die, but a love that strong is kind of romantic. Read another!"

I was just about to when there was a scuffle at the pool table. We looked up.

Scott had pinned a guy to the felt tabletop with one hand, and raised his other fist, ready to punch. "You're about to regret touching my pool stick, Asshole!"

I stood and said, "Oh you've got to be kidding! Let's get out of here, Lin." I pushed her toward the door.

There was a smack as Scott's fist hit the guy's face. Jay announced loudly, "Anyone else wanna mess with us?" He looked our way and shouted, "Where the hell do you two think you're going?" Following Lin, I was almost to the door when Jay came up from behind and reached for me, but grabbed my purse instead.

With surprising courage, I said, "We don't owe you jerks anything. We're leaving."

A huge bouncer wearing a black "Billiards and Beer" t-shirt stepped between Jay and me. I was surprised that his long beard was braided in the front. He said in a super deep voice, like Barry White, "Leave the lady alone, Buddy. The police have been called and you don't want to get in even more trouble."

Jay scowled at me for a moment, then shoved my purse at my chest, knocking me back a little. He snarled like a rabid dog as I ran out the door. The only word I was sure he said was bitch. Lin was already in her running car, so I jumped in and we squealed off.

I tried to catch my breath and said with wide eyes, "That moves up to the number one worst blind date ever." I turned to her, "Did you see Jay grab my purse?"

"No! I wondered where you were. Are you OK?"

"Yeah, I'm fine; just mad that we got into that mess."

"I'm sorry, Pity. We should have left right after dinner."

"Or before dinner. But who knew they would turn psycho?" That was kind of a dumb statement because they did look awful from the start. I looked up at the dark sky and took a deep breath, then I said, "Strange. The temperature has dropped so I should be cold without a jacket, but it feels great out here."

"It's the beer and the adrenaline, or maybe you're turning into a northerner. We can withstand all kinds of cold, don't cha know?"

I looked down at the crumpled paper in my hand. "Oh, shoot. He tore the note! I only have half of it."

"Should we go back to get it?"

I glared at her. "Are you kidding? No way. We'll just try to figure it out when we get to my house." I sighed. "I'm so glad we never have to see those guys again."

She nodded. "Luckily they don't know how to contact us,"

"That's the only good thing about that dating site." I shook my head so my green hair blew in the wind. "I sure won't be using Okie Singles again!" I exhaled and relaxed a little, then stuck my flashing blinker on my crotch and did a little dance in the seat.

Lin noticed and started laughing. "Did he think we'd be impressed by that?"

We arrived at my house, exited the car, and giggled all the way to the door, only to find Ree and Caitlyn's bodies in a tangled heap. I didn't even flinch at the sight. They were just playing Twister and watching TV. But why were they wearing wraps on their heads?

"What in the world? Please tell me you didn't use my other packets of Henna?"

"We decided to make a statement, Mom. Lots of kids dye their hair fun colors, and you said it made your hair feel healthy."

Caitlyn added in her near cartoon voice, "I'm in solidarity with you, Mrs. Kole. Whatever you do is cool with me, so green hair it is."

I grimaced and asked warily, "How long ago did you put it on?"

Ree shrugged, "Maybe 10 minutes?"

Lin winced and said, "Gee Ree, I sure hope that didn't ruin your gorgeous blonde hair."

"Me too, young lady." I turned to the other turbaned teen, "and I hope you didn't change your hair, Caitlyn, or your mom will kill me. "Now, both of you go wash it out right now.

I seriously feared the wrath of Caitlyn's mother, Trish. I had taught music to my daughters and most of their friends at Arrowstar

Elementary, so I know a lot of families. Out of all my students' parents, Trish was the absolute worst.

I don't know how the poor child has survived. Caitlyn's mom was like a helicopter mom, backstage mom, and Joan Crawford combined. Adding to that, Trish's husband is the strictest judge in Tulsa County. They didn't mind letting Caitlyn come to our house as long as everything was under control. With those two parents, this little stunt with the hair color could put me behind bars for years.

The girls left to wash out the henna, and I collapsed into the recliner. "I'm tired, but we have to try to figure out this half message," I took the mangled paper from my purse.

"Give it to me and I'll read what's left of it." Lin took it and read aloud while I closed my eyes to block out the lights.

"No, I'm not mad, but are you sure the doctor is right? There is no mistake? It has to be our secret, but I can help you take care of it. I can't believe "

And that's where the paper was torn. The rest of it was left up to our imagination.

My eyes flew open. "Oh my gosh, she was pregnant?"

"Sure sounds that way. If it were an illness, what could they do about it?"

I stood and paced. "I'll bet the athlete got her pregnant, but the other guy still wanted her, so he planned to kill the jock."

She nodded her head slowly. "We still need to know who it was and when it happened. Why don't you call Kim and see if she can do some research?"

Kim is the middle Kole sister, the one who named me Baby Pity. She's a librarian in Tulsa and has all the knowledge of the world at her fingertips and in her head or so it seems. "Good idea. I'll talk to her." I sat on the arm of my chair. "Hey, I just remembered the garage sale where I bought the desk is going to be open again tomorrow, too. I'll go back and ask him how he ended up with the desk. Wanna come?"

She frowned. "I would, but I have to go to Mom's for our annual pumpkin carving day."

"Is it that time of year already?"

"You betcha. She wants to decorate even more this year because Uncle L is coming to visit."

"You have an uncle named L?"

"Yes."

"Like the letter L?" I asked, cocking my head.

"No, silly. ELLLL," she said louder and in slow motion.

Still hearing L, I said, "Okay, so how do you spell his name?"

"A. L."

"Oh, Al," I said, using an actual short A sound. "I wish you said an *A* like a true Okie because sometimes I still don't understand you."

She frowned. "But that sounds so nasal. Well, anyways, be careful if you go back. The rummage sale man could be the murderer!"

I cringed when I pictured the tall guy with the skimpy mustache who said his wife would kill him if he didn't make some money. "He did seem a little strange. I'll be careful. Maybe I'll ask R.A. to join me. Let's read another note." I opened the second to last paper and read.

I'm sorry you feel ill, baby. Did your mom give you something for it? Maybe you should go to the nurse?

"This must be before he knows she's preggo," I whispered as the girls came into the living room, both with towels on their heads. I wondered if we would ever finish reading the notes with all the interruptions.

I looked at the teens. "Well? Do I need to make a run to get some hair dye remover for you?"

Ree shrugged, "Don't know. It's dark, but it always kinda dark when it's wet."

Lin said, "Oh look, Pity. It's your successor on TV."

I looked at the screen in time to see Todd's girlfriend, Shelly, wearing a witch hat. She was filmed in front of a green screen so she looked like she flew a broom down to her dad's dealership. She yelled, "Time to fly on down to see what's brewing."

We all joined in saying her catchphrase, "Because you'll get the max at Big Jack's Cadillacs!"

Ree said, "Funny thing is, I think she *is* a witch."

I contained my laugh and said, "OK. Enough of that. Go dry your hair and then come back."

The girls left, and Lin and I snickered about Ree's remark. Shelly was awful. It wasn't long before we heard the familiar hum of two hairdryers. I went to the kitchen for glasses of ice water, gave one to Lin, and sat down. I turned my aching head to my friend. "Trish is going to flip out if Caitlyn's hair isn't perfect."

"I know. I was just thinking that" she agreed.

When Harriet barked, I hoisted myself out of the recliner again to let her inside. She ran by me, eyes hidden by her long white/gray fur with only a tongue to indicate which end was which. She made a beeline for Lin, who petted my shaggy girl. I took one look at her tail and shouted, "Marie Elizabeth Peters! What did you do to Harriet?"

Ree ran into the living room, hair still wet on one side, but thankfully the other half was its regular blonde color. What a relief. Hopefully, Caitlyn's hair was fine too.

I pointed to Harriet, whose tail was covered in plastic wrap.

Ree said, "Oops, I forgot. We decided to see if her hair would change color and I knew you would get mad if we messed with her head, so we chose her tail," she explained.

"Didn't ya think I'd be upset if you messed with her at all?" I turned to my friend. "Lin, you might as well go home. I've got a dog to wash and a kid to spank. I'll call you tomorrow with any news."

"Okay. Good luck. Call me ASAP if you find out anything else." She winked and made her way to the door.

Ree backed away with hands up for protection. "Spank? Really?"

"Grrrrr," I growled and acted as if I was going after her. She giggled and fled down the hallway to Caitlyn and her hairdryer.

I washed Harriet's back end in my bathtub, which was a challenge because the dog spent her bath time washing my face with her tongue and trying to jump out of the water. After I used four towels to dry her off, she ran around the house with a big case of the zoomies and smiled her big dog smile. And thank goodness, her tail was still white.

Once the girls' hair was dry, I said a silent thank you that both of them looked normal. I told them to go to their room and not to come out 'til morning, which they did, talking the whole time. What other kind of mess could they get into? Then for my nightly ritual, I drank a glass of milk and headed toward my bedroom.

Before I reached the hall, the front door opened, and Ren entered wearing a Gwen Stefani t-shirt, skinny jeans, and flats. She clutched a movie popcorn bucket and a Coke cup. No matter what she ate, she never gained weight, probably because of all the swimming.

"What's up, Mom? How was the date?"

"Oh, my gosh. You wouldn't believe how bad it was." I shook my head. "No way can you guess the horror of it."

"Hmm. Let me try. Your date got in a fight and Lin's guy put a blinking pin on his crotch?" She laughed and slurped through her straw.

"Good guess!" I smirked. "So, Lin told Jennifer already, huh?"

"The glory of texting. Why is your shirt wet?" she asked.

"Harriet gave me a bath. Ask your sister about that... I'm going to bed." And with my last bit of energy, I pleaded, "Can you tell me about your evening tomorrow, Sweetie? I'm beat."

She said, "Sure," and tossed a piece of popcorn in her mouth.

Garage Sale Tip #5
Go back later for real bargains.

Bang, bang, bang. I watched in anticipation as the man hammered the yard sale sign in the ground. Sweet. Tap, tap, tap. It was a nice big sign. Maybe I would be the first one to the sale! What was taking him so long? Bang, bang, bang. I wanted him to finish, so I could follow him to his house. The pounding continued and then I heard, "Mom!"

Why did the man holler, "Mom?" His voice was unusually high. I opened my eyes to darkness. I wasn't at a garage sale. I was in bed. What time was it? The pounding continued. I moaned, "What?"

The door opened, blinding me with light from the hallway. "Mom, it's nine o'clock. Aren't you supposed to help with the kids' choir at church this morning? And you promised us sugar donuts."

Shoot. I wasn't going to be first at a yard sale at all. Plus, I had overslept. "Oh, yeah" I croaked. "Thanks for waking me." I sat up and tried to discern just which daughter was in my room. Why did I buy blackout curtains for my windows anyway?

Yawning, I said, "You're going to have to wait until we get back to have donuts." I went into the bathroom to put in my contacts but realized I'd forgotten to take them out last night. I tried to focus as I headed to the shower, but my eyes were gummy. Did I even have time for a shower? My eyes finally focused on Ree in the doorway. I said, "Honey if you are going with me, you'd better get ready now."

"Caitlyn isn't feeling so good - she has a rash on her face, neck, and head."

Now that woke me up. "You're kidding?" Crap. She was probably allergic to the henna. I should have figured the little redhead had sensitive skin. I rushed to the bedroom to see the damage and tried to focus on her with my sticky contacts. "Are you OK, sweetie?" Her face was pink. I opened my eyes wide, then squeezed them shut hoping that it was my dry contacts making her face appear so red.

She said, "Yeah, it just looks kinda bad, Mrs. Kole. My mother won't let me use anything on my hair, just in case I have a reaction. Guess I should have remembered that."

Ya think? I pulled her gently into the bathroom to get a better look in the bright light. Yep. There were red welts all the way around her hairline and in her scalp. "Ree, can you go get me some oatmeal, a medium-sized bowl, and a pair of pantyhose?"

"Do you want cinnamon or maple?"

I laughed. "Well, I'm not going to eat it." I realized the last time I'd used an oatmeal poultice on her, she was probably two and explained, "I need you to get the canister of plain oatmeal. We'll make a paste to put on her rash and hopefully, it will relieve the itching."

"What color pantyhose do you want? I didn't know you even wore them anymore," she said shaking her head.

"The hose is to put the oatmeal in, so the color really doesn't matter." She looked at me like I was completely bonkers. "I'll show you what I mean when you get back. But hurry please - and get scissors and a bowl," I added as Ree scurried off.

Caitlyn sputtered, "You're not going to cut my hair off, are you?"

I had to laugh at the way these girls' minds worked. "Of course not. I'd never chop your gorgeous hair. I'm just going to cut the pantyhose. I'll be right back." Her face brightened in relief.

I ran to my room, dressed quickly, and tied a scarf around my head to cover the semi-green hair. I washed my face, put drops in my dry eyes, and applied some make-up before Ree came back. I cut off the pantyhose below the knee, shook some oatmeal in the toe, and tied the top. I put warm water in the bowl and asked Caitlyn to sit on the side of the bathtub. I showed Ree what to do; how to dip the oatmeal ball in the warm water squeeze out the excess and then gently pat it on her skin." I asked, "Does that feel a little better, Caitlyn?"

"Yes, it does Mrs. Kole. You can do anything, can't you?" She looked at me adoringly. It was kind of nice to have a number one fan, but if she knew me as my girls did, she'd run like crazy.

"Caitlyn, why don't you just call me Kitty or Pity?" I asked as I dabbed the paste on her skin. "I'm not your teacher anymore."

"Oh, I could never do that, Mrs. Kole," she said assuredly, then thought about it. "Well, maybe I can when I'm your age."

I handed the job over to Ree and told the girls I'd be back as soon as I finished putting away choir robes.

When I arrived home an hour and a half later, I was surprised to see Ree still carefully applying the poultice to her best friend's head. I guess I should have been more specific that she didn't have to dab all day. Caitlyn had gooey oatmeal in every inch of her hair.

"Well, Ree, I see you took your job very seriously."

"You didn't tell me when to stop, and I hadn't gotten it all covered yet. Besides, we were watching a movie." I recognized one of the Harry Potter movies playing from her iPad propped up against the bathroom mirror.

Caitlyn smiled and said, "It feels much better. Ree is a pretty good doctor, but do I have to wear it like this all day?"

"No, I think you're set for now," which was good because she looked grotesque. "You can rinse it off well in the shower, but don't use shampoo, just warm water. Then, just pat it dry, OK?"

"Sure, Mrs. Kole."

"Ree, while she's showering, ya wanna help make donuts?"

"Yes!"

That was no surprise. Ree always loved to work in the kitchen. I opened a can of biscuits from the refrigerator, punched holes in the middle of each one, and deep-fried them until they were golden. She blotted them on paper towels and rolled them in sugar. Voila! We had a plate of yummy hot sugar donuts.

I figured this was the least healthy meal ever, so I added eggs, bananas, and orange juice to our little brunch.

As the three of us ate, I studied Caitlyn's ruddy complexion. It was always sort of red because of her freckles and the occasional pimple, so the rash wasn't as noticeable on her as it might be on another person, but I was still worried.

"Where's Lauren?" asked Caitlyn before she popped a donut hole in her mouth.

"Oh, on Sunday mornings she volunteers in the nursery at church, so she got up early today. She should be back soon. Make sure to save a few donuts for her," I warned.

"You bet I will. She's so cool. I want to be just like her when I grow up," said the enamored redhead.

Ree said under her breath, "Well, then, we won't get along very well when you grow up."

Caitlyn didn't seem to understand, but I did. Gotta love a sarcastic daughter.

"Do you know when your mom is picking you up?" I asked.

"Oh, she said she'll come to get me at about noon." I looked down at the time on my phone just as the doorbell rang.

I said, "Quick, Caitlyn, go dry your hair on a cool setting, and Marie, get her packed. I'll entertain your mom while you get ready." I took my time getting to the front door. When I opened it, I felt like I'd stepped into an animated Disney movie. Trish looked like Cruella. She was decked out with a long black dress and fur stole. At least it wasn't made of Dalmatian skin. Her stance with a long finger pointed at me, looked like just the wicked character. Of course, her hair had no white streak, but she was horrific all the same.

She waltzed in, scanning the living room for anything that didn't meet her approval. After crinkling her long nose at my headscarf, she shuddered at the sight of the birdcage. "Where is my Catie Linn?"

"She's just getting ready. The girls didn't go to church this morning because Caitlyn had a little rash from a hair product, they tried last night." Why do I have to be so darned honest? I readied myself for the wrath of Trish.

"What? Did you call a doctor? Let me have the box, and I'll call poison control," she said with fervor. "I should have known something like this would happen at YOUR house!" Her face was as red as her daughter's hair. Someday, this lady would explode.

In my calm, teacher-to-parent voice, I said, "Trish, Caitlyn wasn't poisoned. We applied an oatmeal poultice to the rash and she's just fine. There is no need to worry."

"Well, we'll see about that! And how would you know anyway? You're only a teacher. You don't have a medical degree," she said with a sneer. Trish called out with a worried, cracking voice, "Catie Linn, come to Mommy. Let me see my precious baby."

"Just a minute, Mother," returned Caitlyn in a calm voice.

Stalling, I asked, "Did you have a nice evening last night?"

Trish lifted her hooked nose in the air. "Yes, we had a fine time. The Judge and I went to the annual "Evening under the Stars" benefit for the homeless shelter in downtown Tulsa. We made the largest donation, as usual." She anxiously searched the hall for her daughter.

"Of course." I said and added, "Well, I was downtown for dinner last night, too. I'm surprised I didn't see you. I almost donated my purse to a complete stranger."

She lifted an eyebrow so high it almost touched her hairline and looked at me with a curled lip. Caitlyn and Marie came down the hall carrying an overnight bag and pillow, saving me from anymore small talk. Thankfully, they both looked normal.

"Oh, baby, are you OK?" She took Caitlyn in her arms as if she'd been held captive for years and had just been released.

"I'm fine, Mother. Mrs. Kole knew just what to do. She's wonderful, don't you think?"

Oh brother, why did she say that? Trish's face shifted from an irritated pink to a pinched crimson as she prodded and pulled Caitlyn's hair to see if her offspring had any permanent damage. Poor child.

"Look at that! Look at her scalp!" Trish pointed at a tiny spot on the girl's temple. She sounded like a dissatisfied customer who was trying to return a damaged product.

I couldn't help but joke, "I'm sorry, ma'am, but you must have a receipt dated within the last 30 days in order to receive a full refund on this child." I laughed and Caitlyn and Marie snickered. Trish did not.

"I've had enough of your constant sarcasm, Kitty Kole! You…" she huffed. "You are unfit to watch my daughter. She will never come back here! You can bet on that."

Trish grabbed Caitlyn by the hand and yanked her toward the door urgently. You would think the girls would be devastated by this announcement, but it wasn't the first time they had heard those exact words.

Rest assured; Caitlyn would be back soon. Trish and "The Judge" enjoy socializing and schmoozing too much to stay home, and they have no other option to keep Caitlyn company. Caitlyn's young uncle, Andy, used to stay with her when he lived with them for a while, but he recently moved into an apartment when he got a new job. Who could blame him? Somehow, our house always ended up being better than leaving Caitlyn home alone.

In all my years teaching, I'd never known any parent to be so protective. If Oklahoma passed a law against smothering a child, Trish would be a repeat offender.

"See you tomorrow in Math," Marie called just as Trish slammed the door.

Lauren walked in just moments later. "Why was Trish so freaked out? She didn't even tell me my skirt was too short."

I sighed. "Just another bit of drama to add to a crazy weekend. Come have some sugar donuts and tell me about last night's movie."

After eating more donuts with Ren, I called my brother-in-law, R.A. I didn't fill him in on the possible murder but said, "I need to ask the guy some questions about a desk I bought and might want back-up. And they have tools!"

R.A. and my sister, Kim, live in Tulsa, but convincing him to make the 15-minute drive to meet me in Broken Arrow was easy, since he is just as addicted to garage sales as me.

We decided to meet at the QuikTrip near my house and ride together to the garage sale. I got there early and went inside for a drink. So many choices. I finally decided on a mango iced tea.

While paying, I heard the jingle of the door and glanced up to see my sweet brother-in-law walk in, all 5'6" of him, or so it said on the giant measuring tape posted by the door. R.A. was sporting a Yankee's ball cap and neatly trimmed Santa Claus beard. The beard was not a costume. It was real, although at only fifty, a big white beard seemed fake. His whiskers tickled my cheek as he came in for his bear hug.

We've had the best brother/sister relationship ever since he met my sister 25 years ago. Kim is the only Kole girl who found a husband worth hanging on to. My marriage lasted 13 years, and my California sister, Kay, was married several times before embracing single life.

R.A. said, "Let me get coffee before we go." He grabbed a cup and poured his black cup of Joe. After paying, we climbed into his work truck full of electronic equipment.

"I still have my list from yesterday." I gave directions to the house as I sipped my icy tea. "The guy is pretty weird."

R.A. shrugged, "Whatever."

When we arrived, the owners were packing up some of their remaining items. "Just follow my lead," I suggested. We casually approached the yard and looked around. I recognized the tall man from yesterday and nonchalantly picked up a few things before saying, "Hi, I was here yesterday and bought your little purple desk."

"Yeah, I remember you," he said in a gravelly voice that reminded me of Billy Bob Thornton's character in *Sling Blade*. Maybe that's why I thought he was creepy.

"Um, I was thinking of getting another desk for my daughter, and wondered where and when you got it. Is it old?"

"It probably is. I got it at an auction probably 10 years ago when my kid needed a desk. She's gone to OU now and doesn't need it."

An auction? 10 years ago? Could his daughter have hidden the notes? At least I knew where she lived. But the notes looked old and his girl was just now out of high school, so I doubted it. I asked, "Where was the auction?" hoping for more clues.

"Over at the Broken Arrow school warehouse."

So, it was a school desk from my district? So, Jones may have been from here! I was delighted with the information, but I didn't want to look suspicious. I said, "Oooh, I love those school warehouse auctions." I continued with a story, unfortunately a true one; "One time I bid $5 on 500 bright blue blazers there. And I got them! A penny a piece."

The man cocked his head and said, "But why?"

"Well, I figured my school and church choirs could wear them. Unfortunately, that didn't make a dent so I used them for costumes and gag gifts for years. It was nearly impossible to get rid of those darned blue jackets. Goodwill wouldn't even take them. I still probably have 50 don't I, R.A.?"

"Yep. I've even worn a few myself...when I had to," he grumbled as he inspected some strange item with wires coming out of it.

"You don't say," the guy said with a perplexed look.

R.A. added, "Don't get me started on the theater curtains she bought there. It took two truckloads to get that fabric to her house."

I remembered fondly all the costumes I made with the gorgeous gold velvet, and not so fondly how hard it was to get rid of the rest of it. I had rejoiced when I could finally park in my garage again.

"I'll take this," R.A. said and paid the man a few dollars for the odd gizmo. I gave up long ago trying to figure out what he was buying.

I said, "Well, have a good day," and we walked toward the street. I felt good about my investigative skills.

The man called after me, "Hey, would you want the chair that went with the desk? I forgot to put it out yesterday."

I turned with excitement to see him grab a purple chair from the corner of his garage. He said, "You can just have it. They both had the same number stamped underneath, like they went together, so I bought the set. I sure don't need a chair this color. It doesn't match my eyes," he joked.

"Oh, yes!" I squealed and pulled my last dollar from my pocket, handing it to him. "It's the least I can give you for a purple chair."

My brother-in-law carried my new clue to his truck and I told the man, "Thank you so much."

When we got in his vehicle, I turned to R.A. and said, "This is so cool. I have to tell you and Kim the whole story because you won't believe it! Is she free today?"

"Right now, she's busy sewing curtains for Eli's apartment.

I smiled. "Awe. I still can't believe he is out on his own now. I'm so proud of him." My nephew, Eli, had followed in my footsteps and got a music education degree. Now he's a band director in Texas.

R.A. added, "We're going over to the casino for their buffet at 5:00. Want to meet us there?"

"Absolutely, and thanks so much for helping me."

We pulled up next to my car and R.A. said, "I'm glad I came. I've wanted one of these all my life." He held up his prize. I don't know how many times I've heard him say that about something I have never seen before.

He put the chair in the back of Liesel for me, said goodbye, and walked back to his truck. I rolled down the window and shouted, "Hey R.A., do you happen to know when Ken's Pizza started and what year they changed over to Mazzio's?"

He thought for a moment, scratching his beard. "Kens was around in the sixties and I'm sure they changed names in the late 90s. I worked on their sound system when they remodeled.

I smiled. "I knew you were the perfect person to ask."

He squinted his baby blues at me. "Why do you want to know that?"

"I promise I'll explain at dinner."

When I got home, I carried the wooden chair upside down, so I could find the number. In black block letters, it read BAHS, Rm 202 #14. I turned the desk on its side and sure enough, it too said BAHS, Rm 202 #14. I hadn't considered it being a school desk because of the purple color, but it did resemble one, especially with the gunmetal green interior.

Remembering I still had one last note to read, I dug through my purse until I found it. I should have put them all in an envelope so they wouldn't get so wrinkled. The police might actually like to have them in good shape - if I ever decided to turn them in. The final note, or first in chronological order, read:

It's nice to finally have a class together. I'll keep an eye on you.

That sounded disturbing but fit with the school desk theme. I had to get organized and start my investigation in earnest today. The next day, my detective work would be hampered by seven classes of wiggly, singing kids. Although some of them are clever and could be helpful, I knew better than to get children involved in a possible murder case.

I figured Lin was still busy carving pumpkins so instead of calling, I texted her; 'I got a matching chair from BAHS!'

In just a few seconds I got a reply, 'Who is Bags?'

What was she talking about? I looked at my phone. That darned predictive text had changed my message to 'I got a marching chair from Bags.'

Ha! I re-sent the correct message; 'I got a matching chair from Broken Arrow High School'. I wondered if Lin knew what a *marching* chair was, because I sure didn't.

Garage Sale Tip #6
Pay attention to where you are going.

After a shower, I was happy to see the green had faded somewhat so my hair color seemed closer to normal. Thank heavens. With an hour left before leaving to meet R.A. and Kim, I sat on my bed and wrote a list of clues on a pad of paper and put it away.

I hollered, "Girls, come here a minute." Shortly, both girls popped in and sat on my bed with me. It wasn't long before Harriet was up there too, making the double bed pretty crowded. "Have you gals finished all of your homework for this weekend?"

"Yes," they both said.

"Great! And what was your most memorable thing that happened last week?"

Ree said, "Um, when Trish stormed out of the house again?" She smirked as she laid her head on Harriet's back. That dog is the best live pillow ever.

I started, "Well, I don't like to make fun of people, but…" My voice changed to a classic impersonation of Trish. "My Caiti Lin will never step foot in this house again. You can bet on that!" They both laughed and I asked, "What about you, Ren?"

With her elbows on her knees, and head resting on her hands, her caramel brown hair lay across the colorful quilt. "I can't decide if it was the movie I saw, or you turning your hair green."

I made a face and said, "Ha-ha."

Of course, what I remembered most was finding the murder clues, but I wasn't ready to tell the girls about that, so I said, "Well, mine was the horrible date Lin and I endured."

Ree cocked her head, "What happened?"

I realized I hadn't told her about the two disgusting guys. "I'll let Ren fill you in," I said, shaking my head. "Are you excited about Fall Break this week?"

"Yes!" said Ree. "No school Thursday or Friday!" She sat up and bounced on the bed.

"I know," said Ren. "But too bad I have swim practice every day."

I said, "Well, you have to be ready for Saturday's big meet against Jenks."

Ree piped up, "And don't forget I have History Day on Saturday too."

"Well, we'll have to think of something fun to do on our days off. Oh, I forgot, I'm going to meet Aunt Kim for an early dinner in a bit. I'll leave money for you two, if you promise to go somewhere you can get something healthy. And stay out of trouble." They gave each other a sneaky look, making me wonder what they were up to.

"Harriet!" The voice called from the other room. Harriet lifted her head, and we all froze and looked at each other.

"Harriet!" the voice repeated, and the dog jumped off my bed, knocking Ree to the side as she ran into the living room. The three of us started laughing as we realized Edgar was trying out a new voice – mine - calling Harriet. And it worked. Poor dog.

I said, "Well, that's just another reason to watch what we say. Remember the Will Rogers quote your grandpa always says, "'Live in such a way that you would not be ashamed to sell your parrot to the town gossip.'"

The girls nodded their heads slowly as the meaning sunk in.

I had a little extra time before dinner at the casino. So, on my way South, I stopped in Bixby, a small suburb of Tulsa, to find an estate sale that would still be open today, on Sunday. I turned onto Main Street following a huge fire truck going extremely slow. I couldn't pass the guy and before I knew it, an ambulance pulled in right behind me, so I was trapped. Wow, their emergency vehicles sure did drive slow in Bixby.

I focused on looking for estate sale signs as I moved at a crawl. I swerved to miss horse droppings on the road. I knew Bixby was a smaller town than Broken Arrow, but why would horses be on Main Street? I finally got the whole picture when canvas folding chairs and people of all ages lined the street, waving and holding balloons. Oh my gosh! I WAS IN A PARADE!

How embarrassing! Here I was, driving in a recent dark silver VW beetle that wasn't even a convertible. Interesting at best, but not much of a parade entry. Some lady took a photo of me as if I was important. I searched for a way to get out of the line, but all the intersections were blocked with people. I didn't even know the parade theme!

What else could I do but get into the spirit? I rolled down the windows and started waving. I was glad I had taken a shower and put on make-up since I seemed to be a Bixby celebrity. Laughing, I searched my console for candy to throw for the kids, but all I had was a few McDonalds' ketchup packets, dog treats and a bag with only shards of potato chips; none of which would go over well with kids or adults.

After 20 minutes driving at 8 mph, the crowd began to thin. Finally, the fire truck in front of me turned, enabling me to exit the parade route. I smiled, then giggled so hard I had to stop on the shoulder to catch my breath. I was way too late and embarrassed to try to find the sale I'd been looking for, so I headed to the casino.

I made my way past the noisy slot machines to the quieter and less smoky restaurant. It had a wonderful southern-style buffet. Any meal with fried okra, fried chicken, and fried catfish was okay with me. And the bread pudding was to die for. I told my girls to eat healthily, but I had no intention of doing that.

I found Kim and R.A. sitting at a table near the line. They had already ordered my iced tea just right; no lemon, with extra ice. We decided to get our food, then talk. I was too embarrassed to tell them about the parade, but I stifled a few leftover giggles as I ate my salad. Then I made my way back to the buffet to fill my plate with the good stuff.

Sitting down with our loaded plates, my sister demanded with eyes wide, "What in the world are you involved in this time, Pity?"

Between bites of cholesterol-laced food, I started from the beginning and told them everything I knew about the desk, chair, and notes. They were enthralled and yet saddened about the possibility of a murder. They looked over the list of clues I had compiled.

I leaned forward and said, "Kim, can you check old newspapers, etc. to find an…"

She interrupted. "…athlete named Jones from Broken Arrow High who died between 1965 and the late 90s? Sure will."

I brightened at how quickly she caught on. "Right. Thanks! It's too bad none of us went to high school in Broken Arrow. Maybe we would have heard something."

We Kole girls and R.A. went to high school in Tulsa. Back then, Broken Arrow was a small suburb, but now it has a population of over 100,000. I moved there when I got married and have never left.

R.A. said, "Are you gonna go the high school to ask around?"

"Well, I can't leave class tomorrow, but I'll e-mail some friends who work there and ask questions. I thought about asking Lauren to snoop, but figure I should leave her out of it."

R.A. said, "Probably a good idea, but don't go telling too many people about it or you may find yourself in trouble." He warned, "Better yet, why don't you just give your evidence to the police?"

"I know I should, but I want to find out if it really even happened first," I reasoned.

Kim popped a remaining piece of okra in her mouth. "I can see why you feel that way after the movie set incident last spring." She nodded, then said, "Hey, what if it's just a liary?"

R.A. and I spoke in unison. "A what?"

"A diary full of lies – a liary. You know – like a trick to play on someone in case they read your diary."

My eyes shot open thinking that was the most brilliant idea. I could make up my own liary someday full of steamy stories so people thought my life was much more exciting. But once I considered the notes at hand in that way, I scrunched up my face and said, "I don't know. This doesn't seem like a joke."

Kim said, "Yeah. Probably not. Well, if it is true, the killer could still be around the area, so please be discreet while asking questions."

"OK, I'll be careful. Let me know if you uncover anything, Kim."

We walked together toward the exit and each of us stopped to put a dollar in a slot machine. R.A. and I lost ours in no time, but Kim ended up with a ticket that had $4.00 on it. "Lucky you!" I gave them hugs as we parted ways.

I decided to stop by Mom and Dad's house before I got back on the highway. I parked under their gorgeous gold and red maple tree and climbed up the familiar steps of their 1965 brick home, walking directly in the front door as I had done all my life. I say 'all my life' because my parents were actually in the realtor's office signing the closing papers on the house when Mom went into labor with me. "Hello!" I called as I walked through the cozy home with worn carpet from years of busy feet, looking for my two favorite people. I didn't hear Mom's typical response, "Is that my baby?" so I walked to the living room. I kneeled on the striped couch my mother had recovered three times, and looked through the huge picture window into the backyard.

There they were, raking leaves under the big pecan tree. Dad, 82, and Mom in her late 70s, were both pretty active, still doing their own yard and housework. They just celebrated their 53rd anniversary and took yet another trip to Europe to celebrate. I want to be just like them someday.

I pictured my future: *puttering around the garden alongside a nondescript, but loving husband. Our packed suitcases sat by the door, ready to take a long exotic vacation. Several adorable grandchildren skipped around us begging, "Bring me a cuckoo clock from Germany, Papa!" and "I want some French fries from France, Grammie." My gray-haired husband winked at me as I patted the darlings on the head. We were so lucky.*

I snapped out of my tranquil daydream when I heard loud singing: "Mmm mm, Good, Mmm mm, Good, that's what Campbell's Soups are, Mmm mm, Good!" It was Dad's Campbell's soup clock, which hung over the coffee maker in the kitchen. Years ago, when my nephew gave it to him, we all laughed at the noisy clock with the Campbell's Kids riding a spoon pendulum back and forth. But now we are used to hearing the song every hour, and generally sing along.

I sighed. Apparently, my daydreamed future would never happen. At age 45, I'm kind of late to start a 53-year long marriage.

My mother smiled at me. I waved back and headed through the dining room to the family room and opened the sliding glass door. I called to my folks, "Hey kids!"

Dad said, "Hello, sweetheart. Come on down and visit."

"I can't stay," I said apologetically as I walked down the steps and gave him a hug. "I was just in the neighborhood hanging out with Kim and R.A. Sorry I didn't come by this weekend. I've been crazy busy with garage sales, a bad date, dyeing my hair green, getting my car stolen, and trying to find a murderer."

"Well, that does sound busy," exclaimed Mom. "Too bad about your date. I don't care what color you dye your hair, just don't straighten it because I love your waves. I hope you got your car back and found your murderer."

She said all that without taking a breath and remarkably without sounding very interested. She brushed leaves off the chair for me to sit. Does she ever truly listen to what I say or even what she says?

It's not that my mother isn't all there; she's probably the smartest person I know. She just gets distracted on account of the ADD that she so generously handed down to me.

Before I could answer, Mom said, "We went to church this morning, and I fixed a nice dinner for your father. Other than that, we haven't done anything exciting."

I walked over and held a bag as Dad scooped a rake full of leaves into it.

He said, "We had porcupine meatballs and your mother even made me a lemon meringue pie. Where are our sweet granddaughters?" He didn't comment on the murder because he probably didn't hear me. He really needed a hearing aid.

I spoke up. "They're at home getting ready for school tomorrow. Speaking of which, I'd better do that tonight, too, or my 'favorite person in the world' will have a hissy fit if I don't have my lesson plans on his desk before eight o'clock."

Dad said, "Good golly, I just hate that Dr. Love doesn't appreciate all you do for the school. There's nothing you wouldn't do for those children."

I shrugged. "It's alright, Dad. He's just one bad apple. At least most of the other staff members and parents still like me."

Mom pushed her white hair from her eyes and said, "I still say he's jealous because you get more attention than he does."

I changed the subject, mainly because I don't like to spend any of my free time thinking of Dr. Love.

"I got you each something at a garage sale yesterday." I pulled the salt and pepper shakers from my bag, glad I'd thought to bring them along, and handed them to Dad.

"Well, look at those. They are little soup cans." He held them up and said, "I will use these to season my tomato soup!"

"And Mom, I got you some juice glasses." I unwrapped one and handed it to her.

"Just the size I like. Thank you, Pity," she said with a smile.

I collected the items to take inside but turned back and spoke loud enough for Dad to hear. "Hey, I have a question. Since you two have read the Tulsa World all my life, do you recall hearing of a Broken Arrow High School athlete dying between 1965 and the late 90s?"

Dad said, "Well, Pity, that's a really big span of time and there have been a lot of teenagers die over the years."

Mom carried a flower pot from one side of the patio to the other and said, "It's true. We've heard of boys dying of heat exhaustion at football practice, some in car wrecks after prom, and others in hijinks gone wrong. It's just so tragic when someone dies so young. But I can't think of a specific incident from Broken Arrow without more information. Why do you want to know?"

"It has something to do with the murder. I'll explain later."

Dad tied the black garbage bag, then move over to put more leaves into a new bag. Living in an older neighborhood with tall trees, they are always assured of a great annual crop of leaves every fall.

"I should head home and work on my lesson plans for tomorrow." I looked up. "You know, it's getting dark, shouldn't you go inside soon?" As I turned around to leave, my phone rang and Kim's face popped up on my caller I.D.

I answered. "Hey Sis, what's up?"

"I'm at the library doing your research. Are you still in town?

"Yeah, I'm at Mom and Dad's"

"You should come to see what I found concerning your case."

"OK. I'll be right there." I hung up and turned to the folks. "That was Kim. I have to run by her library for a minute."

Mom said, "All right, honey. Would you scope out a good mystery for me while you are there?" I seriously thought about letting my mother take over my mystery, but I decided to just let her have Agatha Christie instead.

"I'll ask Kim to put one aside for you."

"Stay longer next time." said Dad.

"I will. Love you."

As I shut the door, I heard him say, "You know, it's getting pretty dark out, shouldn't we go inside soon?" So cute.

After placing the shakers and glasses in the sink, I left.

I drove through Brookside, a cool retro area of Tulsa, to see Kim. I expected to see the bright neon 'Library' sign that gave her building its character, but it was not lit.

Being Sunday evening, the library was dark and closed up tight; all but the back door, which was propped open by none other than...a book. I snuck through, planning to scare Kim. With no windows in her office, the scene was pretty dark. I stood and watched her for a moment. The glow of the computer screen illuminated her face with similar features to my own. Her hair is the same color as mine minus the green of course and is much curlier. I felt a little pang of sisterly love. I have such a great family. Kim looked up, spoiling my surprise, and said, "Check this out. Broken Arrow High School swim star dies in an accidental drowning. It goes on to say his name is Justin Jones."

I rushed over and positioned myself to read the screen over her shoulder. "Wow. That's got to be him! So, he was a swimmer. Poor Justin. What year was it?"

"February 17th, 1997." Kim looked at me with a frown. "Now you have a school, name, date, sport, and most importantly that someone really died. You were right, Pity."

I shook my head as I read, "They called it an accident." Even though this confirmed my suspicion, I felt sick. "I wish I was wrong."

"I printed the article for you." She handed it to me and said, "He seemed like a really nice boy with a great future."

I studied the photocopy and saw a handsome, trim boy in a Speedo standing by an indoor pool. He wore goggles on top of his head, a towel over an arm, and an impish smile. This guy had his whole life ahead of him. My eyes started to tear up.

"Thanks so much, Kim. This is so sad, but it gives me a lot to go on. Maybe now we can set some things straight and catch the evil person who did this."

She turned to me and said, "Or...you could turn this in to the police and let them do it."

I twisted my mouth. "I'm not ready to give up yet. I want to give them as much information as I can."

Kim sighed, probably realizing there was no use trying to change my mind. "Well, then here are the names of his parents." She pointed a bit lower in the article.

"Yeah, maybe I can call them." I blinked away tears and swallowed the lump in my throat.

I managed to say, "Oh, Mom wants another mystery."

"Speaking of mysteries, what's up with your hair color?"

"Oh, I'm surprised you didn't notice at the casino."

"Well, I did, but I just thought it was a reflection of all the lights."

I explained my henna mess and then we took a minute to find a book, all of which helped lighten the mood.

Kim said, "Please be careful if you go investigating and keep me up to date."

"I will." I hugged her and left for the drive back home to Broken Arrow.

It all seemed to fit. Now what? On the drive, I called Lin to fill her in on the news. "Oh, and can I get Mike's phone number? I mean he is a Broken Arrow Police officer. Maybe he can help."

Next, I called my oldest sister, Kay, in California to tell her about my garage sale finds. I didn't get her involved in the mystery but told her about the purple desk, the chair, and the molds for tiles.

She said, "Wow, you got a lot more than I did." She said she might come to Oklahoma for Thanksgiving, which got me excited.

My last call on the road was to Mike. Aside from having bargaining skills, a police officer could come in handy. I dialed his number and thought about poor Justin as the phone rang. A woman answered, which I hadn't anticipated. "Um, hello, may I speak to Mike?"

"Well, he's a bit indisposed," the woman said with a giggle.

Oh, my gosh! Of course, he has a girlfriend and they are in the middle of something. I said, "Oh, I'm sorry. Could you please ask him to call Pity?"

"What was that name?" she asked, sounding confused.

"Pity. P-I-T-Y." Still embarrassed, I gave her my number. But why wouldn't he be involved with someone? He was a super nice and handsome guy.

Monday morning, I woke on time, excited to start a short week of teaching and investigating. The girls were suspiciously chipper at breakfast and I asked, "What did you do last night for dinner?" I took a bite of Life cereal.

"Lauren has a boyfriend," sang Ree, showing off her adorable dimples.

Seeing those deep divots reminded me of the moment she was born: Just as the doctor delivered her, he said, "Wow, look at that!" My head, naturally being at the opposite end, made it impossible to see what he was talking about. Was the baby deformed? Or did it have a birthmark shaped like Jesus? And, for heaven's sake, was it a boy or a girl? The nurse responded, "Look at the dimples on that girl!" And that's how I found out I had a girl.

"Ree!" Lauren slammed down her spoon, taking me out of my reverie.

I lifted my eyebrows at Ren. "Boyfriend? Oooh, tell me more."

Ree piped up again and explained, "We went to China Star and Chris from the swim team was there with his family. He came over and sat with us for a long time. You should have seen Ren flirt."

"Ree! Can't you keep anything quiet? Just wait until you like a boy - if you ever grow up enough to even look at one."

Jumping in to thwart a full-on fight, I said seriously, "Now Lauren, you're always open with me. You can tell me about your friends, whether boys or girls."

"I know, but she doesn't have to blab." Ren eventually took a deep breath and looked at me with a bright smile. "He's really nice and wants me to go out next weekend."

"That's exciting. I'll check him out Tuesday night at your meet."

"OK, but please don't embarrass me," she said.

"I will try to be good." Then I told myself to really try to be good. I glanced at the kitchen clock and stood. "We'd better get moving, or we'll be late for school."

"Come on, Ree." Lauren put away her cereal bowl and shook her keys." If you aren't in the car in two minutes, I'm leaving without you." Since the middle school is on the way to the high school, Ren drops Ree off every day. My mornings sure got easier once she started driving.

The girls got in her little Corolla, and I got in Liesel. We headed in opposite directions to our schools.

Garage Sale Tip #7

If the house is neat, there's a good chance the items will be nice.

My Monday morning started normally; I dropped off my lesson plan book on Dr. Love's desk and went to my classroom in the prefab to organize a few things before the weekly assembly. I wrote a quick e-mail to the high school media specialist to ask if she could send a 1997 yearbook home with Lauren for a few days. I also asked if any teachers who taught then were still in the system. I said I was looking for information to use in an article I was writing – a fairly safe excuse, and who knew? I could write an article.

Then I made my way to the cafegymatorium and sat at the piano. Naturally, being the music teacher, I lead the music in assemblies. Dr. Love hadn't yet walked to the podium, so I had a few minutes before I needed to start playing. I looked around the large room filled with children sitting in rows on the floor. I smiled and waved back at a few kids as I looked for my three best teacher friends.

There was #1- Jules, the art teacher. She had her long hair pulled up in a messy twist, held in place by a pencil. She sat on a folding chair toward the back of the room talking to #2 – Jana, who wore a gold crown atop her short, dark blond hair. She must be doing a Shakespearian project today. Her Gifted and Talented class sat on the floor beside her. Then #3, Becca, appeared in the doorway. Nobody missed her arrival. The tall blonde entered wearing leopard pants and a shiny gold top, both of which accentuated her shapely figure or, as she says, "fun bubbles." It's not a typical gym teacher outfit, but she isn't your ordinary PE teacher. She's more of a "Sporty Barbie."

Becca said something to the other two girls as she walked by and they both cracked up. I smiled, imagining she said something snide about Dr. Love, or maybe it was about one of her recent dates.

It wasn't until the first graders sitting in front of me started pointing to the stage that I came out of my daze and saw Dr. Love's grumpy face staring at me. I quickly found the keys and played my usual attention-getting ditty.

The annoying principal wore his same ill-fitting suit and tie and peaked over the podium to lead the Pledge of Allegiance. I couldn't help think how he looks nothing like his name. He's not a hot, sexy Dr. Barry Love, but a short, skinny guy with a severe comb-over and pop bottle lenses in 1990's frames. His personality, or lack thereof, was the absolute worst part of him. What a waste of a cool name.

I played the "Star-Spangled Banner" and the character song of the month, <u>COMPASSION</u>. Then Dr. Love took over the rest of the assembly. He grabbed the microphone and spoke in his grating voice.

"Today, we will begin enforcing some much-needed school rules." Oh, brother. It seemed like we just recovered from his uniform policy last year, and here we were again. He began:

#1. **Anyone found on the playground equipment after school hours will be called in and dealt with.** Surely, he didn't mean neighbors, did he? I had brought my kids here since they were toddlers as did everyone else in the area. How could he keep them out? Put up barbed wire around the school grounds and install security cameras?

2. **There will be no Halloween decorations or activities this year and dressing in costumes is prohibited, as it would distract from schoolwork.** There were a lot of groans coming from the kids,

but even more came from teachers at this announcement. Our school had prided itself in having the best spook house for 20 years running and, honestly, one day to wear costumes never hurt anyone.

3. There will be a strict NO TALKING policy at lunchtime. He hissed that the lunchroom was getting entirely too loud and explained that anyone caught speaking will be sent to the lunch detention room where a staff member would be in charge.

Becca, Jules, and Jana, all pointed at me, figuring I would get that duty. I have been on Dr. Love's hit list ever since I dared to raise my hand and ask a question during his first faculty meeting. I shook my head at them, but I knew they were most likely right.

Once the man finished his ridiculous rules, it was time for something positive; the monthly good citizenship award for a deserving student. Every time I see a kid walk up to the stage beaming, I get a lump in my throat.

This time, Chelsea, a little freckle-faced 8-year-old bounced up the steps to receive her award. My lump quickly disappeared when the cold man just handed over a certificate without shaking her hand, patting her back, or even looking at her. Dr. Love doesn't think it's appropriate to touch young people. Honestly, I think he's afraid he'll get cooties. Worst elementary principal ever.

After the assembly, I headed back to my room with an exuberant class of 3rd graders following me. I stopped twice on the 50-foot walk; once to say, "Boys, please walk in Arrowstar fashion," to two students jumping up to hit the flag. The second time I stopped was after the same boys ignored my warning and jumped up and landed on a little girl's toe, which caused the curly-haired diva to throw a tantrum.

In my classroom, we spent the morning using found instruments, like pop bottles, a trash can, and pot lids, including the one I just bought at the garage sale. The kids were delighted, except the two ornery hall-jumping toe smashers who had to forfeit their turns.

At lunchtime, I rushed to the art room with my food to hang out with my three buddies. We're generally called the "Specials" teachers, since we teach Music, Art, PE, and Gifted classes. One teacher called us the "babysitters," since the classroom teachers get planning periods while we teach their classes. Of course, we don't like that term. Students are tested in our subjects as well as the core subjects, but still, it's hard to convince some people that our classes are important too.

Besides being a teaching team, I could write a book about my adventures with Jules, Becca, and Jana.

When I walked into the art room, the first thing out of Jana's mouth was, "How the heck did you get in Bixby's Columbus Day Parade?"

What was she talking about? Oh, no. I felt my face grow hot. So, it was a Columbus Day Parade. I sat at the table staring at my cafeteria tray of chicken nuggets and tried to ask in a disinterested tone, "What makes you think I was in Bixby?"

"Because of the picture in the paper this morning." Jana held out a section of the <u>Bixby Bulletin</u> with a photo of a fire truck, my Liesel, and an ambulance all in a row. The headline read, "Biggest Turnout Ever at Annual Columbus Day Parade." I closed my eyes anticipating a good ribbing.

"Isn't this you waving from your car?" asked Jana.

Becca grabbed the paper. "Ha-ha! Check out your big smile."

"Why were you in the parade? Were you invited?" asked Jules.

I felt my face flush as I said quietly, "I made a wrong turn." There was a brief moment of silence then Becca's hand flew over her mouth. "Oh my gosh, you were looking for a garage sale, weren't you?"

Jules said, "I think you got it right. She's turning red!"

"Now it makes total sense," Jana nodded.

I quickly defended my actions. "I was heading for a really big estate sale, but I accidentally got in the line and couldn't get out, so I just started waving."

I demonstrated my wave, and we all laughed as they made obnoxious jokes. I shook my head, realizing I'd never live this one down. I sure couldn't tell them I'd had my car stolen, too. Just when I thought the joking was over, Becca came closer to me and touched my hair. "That hair color does nothing for you, Pity."

Nodding, I told about that story too. I changed the subject to the new school rules. Shaking my head, I said, "I don't care what he says, I'm still doing my skeleton song with the rattling bones."

"It's just ridiculous," said Becca. "And nobody can go on the playground? What is he thinking? He must have a really little willy and has to prove his manhood by taking charge."

Jules and I laughed, but Jana turned pink. She blushes when anything risqué comes up. But she still hangs around us.

Jules said, "This place is going to feel like prison soon. I wonder when he'll hand out the orange jumpsuits?"

I nodded and moved to another topic. "Becca and Jana, did you know anyone who went to Broken Arrow High School in 1997?" Both of them had grown up in BA so it was a safe bet they did.

Becca said, "My little brother, Jake, graduated in '97."

I didn't have time to tell them why I asked because the bell rang, announcing that recess was over.

As I walked back to my prefab, I decided not to involve these girls in the whole mysterious note project.

When I started class, the first thing out of a 2nd grader's mouth was, "Mrs. Kole, I saw you and your slug bug in the Bixby parade!"

Oh great. I said, "You did? Well, that's nice, Aaron."

"Why didn't you throw me any candy?" he asked, looking hurt.

"I forgot to take any with me." I lied. I shouldn't lie to a child, but what was I to do? I quickly got an idea to help him forget the whole thing. "Since you didn't get any candy from me and because your class is going to be extra good today, I'll let you pass around my apple. You can each enjoy a piece of candy while I tell you what Wolfgang Amadeus Mozart was like when he was about your age."

Yep, that appeased them all. I handed Aaron my big tin apple full of suckers. He walked to each child and waited while they chose one of the Dum Dums while I told the story of the musical child prodigy.

During my planning period after setting up instruments for my next class and working on my lesson plans, I checked my e-mail and found that the high school media specialist had responded. She had found the yearbook, marked staff members who were still employed there, and gave the book to Ren. I could hardly wait to see it.

I pulled out a phone book and looked up the parents of Justin Jones. They still lived in Broken Arrow, so I called the number, not having a clue what to say. A woman answered with a sweet, southern voice. "Hello? Jones residence?"

"Hi, is this Mrs. Jones?"

"Yes, it is. How can I help you?"

"Hi, Mrs. Jones, my name is Kitty Kole. I teach at Arrowstar Elementary school. My daughter is on the swim team at the high school, and I just ran across an article about your son's tragic death." All true so far.

"Oh?"

I continued with my newly formed plan, "The story touched me so much, that I thought I'd write an update in the high school's booster club newsletter. I hope it's not too painful to discuss, but I have a few questions about Justin and what he was like."

I worried that she may resent my questions, but she said sweetly, "Oh, Honey, I don't mind talking to you. We were devastated by his death, but it's been a long time. It's fine."

"Are you sure? I hate to bother you. "

"No, he was such a nice boy, and talking about him keeps him alive in my mind. Would you like to stop by after school today? I just made an angel food cake and would be happy to share it."

"Well, thank you, Mrs. Jones. I would love that. I'm always starving after school." I got her address and told her I'd see her around 4:00. How nice that she was willing to see me so quickly.

During a 5th grade class, I got a note from the secretary saying I had a delivery and to pick it up after school. Oh, no... not Kenny again.

I finished the school day by teaching kindergarteners a pumpkin song. Yes, a real pumpkin song – I peeled off the faces of the pumpkin puppets before letting the kids use them, and I changed a word in the lyrics from witches to bats. Bats are in nature, so I wasn't breaking any rules. I refused to delete a favorite activity for the little guys. They loved the pumpkin song and left the room singing it.

After school, I gathered my stuff and walked to the office to get my delivery. It was a big brown teddy bear with a Mylar balloon, saying, "I Like You a Lot."

As I read the card, I imagined Kenny writing it: *Kitty, I look forward to seeing your beautiful face again soon. Please have a Beary nice day?*

Seriously, what grown man writes Have a Beary Nice Day? Were all these gifts considered stalking or just plain weird?

As I walked out of the school holding the bear and balloon, Makala, a sweet girl with cerebral palsy sat in her wheelchair by the door. The teacher's aide stood by, ready to help her onto the bus. Makala smiled her crooked smile at me. When I handed her the bear and balloon, she made a gurgled squeal. I gave her a hug then headed to my car. Makala deserved a "Beary Nice Day" way more than I did.

I made my way to Mrs. Jones' house. My stomach growled with nerves and in anticipation of the angel food cake.

Her red brick home was similar to the one where I grew up. It had a well-manicured lawn and two large redbud trees. I rang the doorbell, smiling at the hay bales and pumpkins on the porch. A petite woman in her early seventies answered and invited me in.

I wiped my feet at the door and said, "Again, I am so sorry for your loss, Mrs. Jones." She directed me to her flowered couch and I added, "I'm sure you and Mr. Jones miss Justin very much."

"Oh yes, but unfortunately, I lost John last spring. He was ill for a few years. Cancer." Her sadness was evident in her posture.

I frowned. "Oh, my. You've been through so much. I'm so sorry." Scrambling for something more positive to say, I asked, "Do you have other children?"

"Oh, yes. Justin was the youngest of four, but the only boy. My girls are very good to me." Then, holding her hand beside her mouth in a secretive gesture she said, "But you know, they never thought it was an accident."

My mouth dropped open a bit. "What? Justin's death?"

She nodded; eyebrows lifted.

"Why is that?"

"He was the most agile person. Even as a toddler, he never fell down. He could balance himself on anything, so it seemed unnatural for him to slip in the pool and hit his head. But his father and I chose to believe the reports from the medical examiner and the police. I know accidents do happen."

"I see." I so wanted to ask more questions and even tell her about my findings, but I refrained from doing so out of respect.

She stood and said, "How about that cake?"

I followed her into her spotless kitchen to see if I could help. "It sounds like a great treat. I'm just like a kid; I have to have my afternoon snack."

I admired a handmade dish towel and got to the point. "Can you tell me a little about Justin? What was he like? Was he dating anyone? What were his dreams or hobbies?"

She nodded while folding two napkins, then placed forks on top of them. "Oh, I could go on and on. He wanted to swim in the Olympics. I don't know if he was really that good, but he did win a few medals at state meets and was certainly dedicated to the sport." She got an amazing-looking iced cake out of a cake keeper and cut the first slice. "He planned to be a doctor after the swimming ended. Such a smart boy. He had a nice girlfriend, Patty Sue. They spent a lot of time together, but they broke up shortly before the accident."

My stomach lurched at the thought of the girl with the notes. It all felt so real now. The name Patty Sue nagged at me – and not just because it sounded like a name from the 50s rather than the 90s. Then it hit me; the PS in the notes must have stood for Patty Sue instead of postscript? Now I had my second name.

Mrs. Jones placed the first piece on the dainty plate and handed it to me. I picked up a fork and napkin and asked, "Do you know why they broke up?"

"Oh, you know kids..." she shrugged, "probably some little squabble. She was very upset when he passed away and visited me once following the accident, but I didn't see her much after that."

We took our cake back to the living room. I tried to sit ladylike as I held the plate on my lap. "Was Patty Sue a swimmer?" I took a bite. Oh my, the cake was so moist and light.

"No, she wasn't. She went to all of Justin's meets, though."

I heard her, but all I could focus on was the cake. "This is delicious. Could I have the recipe? My daughters really love desserts and I have the worst sweet tooth."

"Well, certainly. It's just a box mix, but the topping is what makes it so good."

A box mix - ahh. Mrs. Jones and I had so much in common — well, except she was sweet, and refined with a house was neat as a pin. I wasn't sure how neat a pin was but figured this must be it. On the contrary, I was pretty goofy, and my house was about as neat as a busted pinata.

I swallowed. "As I said, my oldest daughter is on the swim team. So, I'm a swim mom like you were. It just breaks my heart that you lost Justin that way."

"Thank you, my dear"

I closed my eyes to savor the flavor of my last bite of cake, then I carried our plates back to the kitchen and set them carefully in the sink. "I should probably be going, Mrs. Jones. I was just curious about your son and wanted to see how you were doing."

"Well, aren't you just so sweet? Please call me Linda."

"Okay, Linda, if you want to go to a meet, you can come with me." I gave her a card with my phone number. "Call anytime."

She jotted something on a paper and handed it to me. It was the icing recipe - cool whip, dry vanilla pudding, and crushed pineapple. I could do that.

She walked me to the door. I took her frail hand in mine and looked into the eyes of a strong woman and said, "Thank you."

Once I left, I was too anxious to wait for Ren to get home from swim practice to see the yearbook, so I headed to her pool.

As I drove, I got a call from Mike. I wasn't sure why, but my heart beat faster. He said, "I hope you aren't still in school."

"Oh no, I'm free - I've been out for about an hour. Thanks for calling me back. And I'm sorry I interrupted your evening last night."

"You didn't interrupt anything."

"Are you sure? The woman said you were indisposed."

He chuckled, "Oh, I was at my sister's house on a ladder installing her new light fixture. When the phone rang, I dropped my screwdriver. She didn't tell me it was you until much later."

Well, that explained the giggle. I felt a hint of relief. He continued. "She's very protective. She thinks all women are out to hurt me."

"Why would she think that? That someone would hurt you?"

"Well...I had a pretty bad break-up a few years back. Nothing I couldn't handle." He paused. "Anyway, she doesn't want anyone to know that I'm available. Silly girl."

"Well, I guess you have to be the one to let girls know you are available."

"Evidently. Now how can I help you? Did you need me to get something else from your ex-husband?"

"Not this time. So, is it true you're a policeman?"

"Yes, I'm afraid it's true."

I stopped at a stoplight and took a deep breath, hoping my story didn't sound too lame. "Well, there was a death long ago in Broken Arrow and the official report stated it was an accident. But I recently found evidence that indicates it was actually murder. I need to be sure before I share it officially. Could you look up the case for me and see what measures they took in the investigation? Is that a possibility? Or would you get in trouble for looking into it?"

"I can probably get by with it since I have access to the records room. When was it? Maybe I can find someone who was involved in the investigation."

"Great." I released my breath. "So, it was a Broken Arrow High School swimmer named Justin Jones. He died in an apparent accident at the swimming pool in 1997. I'm convinced it wasn't an accident. And I just left his mom's house and she doesn't think it was either. I'll fill you in on the details once I hear what you find out."

There was a pause and I thought I went in a dead zone. Then he spoke again. "I thought Lin said you were a music teacher, not a private investigator." He said it seriously, but I laughed.

"I know. I'm out of my league, but I just have to know what happened to the poor kid, especially after meeting his sweet mother."

"Alright. I'll check on that tonight when I get to work. Can I call you tomorrow morning?"

"Sure, it'll have to be before 8:30 or during lunch from 11-11:25, otherwise I'll be in class."

"Okay, will do. Wait. You only have 25 minutes for lunch?"

"Yep, they don't want us to slack off and actually chew our food. Thanks a lot, Mike."

"You bet. I'll talk to you tomorrow, Pity," he said. Ooh. This guy was really nice.

Garage Sale Tip #8

Beware of a house in shambles.

Still buzzing with excitement from my conversation with Mike, I arrived at the large Aquatic Center. The word Natatorium had recently been attached above the entrance. Unfamiliar with the word, I googled it, and lo and behold, I discovered it was the name for a building holding an indoor pool. Ya learn something new every day!

I was excited to retrieve the yearbook and entered the humid, noisy pool area, and spotted Lauren right away. She stood behind the starting block, twirling her goggles on her finger and talking to Jennifer. Not wanting to interrupt her, I sat on a bleacher near the door and watched the high schoolers swim laps in all different strokes. I took a deep breath of the thick steamy air and relaxed a bit.

While glancing around the large room, I spotted the records board. Justin's name was listed in three events. Wow, nobody had beaten him in all these years? When I remembered that this was the very place he had died, my eyes filled with tears. I wiped my wet cheeks with my sleeve and shook my head to get a grip.

"Mom, what are you doing here? Is everything OK?"

Where had Ren come from?

"Yes, I'm fine. I just got splashed by some kid doing the butterfly," I lied and wiped my eyes.

"Right," she said sarcastically, "from 15 feet away?"

I looked at my distance from the pool. Must stop with the lies.

I stood and said, "Did you get a yearbook from Mrs. Green? I have something I need to look up and thought I'd pick it up now."

"Yeah. I got it. It's in the car. My keys are over there by my jacket." She pointed a few rows away.

""Hi, Mrs. Kole!" said a scrawny girl from the side of the pool. I tried to place her, but it's always hard to identify anyone wearing a swim cap. "It's me, Danielle Schrivner!"

"Oh hi, honey. I didn't recognize you without your long hair." Danielle was a former student of mine who struggled with popularity. Sweet girl. I always liked her and was glad to see she was swimming. "I'll be watching you tomorrow night! Good luck, Danielle."

She gave a big grin and slipped back in the water.

Ren said, "Well, I've gotta get back before Coach Hamm gets me. "But don't forget to bring my keys back."

"OK. See you at home." I walked over, got the keys, and went to her little green car to find the yearbook. I sat in her passenger seat, amid her school books, Taco Bueno cups, and an empty bag of chips and found the book on the floor. I glanced over the album noticing the librarian had placed sticky notes beside some staff members' photos. Well, look at that...Coach Hamm was there as an assistant coach back then. He would be the perfect one to ask since he had to know Justin.

Yearbook in hand, I went back to the pool area and replaced Ren's keys. A loud whistle echoed throughout the natatorium. I liked that new word and repeated it to myself a few times. Natatorium. Natatorium.

Coach Hamm walked alongside a swimmer shouting directions. The big man, who wasn't a typical swimmer type, wore shorts and deck shoes, which was fitting.

I headed towards the coach, carefully avoiding splashes. I didn't want my new leather shoes to get wet.

"Coach Hamm?" I said in a loud voice to be heard above the din. He sighed and closed his eyes as soon as he saw me, then asked, "Is it time for another fundraiser or swim team party?" His annoyance was fair. Being the swim team booster club president, I usually bombarded him with questions about swim team gatherings. "No. Not this time." I laughed and followed him as he walked poolside. "I understand you've been working here a while. I just have a few questions about a student who swam with you years ago." I tried to keep up with him as he urged a swimmer to speed up. "Can I ask you now, or would you rather wait 'til after practice?"

"Go ahead. Who are you interested in?" He blew his whistle, "Kick, Bennett, kick!"

My eyes crossed and ears rang from the whistle blast, but I managed to say, "Justin Jones. Were you here when he swam?"

I anticipated that he would turn to me when I mentioned the name, but he kept his eyes on the swimmer and didn't flinch.

"Yeah, I knew him. He was a pretty good swimmer." He pointed to the record board without looking up. "Guess you know he died?"

"Yes, I found an article about him. It's just terrible. I wondered if you knew who his girlfriend was? Or if he had any rivals at school?"

He scoffed. "I'm not a nursemaid and don't care about students' personal lives. I just coach swimming. Why do you want to know?"

I was ready with my excellent explanation and recited, "Oh, I'm just checking on previous star Broken Arrow swimmers for a swim booster newsletter. I thought I'd ask people who were close to them a few questions."

He nodded, so I figured I didn't sound too suspicious...until he asked, "Who else are you putting in the story?"

I was totally unprepared for that question and glanced up at the records board. Spotting a random name, I said, "Umm. Hickson. Do you know a Hickson?"

He looked at me, cocked his head. "Hickson just graduated last year," he paused, "but you should know that since you organized his Senior Salute." He smirked.

I stammered, "Oh, of course - I'm just so used to calling him Rudy. Sure, I'll just call up Rudy Hickson and ask him the questions. Well, thanks a lot, Coach. I'll see you at tomorrow's meet." I turned quickly; too quickly, and placed one foot, new shoe and all, in the pool.

I found myself in what must have been a hilarious-looking pirouette. Somehow, I managed to avoid falling in. I casually turned back around and asked, "Do you need any snacks for the swimmers tomorrow night?"

"No, it's covered." I felt him watching me as I left and hoped Lauren hadn't seen that ridiculous display. It must be very difficult to be my daughter.

I got to the car and shook out my shoe. Shoot, I'd meant to ask Coach Hamm if he was there when the "accident" happened, but I was so flustered being caught in the lie about Hickson that I forgot. I just drove home to pore over the yearbook before fixing dinner.

Once settled on my cozy green couch, I opened the yearbook and searched for Justin Jones. I found him right off the bat in the swim team photo and again in his senior picture. I sighed. There was that handsome boy with the sweet smile.

While I sat looking through the staff pictures, Ree came in from her room and stood, hands on her hips, "Where have you been?"

Suddenly, I felt I was back in high school with my parents grilling me for being out late. "Oh, I stopped by a lady's house and then your sister's swim practice for a minute."

She cocked her head. "Well, you didn't answer your phone."

"Oh, I'm sorry, honey. I must have left it in the car. Was there a problem?"

"Yes. Harriet is being held for ransom!"

"What?" I couldn't imagine anyone dognapping our mutt for ransom – although, after last year's incident, it was public knowledge I could imagine anything.

She frowned. "Remember, I had to have Harriet microchipped today for our History Day project? Caitlyn and I took her to the vet and they did it, but since we couldn't pay afterward, they made me leave her there until I bring the money back."

I sighed in relief. I didn't know how I could afford to pay a ransom, even for a dog. "Oh. So, Harriet is collateral. I knew you wanted to have her microchipped, but I didn't know it was today."

"Well, I thought I told you. But anyway, we have to take $45 to them before 6:00, or she'll spend the night there!"

I looked at my watch. Less than 30 minutes to go. "OK, let me write a check. $45 really? This sure is turning into an expensive school project."

"But Mom, just think. Now Harriet can be returned to us if she gets out."

I nodded. "True. Did you say Caitlyn is here? I'm surprised her mother let her come over so soon.

"She doesn't know I'm here." Caitlyn walked in from the hall. "Uncle Andy is going to pick me up and take me home before she gets back from a dinner meeting later."

"You guys are sure sneaky."

This is the third year the two girls have done a History Day project together. It is always a big ordeal, but worth it. Trish won't let them make a mess at her perfectly decorated home, so of course, they would work on it here.

Last year, they built a replica of the Berlin Wall including graffiti and real barbed wire. I can't tell how many pokes and scrapes I got during transport.

The year before, they built a bus for their Rosa Parks project. This year, the theme is technology, so they chose pet microchipping.

"Here is the payment. Let's get our dog out of hock." I grabbed my keys.

"It's okay. We'll walk," Ree said, "but we can't go past Mr. Jenkins' house again. He yelled at us and said if Harriet didn't stop barking at night, he's going to shoot her!"

Caitlyn agreed, "Yeah, he was really scary."

My mouth dropped open. "He said what?" What kind of man threatens two young girls? I have never gotten along with Mac Jenkins, but that just crossed the line.

A few years back, my little old neighbor, Mrs. Garmin, had a piece of the Jenkins' mail delivered to her house by accident, so she took it to him. He yelled at her to get off his property or he'd call the police. Poor little thing was really shaken.

Then last year, the neighborhood wanted to have a block party and close off our street for a two-hour potluck dinner, but he put up such a big stink about it that everyone just gave up on the idea. I ended up having a big dinner for the neighbors and invited everyone except him. It was great even though he called the police on us for being too noisy.

I always felt sorry for Mac's wife, a mousy woman so shy she never looked me in the eye, even when I greeted her. And their poor daughter is even more of a recluse, being homeschooled by the odd woman. I don't think I've seen her outside of the house since she was maybe 8 years old. As much as I worried about the teen, I was selfishly glad I never had to deal with Mac as a school parent.

I shook my head. "Don't you worry, girls. I'll deal with Mr. Jenkins."

The more I thought about it, the more riled up I got. Harriet doesn't even bark at night - she's always inside at the foot of my bed.

Granted, she snores so loud I could shoot her myself for keeping me awake, but when she looks at me with those sweet, dark brown eyes hidden under her mass of white hair, I keep letting her sleep with me.

Ree interrupted my thoughts. "Oh, and I borrowed your camera to capture the procedure for our presentation. Can you get those pictures printed tomorrow?"

"You took my good camera?" Sometimes this kid has gall.

She chewed her lip. "I knew you wanted us to have the most professional project," she debated, "and I was very careful."

"Well, I hope you were. You girls better get going and don't dawdle. Caitlyn, do you have time to stay for dinner?"

"Yes, Mrs. Kole! Thank you so much for inviting me."

Before the door shut, I heard Caitlyn say, "Your mom is awesome. My mom would never let me walk to a store."

Ree responded, "Yeah, Mom's pretty cool most of the time."

I fixed dinner with a smile; happy my girl gave me a compliment.

Everything was almost ready when Ren came in from practice with damp hair. "Mmm. Something smells good. Hey, Mom, what were you talking to Coach about? He was sure grumpy afterward."

"What's new? He's always grumpy to me." I figured I should tell Ren and said, "Oh, I was asking about a swimmer who died there in the 90s."

"Oooh, that's sad. Was it a guy or a girl?"

"It was a boy named Justin Jones. Here, bring the yearbook to me," I nodded to the book on the couch as I set the table. She handed it over, and I found his picture. "There he is." I pointed to the photo on a special 'In Memoriam' page. "He's on your records board. Guess nobody has been able to beat his time in three events."

She studied the photo. "He was sure cute. Why do you want to know about him?"

"It's a long story. I'll try to explain later, but not yet."

Lauren sat down at the table and flipped through the yearbook, pointing out people's hair and clothing styles. It wasn't long before she snickered, "Guess who I found?"

I asked, "Who?" She held the book pointing to a photo of a girl. "Just look," she said.

The face seemed familiar, but I couldn't place her. "Uncover her name, silly."

She said, "It's Trish! Check out her hair."

I looked closely at the picture and could see a definite resemblance. I wondered if Trish knew Justin and who he dated. I'd ask her, but she wasn't speaking to me.

I said, "Too bad the picture is black and white. I'd like to see how red her hair was back then. We'll have to show it to Caitlyn when she gets back."

Ren made a face. "Caitlyn is coming over tonight? Again?"

"I invited her for dinner. I still don't see what you have against her. She's so sweet."

"She's so annoying. Even more so than Ree."

"Well, be nice to her anyway," I warned.

As if on cue, the girls walked in with Harriet on a leash. The dog pulled Ree toward her water bowl and slurped a drink. Ree removed the leash and put it on its hook.

"Hi, Lauren!" Caitlyn called with enthusiasm when she saw Ren. She ran to her side.

With no expression, Ren said, "Hey, Caitlyn."

Standing a little too close to Ren, the younger girl babbled, "How are you? How's the swim team? Do you like your junior year? Are you dating anyone? I'm coming to your swim meet with Ree tomorrow. We'll cheer for you. I sure hope you win your races!"

Ren widened her eyes at me. I understood why Caitlyn annoyed her, but I figured the poor girl just wanted a big sister and had glommed onto Lauren.

"Dinner is ready. Wash your hands."

Ree huffed, "I'm starving. We walked to the vet's office twice, you know." The two 13-year-olds leaned over the sink to wash up. We all sat down and had a nice meal while the girls told Lauren all about mean Mr. Jenkins and how the vet microchipped the dog. Ree jumped up and showed us exactly where the chip had been inserted between Harriet's shoulder blades.

After the table was cleared, Caitlyn called her uncle Andy to come get her. As soon as Ren heard his name, she perked up and rushed away. I knew she thought the older boy was cute. Although he's nice, a guy in his 20s is out of my comfort zone for my 17-year-old. It wasn't long before the doorbell rang. Ren ran to the door first and leaned against the door frame casually. "Hi, Andy."

Now, how did she manage to dry her hair and put on makeup so fast? Interesting.

The tall, handsome young man said, "Hey, Lauren. How's school? Are you a sophomore this year?"

Ren's face fell, and I could tell his question deflated her ego.

I came in behind her. "Nope. She's a junior and is the captain of her swim team. How are you, Andy? I heard you got a job in management. Where are you working?"

"Yes, I just started at Hawkins Construction last week"

I lifted an eyebrow. "You don't know any yokels named Scott and Jay, do you?"

He shook his head. "I don't know many people yet, but I'll keep my eye out for them. Do you want me to say hi for you?"

"Oh no... definitely not. What I want is to never see them again."

He gave a crooked smile. "OK? Sounds like there's a story there."

When Ree came out from her room, Andy asked, "How's the project?"

She smiled. "Good! Thanks for letting Caitlyn come over."

"Hi, Uncle Andy," Caitlyn said as she came around the corner.

"OK, let's go, Kiddo," he said, putting his hand on her shoulder. "Good to see you all again."

When the door closed, Ren sighed and slowly walked to her room.

"Girls, it's time to get homework done. But first, whose turn is it for dishes?"

"Mine," said Ree soulfully as she trudged to the kitchen. I stayed in the living room and relaxed with the yearbook, flipping through other pictures of seniors, hoping to find anything interesting. I heard the clinking of pots and pans in the kitchen. Halfway through the J's, I saw a familiar face. I was surprised because I had thought this guy was much older. It was Mac Jenkins. Imagine that. Our "sweet" neighbor was a senior the year Justin died. Now I could imagine him killing someone. Time to go investigate.

It was only 8 pm and dark, but not too late to be out alone. I left my house and walked to his street without a plan - never a good idea, but it was my usual M.O. On my way, I saw the Bernsteins had an enormous inflated black cat. So lame. Then the cat turned its head to me. Ok. So that was pretty cool.

When I reached the Jenkins' house, I cased the joint. From the street, I could see clearly through the windows, but I moved through the tall weedy yard to get a good view of the living room. Mac sat in an easy chair holding a beer. He barked something at his wife.

I wondered if this could be the couple in question from 1997 - not much love there. What was her name? I couldn't remember. Had I ever even known her name or just heard him call her "the woman"?

I got bold and walked right up the steps of the moonlit porch, dodging empty beer cans and full ashtrays to reach the doorbell. I stalled, looking at the paint chips on the frame of the door, thinking it would be fun to peel them, but that wasn't why I was there. I pressed the filthy bell and heard nothing. Figuring it was broken, I knocked on the door and waited.

After a minute, the homely daughter opened the door and a big waft of cigarette smoke came my way, making me cough. It was difficult to see the girl through the smoke-stained screen, but I could tell her head was bowed down. She turned on the porch light and pulled the screen door open a crack. I still couldn't see her eyes because her long greasy hair covered her face. She said nothing.

In the friendliest voice I could muster, I said, "Hi, you know me. My name is Kitty Kole. I live four doors down?" I ducked my head trying to locate her eyes, but to no avail, and kept talking. "I wanted to know if I could speak to your mother. Now, what's her name?"

After a moment she said, "Susan," so quietly I barely heard her.

"Oh, that's right. Susan. I remember now. You know, come to think of it, could I talk to your father instead?"

The girl actually lifted her face up a little with what I took as surprise. She mumbled, "Hold on." My eyes had gotten accustomed to looking through the screen, and I watched the poor girl lumber across the room with stooped shoulders. She wore a baggy t-shirt and even baggier jeans. When she said something to her father, the big disheveled man got up and walked to the door in large strides.

When he saw me, his unshaven face turned red. As soon as he approached, I could smell his body odor emanating through the screen door. I nearly gagged at the combination of stale smoke, beer, and B.O., but I kept my cool.

He opened his wide mouth and a green fog of funk came out, or at least that's what I imagined would accompany the foul odor. He growled, "Not only do you have an f-ing dog that keeps me up all night, but you interrupt my family in the evening?"

While trying to hold my breath, I said firmly, "Mr. Jenkins, I know we haven't always seen eye to eye, but you have no right to threaten my daughter!"

"I didn't threaten her. I was threatening that mop of a dog you own. Shut that thing up or else." He spit as he spoke, but luckily the screen caught the spittle, so I was spared.

Enunciating each word clearly and with force, I warned, "If you ever touch my dog, threaten, or even talk to one of my children again, I will call the police. Understand, Mac?"

He slammed the door in my face and flipped off the light, leaving me in darkness. Jerk! I let out a shaky breath and started home. At least I had gotten his wife's name.

When I got back, the dishes were done, Harriet snored from her day's excitement, and the girls were in their rooms. I hoped they were doing their homework. I got the yearbook and looked through pictures searching for Susan Jenkins. I found her – Susan Parks, a junior in '97. She was almost unrecognizable as a pretty, confident teen.

I flipped back and forth among the three pictures: Justin, Susan and Mac, wondering if this could possibly be the triangle; what a crazy coincidence if it was. Her name was Susan, and that could be a middle name, so she could be the Patty Sue. The only thing that didn't make sense was the sweetness the writer showed in his notes. I couldn't imagine Mac Jenkins ever saying nice things, and I figured he was even less likely to write notes. But I guess people can change after that many years.

Garage Sale Tip #9
Watch out for policemen.

The next morning, I was dying to hear from Mike to learn whether he found out anything about the case. But I managed to lead the classes in all of their activities despite my distraction.

When Mrs. Shick brought her 4th grade class to me, she grumbled in frustration. "For some reason, these kids have decided they don't need math anymore. They balk every time we start."

When she left, I decided to spend part of my class teaching them a song I had written a while ago about math. To be honest, one reason I wrote the song was to convince myself *I* needed math.

"I hear some of you don't want to learn math. Is that right?"

A few kids nodded their heads, and one boy said, "I hate math!"

I dropped my mouth open dramatically and said, "Ryan, how did you know the name of my song?" I handed out the song sheets and the kids looked at the papers laughing when they read the title, "I Hate Math." I went on to sing the chorus and the first verse.

I hate math. Math hates me
Who really cares what 3 x 3 is?
I won't learn it. No one can make me
Math is a problem and don't mistake me

Count me out. It makes me sick.
Don't teach me arithmetic 'cause
I'll never use it. Yes, I refuse it.
Math is a problem I don't need.

I think I'll take a little vacation,
to get away from multiplication
Now how much is that gas,
If I want five gallons, how long will it last?
How fast are we going? How much longer will it be?
This sounds like math I'm turning green

The song went on to include other examples of why we needed to learn math and ends by admitting math is OK.

The kids picked up the tune quickly and sang it to Mrs. Shick when she came back to get them.

At first, she glared at me like...*You're teaching them a song called "I Hate Math"?* But after listening to the rest, she said, "You scared me for a minute, but that was clever. Thank you."

As the group left, a girl said, "I like your song a lot," and she gave me a hug. This is the best perk of being a teacher: hugs, lots of hugs. See what Dr. L is missing?

After my playground duty, I sat in the art room with my buddies, gossiping about the new hunky student-teacher n Mrs. Ball's class.

Becca said, "I wouldn't get any teaching done if he was in my class all day."

I ate my bland pizza from my tray while Jules made samples of line drawings on the whiteboard for her 5th-grade art class. I could watch her draw for hours. Such talent!

Then I remembered the yearbook. "Hey, I brought this BAHS yearbook from 1997. Becca, do you remember any of your brother's friends?" I held the book out to her.

Becca put down her protein drink and squealed, "Oh, let me look!" She leafed through the yearbook, her super long earrings touching the page. She pointed to her little brother.

Jana looked over Becca's shoulder. "Look at Jake's face. He's such a baby. And to think he's got four kids of his own now."

Jules was still busily drawing masterpieces on the board, but turned her head toward me and piped up, "Why do you want to know who went to the high school in '97?"

"It's a project I'm working on for the swim team booster club." A natural-born skeptic, Jules probably didn't believe me, but she was so busy working on her artwork she didn't say anything else.

I asked Becca, "Jake wasn't on the swim team, was he?"

"No. He played trumpet."

"Ahh, now there's a boy after my own heart," I said, having spent my whole school career in band.

She flipped to another page and said, "Eew. I hated that guy." She shuddered. "He was always so creepy. He came over to our house to work on English projects with Jake. I was just sure he would rape or kill me in the night."

"Which one is he?" I said, wondering if it might be Mac Jenkins. I moved over to join the two looking at the book.

"The guy with the long greasy hair, Marcus Fisher." She pointed to an odd-looking boy. I typed the name Marcus Fisher onto my new phone list titled "Suspects" just underneath the only other entry, Mac Jenkins.

"And I was right, too." Becca added, "He ended up going to prison in Okmulgee for rape and aggravated assault. Just think, it could have been me he attacked." She shuddered.

"Oooh," I said, a little creeped out. It sure made me wonder if he could be the one.

When my phone rang and I saw the caller, I jumped up so fast my thigh banged the short table. I rubbed my leg and hobbled outside to take the call. I knew three sets of eyes were following me as I left.

"Hi, Mike. What did you find out?"

"Well, after reading the reports and talking to some of the older officers who investigated the Jones' death, it sure looks like it was an accident. It seems Justin was earning extra money by cleaning the pool after hours. So, a few days after the state meet, he was at his normal job cleaning and apparently slipped into the pool. He hit his head on the deck and drowned. The only thing that seemed odd was that there was usually a janitor or coach there while he worked. But on that night, he was alone in the pool area."

"Did they interview the coaches? The janitors? The girlfriend? Other students?"

"Yes. Nobody seemed to be suspect. No mention of a girlfriend."

"Oh," I sighed. "I hoped for a clue. You didn't copy the report, did you?" I made a hopeful face that of course, he couldn't see.

"I did, but I can't give it to anyone. Maybe you could just happen to glance at it over my shoulder at say... early dinner tonight?"

Oooh, that sounded good in two ways. "Tonight would be great. My daughter, Lauren, has a swim meet is at 7. Would 5:30 work?"

"That's great since I have to work at seven. How about Goldie's?"

"I love Goldie's - especially the pickles, and the cheeseburgers, and the okra. Do you usually work nights?"

"Yes. 7-3. It's not my favorite, but I'm used to it. Being single, I don't have to be home in the evenings for anyone, plus my days are free to be outdoors."

"I see. Well, I'll meet you there at 5:30. Oh, and I have a neighbor problem I need to discuss with you, too."

"And you'll actually tell me what you're involved in?" he asked.

"Of course. See you then." I walked back in the art room with a smile that I forgot to wipe off and all three girls stared at me.

"Who was that?" sang Jules. "Look, Pity's all flushed."

"I think she's got herself a man," teased Becca, who had more than her share of men interested in her.

"It WAS a man," I said and struck a provocative pose and batted my eyelashes. "But he's just a friend."

"Sure," said Jules sarcastically.

Jana joined in, "Just like Kenny?"

My face sank. "Oh my gosh! Speaking of Kenny, he sent me a teddy bear yesterday and wrote *Have a Beary Nice Day*. I don't know how to get rid of him." I shook my head. "But this guy is a policeman friend of Lin's. He seems nice and normal."

"Oooh, a policeman? Watch out, he could arrest you," said Jules.

Becca added, "Or handcuff you!" When she made a suggestive gesture, Jana looked down at her lunch.

I endured five more minutes of the taunting and was thankful when the bell rang, so I could leave.

Back in my classroom, since we were caught up on the lessons I had given, I decided to use an activity that would give me a break from standing, singing or dancing all afternoon: Surprise Puppet Day. I pulled out my giant box of puppets and once the first class arrived, I told the kids to prepare a song, to be "sung" by a puppet. Some shy children won't sing by themselves, but they will let their puppets sing. It's really fun to watch the transformation.

I put the kids in groups and had them practice their routine for 15 minutes while I observed them. I made notes in a notebook — mostly about the students, but I also jotted notes about the case.

The majority of the singing puppets sounded pretty bad with unrecognizable songs – even after disclosing the name, but the kids had fun. Some were very good. One cow puppet sang "Somewhere, Over the Rainbow" so beautifully, I wished I recorded it.

When a third-grader, obsessed with The Beatles, had a fluffy dog puppet sing one of my favorites, "Yesterday," I actually teared up; partly because the dog reminded me of Harriet, and also because I couldn't help think of Justin.

After school, I stopped by Walgreen's to pick up Ree's photos

When I walked into our living room, Ree and Caitlyn sat in the middle of the floor surrounded by posters, markers, papers, rulers, and Harriet. They were arguing about which girl had the best handwriting and, hence, who should do the lettering.

"Here are your pictures," I said, handing them the packet.

"Thanks, Mom!" they said together.

"I mean, Mrs. Kole," Caitlyn said with a slight apologetic lift of her shoulders.

I smiled at her flub. "Does your momr know you're here today?"

"Yes, she said I could ride the bus home with Ree, so we could work on the project. She also knows I'm going to the meet, but reminded me again that I won't be swimming next year and that I shouldn't even think about it."

Ree made a puzzled face. "Why won't she let you swim?"

"She's afraid the chlorine will damage my skin, or that I'll get too tired. I'll be lucky if I get to join the debate team." She furrowed her brows. "I can't get hurt on a debate team, can I?" We shook our heads.

Changing the topic, I said, "If you two need anything for Halloween costumes, let me know soon so can look at garage sales. Or are you too old to go trick or treating?"

Ree answered, "I'll never be too old. I want to trick or treat until I have my own kids. And when they have kids, I'll take my grandkids."

I couldn't help but chuckle at that. "Hey girls, I'm going to go meet a friend for dinner. You can come with me or stay here and find something to eat." I counted on them wanting to remain at home. "Can we make biscuit pizzas?" asked Ree, lifting her eyebrows. "Only if you remember to take them out of the oven and turn it off, so we don't get another visit from the fire department."

"If you remember, Mom, that was you who left the roast in the oven to burn when you went to a garage sale." Ree pursed her lips.

It was true. My neighbor, Mrs. Garmin, saw smoke billowing from the windows and called 9-1-1. I'd never had so many handsome men waiting for me when I got home. But I had to get a new front door since they broke it down to get in. "OK. Fair enough. I'll be back by a quarter to seven to pick you up for the meet."

I left them to discuss microchipping, costumes, and pizza while I went to put on mascara. I studied my reflection in the bathroom mirror: a so-so complexion and distinctly wide German Kole nose but overall, a pleasant face when I smile. Must remember to smile more. I lifted my bangs to see if I could ever live without them. Nope. When I'm 90 years old, I'll still have bangs. Then there was the slight green tint to my hair. It was not so bad now, but still visible.

I stepped back from the mirror to see if my jeans were too short. Finding pants long enough for my 5'10" frame was a challenge. That's why I prefer summer when I can wear shorts and skirts.

I always coordinate my earrings with each activity whenever possible. Since I was going to a swim meet, I wore earrings with dangling swimmers. If had pickle earrings, I'd wear them to Goldie's. Who knows? Maybe I'll find a pair at a garage sale someday.

When I arrived at the restaurant, Mike stood beneath the Goldie's Patio Grill sign. He was striking in full uniform, complete with a weapon, and sunglasses. For some reason, he looked familiar in the uniform. He smiled, then opened the door for me. A gentleman! Nice. Quite a switch from the last guys I joined for dinner.

"You didn't have to dress up just for me," I said, jokingly.

"I even brought handcuffs; in case I need them."

My eyebrows flew up like, "What?"

He quickly clarified, "In case I have to arrest you...I mean somebody." His face turned pink. "I mean, I have to go to work and wouldn't have time to change," he sighed, still a little flustered.

"I kind of figured," I said. We laughed uncomfortably as the hostess led us to the green vinyl booth nearest the pickle bar. I asked, "I'll get the pickles. What kind do you want?"

"All of them," he said and sat down.

I went to the long bar of pickles and filled four small, brown plastic bowls, each with a different type of pickle, heaping one bowl especially high. "Here ya go," I said. I sat across from him and began munching on the bread and butter pickles, the only kind I eat. I love the cool sweet, salty crunchiness of the corrugated slices.

The server arrived, and I ordered iced tea with extra ice, the Goldie's Special with cheese, well done, and fried okra for my side. Mike ordered the Special with onion rings and a D.P.

I smiled at him. "Well, here we are. But before we begin..." I looked up at Mike, "...I should address the elephant in the room."

He cocked his head.

"Please disregard my hair color. That bag of goo you saw me with when you stopped by the house didn't do what I hoped."

He shrugged and studied my hair. "Well, it's a little different, but who wants to be like everyone else?"

I blew out a sigh and bit into a pickle. He crunched on a dill slice and said, "I don't know what you know about Justin's death, but the police interviewed everyone and they found nothing fishy.

"Well... the pool was chlorinated."

Mike narrowed his eyes, then groaned at my terrible joke.

I put my hands flat on the table. "OK, I guess I should explain." I told him what I had found in the desk then took the crinkled papers from my purse, and handed them to him. "Can I look at the report over your shoulder now?"

He opened the manila folder and set it beside him. As I moved across to sit next to him, I noticed his fresh scent. Was that Irish Spring? Hmmm. It WAS manly, and I DID like it too.

We both read in silence. I checked the names of the people who were interviewed. According to the coaches, Justin had told them he wouldn't be long cleaning. since nobody had swum there in a few days, so they just left. The custodian who found Justin assumed a coach was with him or would have been in the pool area. A few teachers were interviewed, but they gave no new information. His friends were devastated by his death. Nothing else seemed unusual. I propped my head on my hands and imagined the 1990s scene:

Justin waves to the coaches and goes back to work, singing "Whoomp! There It Is, Whoomp! There It Is", while scrubbing the tile around the pool in rhythm.

Not long afterward, Mac Jenkins enters (I needed a face to go with my imagined story) and says "Justin, you got Patty Sue pregnant! You're gonna pay because I love her!"

Justin turns in surprise. "Pregnant? I don't know what you are talking about." He moves toward Mac and tries to calm him down. "I know you have a class with her, but I didn't know you loved her."

(Ok, so my imagined dialogue is really lame, but it's the best I can do from the info at hand.)

The perpetrator pushes Justin's feet out from under him, causing him to hit his head on the side of the pool. Mac watches as Justin sinks further into the water, then turns to leave.

I winced at the gruesome scene I had just pictured.

Mike said, "You know you should turn these in officially." He looked at me with concern.

"So, you think the clues are real?"

He nodded slowly. "And it looks like they are pointing to this particular case."

"Right?" I was excited to have him confirm my suspicions and said, "And I am even more convinced after speaking with Justin's mother today. But I want to do a little more checking before I hand it over. Is that illegal?"

"Withholding evidence in an active case would be illegal, but since it's closed, it probably isn't. However, you could be in danger if you poke around the wrong person."

"Everyone keeps telling me that," I nodded, "but I doubt anyone who was involved is still around." Of course, Mac Jenkins was still stuck in my head, as little as I wanted him to be there.

"You never know," he warned.

The waitress arrived with our food, so we pushed our papers across the table from us. I don't know why I didn't move back to my original side, but Mike didn't seem to mind sitting by me. I took in a deep whiff of the yummy food and dipped my burger in the ketchup on my plate and took a bite. Delish.

Wiping ketchup from my lips, I said with food still in my mouth, "I actually have an idea of who it could be."

He looked at me, and his eyes widened, probably disgusted by my bad manners. So, I swallowed, took a drink, and told him all about Mac Jenkins, including the confrontation over Harriet and the fact that he was in Justin's class in 1997. "I used to think he was just creepy, but now I think he could have killed poor Justin. What do you think?"

"Well, it sounds like we need to keep an eye on him no matter what since he threatened your dog. You know you can file a complaint." He looked at me as he took a drink of his Dr. Pepper.

"I'll wait a while. I may have scared him with my counter-threat." I ate the bonus fry on my plate.

He shook his head, "I doubt it." He looked squarely into my eyes and said, "I can't believe you just walked up and confronted someone like that."

Gee, when did Mike's eyes turn so blue? Amazing. Must be the dark blue uniform. I blinked and responded, "Yeah, I have a slight problem. They say I'm impulsive."

"Well, that trait could get you in hot water someday," he warned, not knowing how much of my life I'd spent in warm to boiling water.

I asked, "What should my next step be?"

He gave me a crooked smile. "Hand it over to the police and go back to being a music teacher. That's your next step."

"Well, that's not going to happen. Not yet, anyway. Maybe I can get a class list?"

"You are impossible." He frowned, then chuckled. "Well, be careful and let me know if you need anything. And keep your cell phone with you at all times."

"I will." I noticed onion ring crumbs on his face so I reached over and wiped them off. He gave me a cute smirk.

Embarrassed that I'd touched his face like that, I apologized. "Oh, sorry. Too much time with kids".

"That's OK. You can wipe my crumbs off anytime."

Was that a flirt? Hmmm. I dismissed it just in case that wasn't what he meant and said, "Well, I guess I need to go pick up the girls for the meet." I started collecting my notes and purse.

"Kitty...," he said, "or should I call you Pity?"

I stopped fiddling with my keys and looked at Mike's rugged face then shrugged. "I don't care what you call me." I refrained from adding 'as long as you call me'.

He said slowly, "Well..."

I knew it. He was going to tell me I was a crazy person and should leave him alone. I readied myself to hear the final goodbye.

"I was wondering... if you might like to go with me to the giant flea market in Sand Springs this weekend?"

What? He wants to go somewhere with me? And not only that, to Junquefest? I've always wanted to go there, but I decided to play it cool and not get overly excited.

I tilted my head casually. "I think I have Saturday morning free," I nodded. "Mind if we go early, so we can get the best stuff?" I spoke a bit faster, "It sounds like fun." Even faster and louder, "Can we take your truck in case I find something big? I've always wanted to go to Junquefest." I let go of a "Yahoo!" So much for hiding my excitement.

He laughed. "You bet. We'll go early and take the truck. I'll call you later to shore up the plans."

I could barely contain my excitement as he paid the bill. As we walked to the car, I said, "Thanks for helping me, Mike, and for the yummy meal."

"You are most welcome." When I unlocked my car he said, "Do you like your bug?"

"I love it. I've wanted one for years and finally got her. Her name is Liesel."

He nodded as if that made sense. "Well, have fun at the meet, and don't get into trouble."

"OK." I wondered if I should hug him, or maybe shake hands, but nothing felt right so I just gave a little wave, and said, "I'll try to stay out of trouble. Can't wait to go to Junquefest on Saturday." I hopped in my car feeling giddy. Was it in anticipation of Junquefest or having a new male friend? I mean, I love my girls and girlfriends, but there is something about spending time with a guy, especially one that's nice, handsome, and smells amazing.

Garage Sale Tip #10

It's OK to buy something just because you might need it someday.

Back at the house, I was glad to see the oven was off, so no firemen greeted me. All was right with the world and the three of us took off for the swim meet.

I was glad the first meet of the season was at home, so I could check out the scene of the crime again. When entering the pool area, I was instantly hit with the thick humidity. I found it hard to breathe and could actually feel my hair begin to frizz. I glanced at my camera and frowned to see the lens had fogged over.

I usually sat with Lin at the meets, but she had to work on an apartment tonight so the girls and I found seats about five rows up in the middle. The concrete bleachers are never comfortable, but each row is tall enough that people's heads don't get in the way, so at least we had a great view of the entire pool. I scoped out the scene and found Lauren standing with her teammates. One boy stood extra close to her. That must be Chris, I nodded. Oh, sure, I knew which one he was. A nice kid. I picked up my camera and was glad to see the lens had already cleared. I took a few shots of the two. Then I photographed the pool and the records board, just in case I'd need them later.

Caitlyn and Marie were busy pointing and giggling - probably at the boys in their Speedos. Coach Hamm glanced up at me, so I gave a little wave, but he looked away.

I heard a cackle and turned to find Todd and Smelly Shelly sitting to the left of us. At least they were up a row, so I wouldn't have to see them every time I looked at the pool. Shelly was all decked out in a short red skirt, a black flowered low-cut top, and her signature big hair. Who gets dolled up for a swim meet? Obviously, Shelly does.

The crowd stood as the Star-Spangled Banner played. The recording had a warbled echo as if it had been recorded in the pool underwater. Maybe I should try to find a better version of the national anthem that didn't sound so awful.

Then, sitting back on our cold, hard concrete seats, we watched the first group of swimmers step onto their platforms. They positioned their goggles and readied themselves for the first race. The gun fired and the girls dove as far out as they could, hitting the water with a splat. The splashing began. Being mostly junior varsity swimmers, this wasn't a fast heat. It took quite a while for some of the young girls to reach the other side of the pool, make their awkward turns, and head back.

The real excitement is always when the varsity boys compete. The water churns as if it's boiling. It's so hard to believe how strong they are. But, of course, my favorite races are any that Ren swims.

I shouted, "Go Danielle!" when I realized my little friend was swimming. I snapped a few photos of her. Although she came in second-to-last, she was still going faster than I'd ever seen her move – even on land. Good for her!

I looked up at the records board and saw Justin's name again and hoped that his records would stand for many more years. His mother really should come to a meet, if for nothing else but to see the board.

Across from me, I recognized an older woman with flawless dark skin and a headscarf tied around her hair. It was Mrs. Bates, Ren's math teacher from last year. The more I looked at the pretty scarf, the more I thought it a great idea to cover my green frizzy hair, but I didn't want to be accused of cultural appropriation.

I remembered Mrs. Bates had taught at Broken Arrow High School a long time, I headed that way to talk to her.

"Hi, Mrs. Bates? I'm Kitty Kole, Lauren Peters' mother," I said, and sat down next to her.

She looked up and with a super high, babyish voice, said, "Oh yes, hello. That's right, Lauren is a swimmer, isn't she?" I remembered how Ren used to imitate Mrs. Bates' high voice.

"Yes, she's the captain of the girl's team," I bragged.

"Well, isn't that nice? She's a very sweet girl, but she had trouble with her equations," she squeaked at a fast pace except for the last word in each phrase, which she drew out.

"I know. Unfortunately, she takes after me on that." Gee, my voice sounded like Darth Vader's after hearing this woman speak. I continued, "I was wondering how long you have been teaching at Broken Arrow High."

She calculated in her head, a skill I've never had, and answered, "I've been at the high school for 28 years. I'm retiring next year!"

"Lucky you. I'll be teaching at least another 15." I made a face. "So, did you happen to know Justin Jones?" I pointed up to the large black board sporting names, numbers, and dates.

Her face sank a little. "Yes, I had Justin in my class for two years." Her voice was still high, but softer. "He was very bright and sweet, but he could be a pest. He cracked a lot of jokes in class, but, honestly, he was so funny I didn't even mind."

"Oh, I see. Do you happen to know who taught in room 202 back then?" I knew that sounded odd, but she wasn't fazed.

"Well, I've been in room 206 since I started. Room 202 is just a few doors down on the right." She paused and cocked her head, "I'm pretty sure it was Mr. Murphy, because my son, Steven, was in his class with Justin." She said, "Why do you want to know?"

Crap. Why would I want to know that? "Well, it's rather silly. I just bought a chair at a garage sale and it said BAHS room 202, and I was just curious." Lame, but true. I continued, "Is there a way to find out who else was in his classes that year?

She squinted. "So now you want to find out who actually sat in your chair?"

I laughed. "Oh, no. Of course not!" Even though that was exactly what I wanted to know. "I'm writing an article about Justin." The more I talked about the fake article, the more I considered actually writing it. "Was Steven friends with Justin?"

"Yes, they were very close. They were on the state championship 400 freestyle relay team together." She pointed to the records board. S. Bates. "That's why I still come to the meets. I just can't get swimming out of my blood."

"Do you think I could speak to your son?"

She smiled and sounded like she had sucked in some helium. "Of course! Steven lives in Dallas now, but he'd be happy to talk to you." She jotted his number on a deposit slip and handed it to me.

I smiled. "Thanks so much. I look forward to speaking with him. Oh, is Mr. Murphy still teaching?"

"No. He retired about four years ago."

I looked at the pool. "Oh, Lauren's getting ready to swim. I handed Mrs. Bates a business card. "Please contact me if you think of anything else."

I thanked her again and went back to my seat to make sure the girls were paying attention. Surprisingly, Ree and Caitlyn were watching the action way more closely than I had been. I focused my attention and my camera on Ren as she got ready for her 200 Individual Medley swim. She took off with her usual graceful dive. I worried that she wasn't kicking hard enough in her butterfly, but she kept pace with the others and even inched ahead with her flip turn.

Caitlyn asked, "Why did she change the way she's swimming?"

I started to answer, but Ree explained, "This is the individual medley. Each girl swims four different strokes - one whole length of each. This is the backstroke." I was impressed that Ree knew what was going on, since she usually reads a book during the meets.

"Yeah, I can see why it's called the backstroke. What's next?" asked Caitlyn.

"The breaststroke," I said. "It's her best event."

Sure enough, as Ren made the turn into the breaststroke, she pulled ahead swiftly and took the lead. Last came the freestyle, which I still call the American Crawl, since that's what I learned at Girl Scout camp. I was a pretty good swimmer but never swam competitively.

I held my breath as I often do while watching my daughter swim.

"That other girl is catching up!" yelled Caitlyn.

"GO LAUREN!" we all shouted, which is funny because I'm pretty sure she can't hear anything while underwater.

I watched anxiously as the girl from Owasso beat Ren by only the length of a hand. That's OK, I told myself. The time was Ren's personal best in the IM. We stood and clapped as she pulled herself out of the pool. She bent over to catch her breath as water dripped from her suit. She took her goggles off, looked up at us, and shrugged. I'm sure she was disappointed, but when I pointed to my watch and gave her thumbs up, she smiled. The coach came by and said something to her, and her shoulders drooped. What had he said?

I was having a good time until Todd and Shelly stopped by on their way to the concession stand. "Hey, squirts," said Todd to the girls. He handed Ree $5 to get snacks. They ran off, giggling.

I wasn't sure if they were happy to get the snacks or because a couple of middle school boys were hanging out by the snack bar. "Well, lookie," said Shelly in an obnoxious singsong tone. "I guess the hair products at Walmart don't work so well. What an unusual color," she cackled as they moved on.

I considered tripping her to see if she would bleed red or some alien color, but I took the high road and gave her the finger behind her back instead. Of course, I didn't, but I sure thought about it. That's the kind of thing you must refrain from when you're a mother, a school teacher, and a part-time church choir director.

My phone rang and Kim's face popped up. I answered it and said, "I'm at a swim meet. Hold on." I climbed down the bleachers and went to the lobby, so I could hear. "What's up?"

"Just checking to see how your investigation is going?"

"Actually, I do have some stuff to tell you. Can you and R.A. come over tomorrow at 6:00 to celebrate the beginning of Fall Break and have beer and pizza? I'll tell you then."

"Sure. We'll be there, and I'll bring a salad."

"Great. See you then!" I could always count on Kim to add the green to a meal.

I went to the bathroom before heading back to the stands. While I was in the stall, I heard Shelly's voice on the phone from another stall saying, "And her hair was frizzy. I swear it was the worst color, sort of green. I don't see what Todd ever saw in that plain Jane. And what kind of name is Pity? She's just a stupid nobody."

I waited, trying not to make a sound until she was gone. My face fell. I tried not to feel hurt. After all, it was Shelly speaking, and I've probably said worse about her, but nobody wants to hear that. I vowed right then and there in the bathroom stall, not to talk behind people's backs from now on if I could help it.

When I returned, I had trouble getting in the spirit of the meet, but I pepped up when Ren came in first in the 100-meter breaststroke. Just looking at her happy face made me smile. Her teammates slapped her wet back, and I felt proud.

Ree said, "I knew she could do it. Next year, I'll be down there." I raised my eyebrows at my little one. That was the first I had heard she was interested in swimming.

"I wish I could join the swim team, too," said her buddy. I felt sorry for Caitlyn again.

Before we left, Ren brought Chris by to meet me. He seemed nice enough.

I warned, "Don't stay out too late. You have school tomorrow."

"I know, Mom. Everyone has school. I'll be home by 11:00. And yes, I already finished my homework," she said with an excited smile.

As the younger girls and I crossed the parking lot to the car. Ree grumbled, "Mom, you got another parking ticket."

"Oh, great." That's all I needed. I looked around the car, wondering if I'd parked in a handicapped spot, but I was in the clear, and furthermore, I couldn't see any other parking violations. I took the ticket from underneath the wiper blade and sighed as I read:

This citation was given for the following infractions:
1. proceeding through life in a reckless manner
2. distracting an officer before the line of duty
3. failure to allow plenty of space between you and your dinner date.

I smiled as soon as I read infraction #2 and continued reading.

4. exceeding the limit of sweet and sour pickles in one sitting
5. parking your nose in places it probably shouldn't be
You are summoned to appear at Junquefest on the date of October 19 at 7:30 a.m. Failure to do so will be grounds to revoke all garage sale privileges.
Signed, Officer M. Potter

I beamed, realizing my new friend was a clever son-of-a-gun. I reread the ticket and sighed. Finally, a guy who wasn't boring or disgusting.

Ree opened the door and grumbled, "Are you going to just stand there? We have school tomorrow, you know."

"Oh yeah." I got in and started Liesel. After we dropped off Caitlyn at her house. I turned to Marie, "You'll be a great swimmer next year."

She grinned all the way home. I grinned too, but for another reason. Someone didn't think I was a nobody.

I had trouble sleeping, still buzzing from my interactions with Mike and thinking about all I'd learned today that might help my investigation. Tomorrow, I would try to find a former teacher named Mr. Murphy and call a friend of Justin's named Steven Bates. Once my list was secured in my brain, I could relax enough to sleep.

On my way to school the next day, I saw an estate sale at the end of my block. Although it looked intriguing, I used my willpower and kept driving.

The morning was uneventful, except a kid in my kindergarten class threw up on his tambourine. Luckily it was a plastic one and easy to clean. The boy was fine – he said he just ate too many pancakes, which is probably why my room smelled like maple syrup the rest of the day.

At lunch, my buddies asked me about "The Policeman."

They quizzed, "How old is he? Has he been married before? Does he have any kids? Where's he from? Where did he go to school? How long has he lived in Broken Arrow?" Those were just a few of their questions and I didn't know the answers to even one. I figured I should grill Mike when I see him next time.

I finally had time to tell the girls about my horrible blind date downtown. They shook their heads, and Jana said, "Pity, I can't believe you actually went to the bar after such a terrible dinner."

I shrugged.

Becca said, "I would have dumped them at the first burp."

Jules said, "I have no desire to be 'out there' again."

During my planning period, I called my friend, Carol Hobbs, who works at the high school. She was our secretary at Arrowstar for years, and everybody loved her, but she couldn't stand working for Dr. L., so she got a new job at the high school.

I asked her if she happened to have the roster from Mr. Murphy's class in 1997. She said, "We don't have those kinds of records here. Certainly not from that long ago. Why in the world do you need that, Pity?"

Again, with my faux but maybe real article, "I'm working on an article about a boy who died. I want to interview his classmates and friends."

"Well, why don't you ask Mr. Murphy himself?" she suggested.

"Is he still there?" I was surprised since I thought he was gone.

"He retired several years ago, but he subs for us sometimes."

"Is he there today?"

"I'll check." I heard her clicking keys. "No, but I can call you when he comes in. I can't give you his contact information without his permission."

"Sure. Well, thanks anyway."

Her voice got quieter, "So how is the slimy squirrel?" Of course, she meant Dr. Love.

"Oh, he's still just as bad." I went on to tell her about the new playground rules, but I tried not to use any rude comments after I realized how much it hurt. She said she couldn't believe the rules, but then again, she could. We chatted a bit more before hanging up.

Later, I was in the middle of a lesson teaching eighth notes to third graders, when I saw the short, balding principal peek through the window of my door. I cringed as he stepped inside. He watched for a moment, cleared his throat, and called me to the door. I asked the children to practice their tas and titis with a classmate. I know, to a layperson that sounds a little kinky, but it's just a method of counting rhythms.

He whined, "Exactly when did you get permission to use bats in a song, Ms. Kole?" When he said my name, his nose wrinkled as if he detected an odd smell.

"Oh, it is just a little pumpkin song I teach the little kids every year. I changed the lyrics from witches to bats, assuming it would be fine since bats are a part of nature. Is there a problem, Dr. L.?"

"I certainly don't like the idea of the children being frightened in music class...and my name is Dr. Love, not Dr. L," he said stiffly.

I hadn't even realized I had shortened his name out loud. Good thing I didn't call him Dr. Dread. "I'm sorry, Dr. Love," I corrected myself and now was worried. "Was a student scared by the song? Did someone complain?" I was concerned because I thought they all loved the song.

"I heard a child singing it in the hall, and I asked where he had learned it. He told me it was in your class. Let's not let this happen again," he said with a stern warning as if I was a fifth-grader who had just been caught cheating on a test.

Then he added, "Oh, and you will be starting the new lunch detention on Tuesdays and Thursdays since you have an extra 10 minutes at lunch on those two days." Bingo - I knew it! I knew he'd stick me with that. Well, not for long, I thought.

He continued, "You can enjoy your lunch in the library while watching the young delinquents." He said it as if it was a bonus to eat with kids in the library.

I was outraged for three reasons:

First, because he called the students who make a peep during lunchtime delinquents.

Second, the only reason I have an extra ten minutes for lunch on those days is that he assigned me to tutor during my planning period. Those ten minutes were my only break.

Third, because I'd have to miss my lunchtime with Jules, Becca, and Jana - but I sure wasn't going to tell him that one.

Think, think, think of what to say...I looked toward the students, then turned back and said sweetly, "OK. Good! So, you have found someone else to tutor for me on Tuesdays and Thursdays?" I said that with a smile then I continued, "I know you want Arrowstar to comply with the Teachers' Association by allowing for the agreed-upon daily prep time and duty-free lunch for each teacher. Whatever you decide will be fine with me, Dr. Love." I nodded, attempting to be overly agreeable.

His eyes flickered a bit as he stared at me. Just then, one of my special needs girls came up and hugged me around my waist. She reached out for the principal, but he jumped back as if a snake tried to bite him. The little girl came back to me, unfazed, and snuggled against my leg. So what if snot ran freely from her nose to chin? I usually changed clothes when I got home anyway.

Dr L. left in disgust before he could make a good comeback. I wondered if I could bribe the snottiest kid in the room to do that every time he came to visit just to get rid of him, so I could teach. Despite his quick departure or maybe because of it, I expected some sort of retribution for my clever reply. Argh.

Once my last class was gone, I let out a big breath. It was Fall Break Eve. I checked my computer again and found an e-mail from Mrs. Bates. As I read, I could hear her super-high voice. "Kitty, I looked through my files from when I was the team leader for Math and English in the 90s. Remarkably, I found the class rosters of the English teachers for 1997. See, it pays to never throw anything away." Funny, that's what I believe, too. I never throw anything away, and my house and school room show it. She said, "I've attached Mr. Murphy's spring class list. Hope you find what you are looking for." I thanked her and printed the names she had attached and put them in my bag. I decided to go see Lin on the way home. As I drove down the street, I realized I could stop at the estate sale. I parked legally, held keys in hand, and walked to the door, making sure it was the right house. Not going to make that mistake again. Estate sales usually made me sad, especially if there were walkers or wheelchairs throughout the house. I hated to think someone died and their possessions were being sold, erasing their existence.

But this sale was run by three fun sisters who held the sale themselves, rather than hiring a company to liquidate. There was not a single walker in sight.

One sister told another customer, "Our parents collected so many things. We've kept as much as we can handle but have to get rid of all this." That would be my girls one day.

The gals were sweet and obviously loved the items in the house, which made me less sad. I bought a little pitcher to put on my window ledge and went to the last room. It was full of electronics; stereos, printers, turntables, and televisions. An old 13-inch square tube television was on and tuned to a police show – probably to prove it worked. Everyone on the screen sat in a squad room discussing a murder case. Hmmm. Now there's an idea.

Garage Sale Tip #11
Shop with a friend for moral support.

I found the house Lin was staging and knocked. When she answered, she blew hair from her eyes and said, "Just in time to help move this table."

I was amazed at what she had done with an empty house. It looked gorgeous. After we moved the table, she said, "It looks pretty neece, eh?" I nodded but chuckled. She hadn't acquired our Okie twang even after all these years.

She said, "What are you so tickled aboot?"

"Pretty neece? Don't you know in Oklahoma it's 'perty nahce?'"

"You're bad, Pity. So, give me the scoop or I'll just have to wring your neck. How was your supper with Mike? Did you find out anything else?"

"I don't have time to tell you about it now, but can you come over to my house at about 6:00? Kim and R.A. are coming over for dinner, and I thought we could set up a command center as they do on TV. Pizza and beer!"

"Ya said the magic word, beer. Are ya gonna invite Mike?"

I cocked my head at the idea and said, "Well, I guess I can if he's off tonight. He knows what I'm involved in and he does have a different perspective."

On the way home, I called him. "Hey, Mike. I got your ticket. The fine seemed pretty light for all the laws I broke. Thanks for going easy on me."

"Well, it was the first series of offenses I've observed, so I decided not to throw the book at you yet."

"Hey, Mr. Clever Man, are you working this evening?"

"Nope, I'm off tonight."

"Good. My sister, brother-in-law, and Lin are coming to my house at 6:00 to discuss the case, and we could sure use your help. I'll have pizza and beer. Wanna join us?"

"That sounds great. Can I bring anything?"

I almost said just your big beautiful face, but instead, I said, "Just your expertise."

"OK. I'll be there," he said.

I bought more beer and pop on the way to the house. When I arrived, Lauren was sitting on the couch in the living room with Chris by her side. I said, "Hello." and was very cordial to the boy, then asked, "Ren, can I see you in my room for a sec?"

She followed me into my bedroom, and I whisper-yelled, "I believe I had my phone with me, Lauren. You didn't think to ask me if you could have a boy over when I wasn't home?"

"Mom, we weren't doing anything," she protested in a quiet voice. "Marie and Caitlyn are here anyway."

"You know the rules. If you have anyone besides Jennifer over without me here, you are to ask. And remember, I used to teach middle school in Tulsa. One year, three girls got pregnant by the same boy at parties after school."

"Are you comparing me to those kids?" she said in disbelief. "Don't you know me by now?"

I softened, "I know, honey. You know I trust you. I just don't know this guy very well. So, please let me know anytime you have someone new over - or any boy, OK?"

"OK," she said rolling her eyes.

I reminded myself: kids need rules.

Back in the living room, I spoke in a more normal voice. "I'm having Kim, R.A., Lin, and a new friend over for pizza. You two are welcome to join us for dinner, but we'll be upstairs working on a project. Chris, do you like pizza?"

"I wouldn't be a normal guy if I didn't."

But all I thought was, 'You wouldn't be a normal guy if you didn't try to put the moves on my daughter either.'

I said, "Good, I'll order plenty," and dialed Mazzio's.

I went to the garage and ducked under the hanging ladder to reach the big whiteboard and markers I bought at an auction. I hauled it upstairs to get ready for the meeting. Last summer my girls asked me why I needed a big whiteboard. Ha! I knew I'd use it someday. I also grabbed my small bulletin board off the wall and hung it over my sewing machine in place of the thread rack. After I pinned the notes to it in chronological order, I wrote the names of suspects on the whiteboard, moved around a few chairs for my "squad room," and got out a stack of clipboards and paper. I was all set.

Ree came in and said, "Mom, come look at our project."

"Your expensive project," I clarified, and followed her down to her bedroom. It was like Caitlyn lived with us lately, but that was normal every year prior to History Day.

"We're almost done," she said and opened the door. "Ta Da!"

I was astonished by the transformation of the plain white tri-fold board. The colorful informative display included the photos of Harriet with the veterinarian, facts about microchipping, its history and the statistics on its benefits. They even had a tiny microchip encased in a plastic box amid articles and beautiful lettering.

"Wow! I'm impressed." I truly was.

Caitlyn said, "We hope the judges will be, too. But you have to OK the key part of our presentation."

I waited for the big ask. "Yeah? What do you need?" Ree answered. "We need to take Harriet to History Day as part of the display." She winced as if I would say no right away. She continued excitedly, "The vet is loaning us the microchip scanner, so we can demonstrate. Please!!! It will be so cool."

I smiled. "That would be pretty neat. It's fine with me to take her as long as it's okay to have a live animal in the facility, and you make sure she has water and gets potty breaks. You are in charge of asking permission and you had better be quick. Saturday will be here soon."

"Only three more days!" the girls squealed in unison as if they were going to a rock concert.

I shook my head at the sillies. "Looks like you are all set. Good going!"

Ree smiled, "Well, we still have to add music and another surprise."

After I told them about my meeting upstairs, Ree asked, "Can you order a cheese pizza for us?"

"Already did. I'll call you when it's here. Oh, you are to stay downstairs and keep an eye on Ren and Chris." The girls snickered as I left the room.

I changed out of my dirty, snotty school clothes, put on fresh jeans and a comfy sweatshirt, and looked in the mirror at my plain Jane outfit. Detectives were usually pretty boring in their meetings anyway, so I shrugged.

I started setting up for dinner. Just as I got plates, pop, and beer set out on the counter, the doorbell rang. It was Mike. I introduced him to Lauren and Chris. Then Kim and R.A. walked in and the introductions continued. Kim followed me into the kitchen while the men visited. I overheard them talking about Edgar. R.A. told Mike how I had refurbished the player piano, but I stopped listening when they started in on the World Series. Mike is so nice, and R. A. gets along with everyone, so I knew they would be buds in no time.

"OK, so who is that?" Kim's eyes were huge as she pointed to the tallest man who had ever graced my living room.

"He's my new policeman friend," I said with a grin.

"Oh yeah? You didn't happen to mention a 'new policeman friend' to me?" she said with a surprised and hurt look on her face.

"I know. Well, he's really new – like this week new. I can't believe I haven't talked to you, but it's been a crazy few days."

"Jeez Louise, you could have found time to tell me that." She urged me on for more information, "So is he just a friend?"

I shrugged, then smiled, "For now. But he is taking me to Junquefest in Sand Springs on Saturday," I said with a little dance and a "whoop whoop."

She slammed her palm to her forehead. "Oh, no. A guy who encourages your habits? Now that's bad."

Lin appeared in the kitchen and asked, "Sooo? What did you find out when you ate with Mike at Goldie's?"

Kim's eyes widened, and I explained sheepishly, "So we went there on official business. I thought he could help with the investigation. And the reason Lin knew about him is that she introduced us. He's her neighbor." The doorbell rang, and I sighed, happy to escape more of Kim's questions.

I got my purse and went out to the living room, but the door had already shut. Mike and R.A. walked towards me with pizza boxes. I held out my debit card, "Hey, I need to pay that guy."

"We took care of it," R.A. said as he set the boxes on the dining table.

Mike agreed, "Yeah. You got the beer. It's the least we could do,"

I turned to Lin and Kim. "Now, that's what I'm talkin' about."

I called the kids to come to get food and introduced the other girls to Mike. Ree eyed him curiously until she saw the pizza, and both girls stacked their plates high with slices of the cheese pie, while grabbing drinks. Apparently, he was already forgotten.

The adults filled plates and headed up to command central with beer. Kim was the last one up the stairs because she had to visit with her nieces. Kim and Ree usually discuss books, whereas Kim talks sewing to Ren.

Once upstairs, I invited them to sit. They could choose from mismatched, but comfy wooden folding chairs or two movie seats, that I picked up for only $20 at an auction.

Mike looked around at the eclectic decorations with interest and said, "Well, I guess you really do teach music."

I nodded. The whole west wall of my large room featured musical instruments attached from top to bottom. From the left was the string section, then brass. The woodwinds were on the right. I had bought most of the old instruments at school auctions and garage sales for no more than $20 each. Lin took down a French horn and blew, making a horrible blat. I held my ears, and she put it back.

I said, "I did not teach her that."

The south wall was short, due to the sloped roof of the former attic. It only had room for a television and Iggy's enormous, heated reptile aquarium. Half the slanted ceiling was covered with record jackets from my favorite musicals. The north wall had built-in cabinets full of craft supplies. I loved this room so much.

The last side of the large room is where I spend many a late night working on music, scripts, and costumes. It held my electronic piano, the computer, and my sewing machine.

Mike balanced his plate on his lap and put his beer on the glass top of the bass drum coffee table. Of course, I hadn't left out the percussion section.

I stood in front of the group, picked up a yardstick and pointed to the notes on the bulletin board. "Uh hem." I cleared my throat and began winging it. "Here is Exhibit A - the notes in what I assume to be chronological order. Exhibit B is the purple school desk. It is downstairs in the kitchen in case you want to check it out. "

I tried to act professional as if I was a police captain leading an investigation. I strode over to the white board. Aiming my ruler, I pointed out dates, places, and poor Justin. When I told the group that PS was probably Justin's girlfriend, Patty Sue, I actually heard a gasp from Lin (no, I didn't pay her for that enthusiastic reaction, but I loved it). Next, I pointed to the name of the felon, Marcus Fisher, and then to my main suspect, our rude neighbor, Mac Jenkins. I told them I ruled out the seller of the desk because he only bought it ten years ago when his daughter was probably seven.

I filled the group in about my visit with Mrs. Jones, my call to the high school and the police report. Then dramatically, I announced, "I have here in my hands, Exhibit C. The rosters from Mr. Murphy's classroom in 1997. I believe this was where the notes were written." I pinned the roster to the board.

I had no idea what we could accomplish from this evening's pow wow, but it sure wasn't like the one I had seen on TV at the estate sale. I'm pretty sure most investigators don't smile and eat pizza during debriefings, but then again, formal investigations don't usually involve beer and bass drums.

It was time to pull out the big guns, "And here...is Exhibit D." I held up the yearbook and showed them the pages marked with staff members, then the students who knew Justin, and finally, for dramatic impact, I turned to the 'In Memoriam' page. I was disappointed not to hear the oohs and ahhs you might get in a dramatic court scene, but at least their smiles dissipated while viewing Justin's picture. Lin shook her head.

I redirected the crew with, "OK, let's break into teams and brainstorm. Feel free to take your dinner with you." I turned to the girls, "Kim and Lin, can you go through the lists of students and the yearbook to look for other possible matching suspects? And see if you can find a girl who could be our Patty Sue. Since the yearbook isn't mine, please use sticky notes instead of writing in it."

I turned to Mike and RA. "Can you two come up with a timeline, and brainstorm questions about anything related to the case?"

"And I will call Justin's high school friend, Steven Bates." I clapped my hands, meaning "Let's go!" and, believe it or not, the girls stood and walked to the table with the yearbook and list, while the guys went to the board and started drawing a diagram that sort of looked like a baseball diamond. I hoped they weren't just discussing the Yankees, but they *were* volunteers. Whatever.

I sat at my computer desk and dialed Steven's number, playing a few silent notes on my keyboard as I waited for someone to pick up. "Hi, may I speak to Steven Bates?"

"This is he," a deep male voice said. I was so relieved that he hadn't inherited his mother's helium-induced voice.

"Hi, my name is Kitty Kole. I spoke to your mother yesterday. I'm a fellow teacher, and my daughter is on the swim team."

"Yes, she told me you would be calling. This is about Justin Jones, right? You're doing some sort of story about him?"

"Yes, that's right." I looked around as if my cohorts could hear what he said through the phone and I'd have to explain my lie to them, but they were busy. I said, "I understand you were pretty close to Justin. Can you tell me anything about the time leading up to his death?"

"Well, it was a long time ago, but from what I remember, he acted pretty normally, except he broke up with his girlfriend and was upset."

"Can you tell me her name?" I held my breath.

"Yes, it was Patty Sue. I don't remember her last name."

Although disappointed, I probed further. "Can you describe her?" I crossed my fingers.

"I didn't know her well. She was pretty and fairly tall. I guess her hair was dark."

I figured that description would fit a lot of people, including me, but I wrote it down.

"OK. Did you know anyone who didn't like Justin?"

"Would you really put that in an article?"

Oh shoot, I might as well tell him the truth. "Well Steven, to be honest, I'm actually doing a little investigation. I'm not so sure his death was an accident."

"Really?" He sounded more interested. "You know, I have always thought that myself. You didn't know Justin, but that guy was incredible. How could he just slip and crack his head on the side of the pool? He was like the perfect athlete: smooth, coordinated, and agile. It never made sense to me."

I nodded as he continued, "I honestly don't know of anyone who didn't like him. I'm sure there were some other guys at school that were jealous because he was pretty damned perfect. And he annoyed a few teachers because he joked in class a bit, but no more than most other guys. I can't think of anyone who would want to hurt Justin."

"I see. Do you remember a Mac Jenkins or a Marcus Fisher?"

"I didn't know anyone named Mac, but Marcus Fisher was a freak," he confirmed.

"Did Justin have any interaction with Marcus?"

"Not that I recall, but everyone thought Marcus was strange, so I'm sure he thought so too."

"Well, if you have a chance, could you look through the yearbook? If you see anything that jogs your memory...or if you remember Patty Sue's last name, please give me a call. I'd really appreciate it. I'll give you my number."

"That's OK, I have it on caller ID. Sure, I'll think about it. What will you do if you discover his death was really foul play?"

"Turn the information into the authorities, I guess."

"Well, I'm a criminal lawyer, and I would certainly do anything possible to help my friend's family."

"Wow, thanks, Steven. You've been very helpful already. Have a nice evening."

"You too, Ms. Kole. Goodbye."

I rushed over and interrupted the groups. "Steven didn't think it was an accident either." I mentioned his description of Patty Sue and his offer to help us. We were all a little stoked.

Then I joined Kim and Lin, who intently studied the yearbook. They hadn't found a Patty Sue but there was a Patty, a Susan, a Susie. and two Patricias in Mr. Murphy's classes – so many possibilities.

Kim flipped through the photos and said, "The only blonde is a Susie, so we can take her out of the equation. I put removable star stickers on the photos of those who might qualify – my mousy neighbor, Susan, being our main suspect."

Lin said, "As far as the boys are concerned, we didn't find anyone questionable aside from Mac Jenkins. We put a star on the picture of Marcus Fisher since he was in Mr. Murphy's class too. We also found your Steven Bates."

She showed me his picture. He was a nice-looking kid with hair in twists or dreadlocks. Printed under his name was 'Most Likely to Succeed.' I guess he did since he's a Dallas criminal lawyer.

I called the group back to order and said, "Anyone got anything?" I sat on the floor and took a swig of warmish Stella, along with a bite of cold pizza.

Mike said, "The police report said the pool area was always locked. The only people with keys were the two coaches, the custodian, and the secretary. The head coach let Justin in that day."

R.A. said, "So we have to assume Justin knew the murderer and let him or her in."

Kim said, "In order to move forward, we need to find out who Patty Sue is. I assume she's still alive and could be in the area."

I nodded and asked, "Any other ideas?" Everyone just sat with stumped looks on their faces. "I know you're all tired. I'll look over the list of the possible Patty Sues tomorrow and let you know if I find something." I took a drumstick and hit a snare drum end table, as a replacement for a gavel and announced, "The meeting is adjourned."

They shook their heads, probably wondering how I got so weird. Harriet scratched at the door, and we let her in. She became the center of attention as usual and maybe even scored some crust. We finished up by chatting about the pizza, the iguana, and Ren's cute new friend.

We left our investigation information in its place and headed down the stairs. Chris and Caitlyn had both gone home and my girls were in their rooms. I walked my team to the driveway and thanked them for their help.

I followed Mike to his truck and asked, "Hey, if you aren't working tomorrow, do you want to come over for that tour of the backyard? It's our fall break, and I actually have Thursday and Friday off."

"Oh my, more free time for you to get in trouble?"

"I'll make you a deal: you come over, and I'll try to be good."

"Anything to keep you safe. I am curious about the bottle trees. I'll come by before I go to my sister's house. How about 2:00?"

"All right, see you then. You're in for a real treat." I joked. When he drove off, I let out a big breath, feeling my evening was successful.

I suggested my girls not go upstairs for a few days because I was working on a project.

Ree said, "How can I feed Iggy?"

"I'll take care of her."

She shrugged her shoulders happily and I asked, "You guys want to watch a movie?"

Of course, they said yes. We cleaned up the dinner mess, popped some popcorn, and got comfy to watch *Wait Until Dark*, happy we could stay up as late as we wanted.

Garage Sale Tip #12
Well-made signs don't ensure a good sale

The next morning, during a late breakfast of Eggo waffles, Marie said, "I forgot to tell you — yesterday, after orchestra, Matt Mason ran into my violin case and broke another string," she said, rolling her eyes. "He's so clumsy and stupid."

I said, "Let's try not to call names. At least he didn't sit on it like last time."

"I guess," she groaned.

Her sister teased, "I'll bet Matt was flirting with you." More than likely, Ren was right. Ree is a beautiful girl who is tall and thin with a heart-shaped face. I'm sure there are lots of boys interested in her, but she's just got so much on her mind that she doesn't even think about them seriously yet, which is totally fine with me.

Ree said, "Eew, gross!" She looked as if she smelled burnt broccoli - or any broccoli, in her case. She continued, "If the destruction of my property is how he'll get my attention, he's wrong."

"Good girl, Ree." I rinsed my plate, put the syrup away, and asked, "Which string was it?"

"D."

"OK, I'll see if I have one." I ran upstairs to my instrument stash, where I have kept my instrument parts ever since I taught band and orchestra at a middle school when my girls were tiny.

I looked around at command central and smiled to think how I have friends who would actually help me to solve this mystery. They could have just blown me off. The list of possible Patty Sues lay next to the yearbook. I would study them when I got home from my second job tonight.

I dug through the instrument repair drawer, past cakes of rosin, tiny screwdrivers, reeds, key pads, valve oil, and other instrument parts. I finally found a packet with a coiled D string. I purchased most of the stuff from a music store that went out of business. It was sad to lose the store but good for my supply.

Back downstairs, I held the violin at arm's length and squinted as I tightened the new string. If you've ever been popped in the face with a taut wire string, you learn to be careful. After I tuned all four stings with the piano, I said in a hick accent, "Here's your fiddle, kid. You should have plenty of time to practice over this long weekend."

"Yeah, I will," she said, but I knew I'd have to prod her to get it to happen.

I added, "Since I'm working at Tulsa Opinions tonight, are you going to Caitlyn's or your dad's?"

"Both. Can you take me to Caitlyn's after lunch, so we can finish a few details? Dad's going to pick me up there for dinner."

"Sure, I'll take you, but only if you were invited. Oh, did you find out if you can take Harriet on Saturday?"

"Yes, Trish said I could come over and, yes, I can take Harriet! But she has to be on a leash the whole time and can't make noise or a mess." She gathered her materials.

"Well, that should be no problem. She's a very good girl." I reached down and patted the shaggy pup on the head.

Ree sat beside me on the piano bench. "Do you really have to work two jobs?"

I said, "Well, I could get by with one, but money would be tighter, and we wouldn't have many extras." I brushed a blond strand of hair from her eyes and put my arm around her thin waist.

Ren appeared and joined in, "And we couldn't take our trip each summer. You know Mom's extra job pays for that."

Ree's eyes widened. "Oh man, where should we go next summer? I am ready to go back to New York City."

"I doubt we'll have money for that kind of trip for a while, but we have plenty of time to make a plan. It's only October."

We lazed around the house the rest of the morning - something we all needed, then got ready for the day. Ren went shopping with Jennifer, and I took Ree to Caitlyn's.

I stopped at the grocery store on my way home to get a few items. While looking at bananas, I spotted my admirer, Kenny, standing by the bakery counter a few aisles over. He wore an expensive-looking argyle sweater, khakis, and loafers, all probably handpicked by his mother. I suspect he still lived with her. When he turned his head my way, I ducked behind the display of bananas.

I started to peek up at him when a little boy appeared and exclaimed in amazement, "Hi, Mrs. Kole! What are you doing here?" It's so funny that kids are shocked to see teachers outside of the classroom. They must think we all live in the school building.

I kept my eye on Kenny and whispered, "Hi, Mason. I shop here. I'm buying some fruit. Hey, do you see a man over by the cakes?"

"Yeah, I see him," he announced loudly.

"OK, can you tell me when he leaves?" I whispered, hoping he would catch the hint and keep his voice down.

"Sure," he said, a little quieter.

"Mason, what are you doing?"

I looked up to see Mason's mother looking down at both of us with eyes narrowed. I felt a bit stupid kneeling for so long and was going to pretend I was tying my shoes until I realized I wore slip-ons. The first-grader saved me by pointing and saying excitedly, "Mrs. Kole, the man's going."

I peered over the bananas and watched Kenny carry a box toward the check-out.

I stood. "Mrs. Dixon? Hi, I'm Mrs. Kole from Arrowstar." I thought about asking her why she had named her child Mason Dixon, but I thought better of it. "I just dropped my grocery list." Enough with the lies, Pity. Then to distract her, I said something really true, "Your son is so good in my class. I think he has some musical talent." He really does sing on pitch consistently.

She looked proud and said, "I always thought so, but it's nice to hear you say that. Mason, we need to go get some bread. Tell Mrs. Kole goodbye."

"See you on Monday!" he waved his hand as she pulled him towards the bread.

"Nice to meet you, Mrs. Dixon." Then, with no sign of Kenny, I walked to the register.

I got home in plenty of time for Mike's scheduled tour. When the doorbell rang, there he stood in jeans and a snug t-shirt that emphasized his fit physique. I was glad that I had taken the time to fix my hair, since the last time he was here, my head was in a bag.

"Welcome again to our humble abode," I said in my best hostess voice. "Would you care for a coke before we take the tour?"

"Sure."

What would you like? We have Dr. Pepper, Diet Mountain Dew, and La Croix."

"Oh, so no Coke?"

"Oops. Sorry, I don't. I just call all pop coke."

"Okay then. I'll have a DP."

Once he had his drink, I spoke in a dignified voice of a butler. "Please walk this way, Officer Potter." I let him out the back door.

Turning to the right, I pushed a lever with my thumb. "In case you are still parched, here is refreshing water, straight from a drinking fountain purchased at one of the finest local yard sales." I pointed at the fountain and waited. He didn't react, so I nodded toward the arc of water indicating he should try it.

Mike caught the hint and despite holding his pop, he leaned over and took a sip from the fountain. He opened his eyes in surprise. "That's good water and really cold!"

"I know." I nodded my head and ditched butler mode. "Next is Harriet's periwinkle blue dog house." The dog heard her name from across the yard and bounded across to join us.

Mike ruffled Harriet's fur and said, 'So has she done anymore disappearing acts?"

Confused, I said, "What?" Then it hit me. That's why he looked familiar in his uniform. "That was you who filled out my stolen dog report last spring?"

Mike smirked. "I wondered if you'd ever remember me."

I blushed from embarrassment over the incident and said, "All I remember is that the policeman was tall and handsome, just like you." I turned even redder when I realized what I just said.

He gave the cutest smile. "Shall we continue the tour, Ms. Kole?"

I cleared my throat and went on, "To the left of the patio is my unique wall of glass shower doors you noticed the other day." The doors stood upright and were staggered like giant clear dominoes. "The sun shines through for the flowers. Artsy, huh?"

He stepped behind one of the doors and pretended like he was soaping up in a shower. I laughed and snapped a picture with my iPhone and checked the photo – yep – I got his biceps.

I walked past the bowling pins without comment. I didn't need to show off every little thing and said, "In the back corner is the girls' old wooden swing set, re-purposed as a shed to hold my garden tools. Do you like the snow skis outlining the wood?"

"Yeah, but what's the refrigerator door for?"

"Open it!"

He pulled the lever on the vintage fridge door, and it swung open to reveal hammers, pliers, and garden tools inside the door and on the wall behind it."

He nodded. "Now that's practical." I was glad he saw some redeeming qualities in my backyard madness. He looked up. "I like your pine trees. So much shade."

"I know. But when three of the 20 pines died, R.A. cut them down halfway to make bottle trees." I pointed to the multi-colored trees. "I like how the sunlight shines through the bottles."

He said, "You must have drunk a lot of wine to make so many bottle trees.,

"Indeed, I did." I nodded my head at each word.

I walked him to the pond. "Have a seat on my surfboard bench." We sat down on the smooth orange and red checkerboard surfboard. I said, "My teacher friends gave it to me. Oh look, Dave and Buster came to see you." Their bright orange and yellow heads started nibbling on bubbles in the water.

"The day we put the pond in, a whole herd of frogs appeared. We have no idea how they found the water so fast. They are kind of fun but croak so loud outside my window in the summer I can hardly sleep."

Mike shrugged, "I'm not sure a group of frogs is called a herd. You know, this is pretty relaxing and surprisingly tropical."

"That's what I was going for, but in Oklahoma, it's not easy. In about a week, I'll have to drag in those cannas, banana trees, and elephant ears for the winter, or they'll freeze." I made a face. "That big tall clump over there is bamboo. Luckily, it stays outside all winter."

"Nice," he said.

"Since frogs miraculously appeared when we got a pond, now we wonder when pandas will arrive to eat the bamboo."

"Ha! Good question. Please call me if they show up."

I led him back inside. "Thanks for enduring my tour, Mike."

"My sister took me on garden tours before, but none were as cool as this."

I beamed as we walked to the front porch. He turned and looked down at me - not in a demeaning way, but because he's considerably taller than me. "I'll pick you up Saturday for Junquefest. 7:30?"

I said, "Sounds great," and gave him a quick light hug. The mention of his sister reminded me of all the questions my friends asked about him. I blurted out, "So, Mike, how old are you? I mean, how long have you been a policeman? Does your sister have a name? How long have you lived in BA?" Jeez, Shut up, Pity. I sounded like Caitlyn bombarding Ren with questions. I sputtered an explanation. "Well, you know everything about me, and I hardly know anything about you."

He smirked. "OK…that's fair." He paused to think. "I am 49 - hitting the big 5-0 in a month. I've been in police work for about 20 years. My sister's name is Maggie, and I moved from Denver to Broken Arrow five years ago. What else do you want to know?"

I went blank - forgetting all other questions. I shrugged. "That's all for now. I'll ask more when I think of something."

He smiled, stepped into his truck, and waved as he pulled away.

I floated inside, and before I got ready for my job, I texted the picture of Mike behind the shower door to Becca, Jules, and Jana.

Then I drove to Tulsa for my second job. Working as a focus group hostess at Tulsa Opinions is fun, but I'm usually exhausted when I get home late at night, especially after a full day of teaching, too. I only work the extra job once or twice a week and try to coordinate my days with the girls' visits with their dad. Ren and Ree know they can always text me while I work, so I'm never out of reach.

When I arrived at the office, I looked over the client checklist to see what was needed for the market research sessions. Focus groups are a great way to have people evaluate new food or products, rate songs, or participate in a mock trial. It's always something new. Like teaching, it's never boring.

Participants were only invited if they fit the target audience. Tonight's respondents were men, ages 30-50, who chew tobacco. (yuck) The client wanted them to give their opinions about a new tobacco tablet. It was a good thing they didn't ask my opinion since I think chewing is a disgusting habit. But these guys liked it and would get paid $50 for two hours, so it wasn't a bad gig for them.

After I laid out sandwiches for the respondents, I ordered dinner from a nice restaurant for the tobacco company reps. The clients were often demanding. As if to prove that point, no sooner had I hung up the phone from their food order, than a woman in a tailored black suit marched to my desk and announced in a New York accent: "Your soda is expired."

She shoved a can of Diet Coke at me. I turned the can over – surprised to find out pop cans even had expiration dates. Wow, it was one whole week out of date. Tragic. But I quickly apologized and went to another refrigerator and found some newer cans. Since the clients paid a lot for us to conduct the study, I gave them anything they wanted and did it with a smile.

Once everything was set up and the clients were seated behind the two-way mirror with fresh Diet Cokes, I heard a buzz coming from under my desk. I found my phone and saw a text from Becca:

"Woohoo! Is that your policeman? Already got him in the shower! You go, girl!" I smiled.

The door jingled, and the first respondent entered the lobby. He was a short, balding man. For a second, I thought it was Dr. L, but his friendly smile assured me it was not. According to my notes, he was a 45-year-old non-smoker who used Skoal twice a week. I asked him to show me his ID, and I signed him in. After giving him his name tent, I offered him food and asked him to have a seat in the lobby. When he turned, I noticed the Skoal ring on his back pocket. Probably all of the men tonight would have one.

Men of all sizes and shapes arrived; most wore cowboy hats, jeans, and boots. A few were missing teeth. Was that coincidental or a result of too much chewing tobacco? One guy was actually chewing when he walked in the lobby. He spat in the wastebasket right next to my desk. I watched the brown slime ooze down the side of the plastic liner. It reminded me of my hair dye dripping down my cheek. The sight of the spit coupled with the disgusting wintergreen tobacco smell made me sick to my stomach. And to think I had to touch that trash bag later. I immediately moved it a few feet away.

The men kept coming in until only two names were left on my list. I looked over the group as they ate their sandwiches with gusto. They sure were rough around the edges compared to last week's prim 40-to-60-year-old ladies who tested a new cutting-edge broom. I wish I could have tried it, since they raved about it on their way out. What in the world did a broom do that was so special? Sweep?

The door jingled again, and I looked up. Damn! In walked Scott and Jay, the two jerks from Saturday night. What were the chances of them getting invited? Thinking back, I had seen their Skoal rings.

I considered ducking under the desk, but I knew I couldn't hide for long, since someone had to check them in. I forced a smile and hoped they wouldn't recognize me - after all, they had been drunk then, and I could only hope they were sober tonight.

The two hicks talked to each other as they walked up to the counter. Jay said, "That bastard still owes me a new tire."

Scott turned to me, squinted, and said with his head cocked so the fluorescent lights spotlighted his face under his Valvoline hat. "Don't I know you from somewheres?"

I replied professionally, "Let me think...have you been to Tulsa Opinions before?"

"No." He wrinkled his weathered face as he tried to remember.

Then Jay said with a puff of alcohol-laced breath, "You's that teacher we bought dinner fer last weekend, ain'tcha?" That was more than he had said that whole night.

"Yes, but I also work here." I lifted my eyebrows and got to business. "I'll need to see your IDs. Then sign in beside your names and feel free to have something to eat and drink."

"I ain't showing you my driver's license," Scott shook his head.

"Well, then. I guess you won't get to participate... or get paid."

"You are such an uppity bitch," Jay said, revealing his nasty brown teeth.

One of the other guys in the waiting room stood up - all 6'3" of him. "Is there a problem, ma'am?"

I looked Scott in his eyes and said firmly, "I need these men to follow the procedure to get signed in."

"We ain't signing nothin'!" Jay barked.

The moderator entered the lobby and walked to me. He said softly, "The clients can hear a disturbance through the microphones. Is everything OK?"

I said, "These gentlemen," (ha- gentlemen) "refuse to show me their IDs or sign in."

He turned to the guys and said calmly, "We can only use people in this study who are willing to cooperate. If you aren't interested in being involved, we can pay you $20 each for your time, and you'll be on your way. But we still need to see your IDs even for that."

They looked at each other and then turned to us. Scott said, "Screw you all, especially that bitch!"

They turned and strode to the door, slamming it behind them. I told the moderator I was fine, and he went back to the clients, shaking his head. But I couldn't believe how shaken I was. Those two acted like they wanted to hurt me.

The other men were very sweet as I led them into the focus group room. Once they were situated with folded cardboard name tents on the table in front of them, I went to the backroom and started the video recorder. As soon as the clients' food was delivered, I locked the front door in case the creepy guys reappeared. I served their Caesar salad, Portobello mushroom pasta, and chicken scaloppini meal buffet style, and I hoped there would be some left because I was hungry. There were always leftover sandwiches in the lobby, but I get tired of them, and, of course, I preferred the good stuff.

I busied myself writing checks for the men and getting set up for the 8:00 group. When the doors opened, I paid and thanked each of the guys for their time and for being so cooperative. They seemed to enjoy themselves. A few commented on the earlier event and said they were sorry I had to put up with such jerks.

I cleared the client's dishes, happy to find extra chicken scaloppini in the large pan. Nice! I made a little plate for myself and stored the rest in the employee fridge for the staff to eat tomorrow.

When the next group arrived, I signed the men in and took them back at the appropriate time. With a sigh, I sat down at my desk and finally ate a few bites while googling the name for a group of frogs. I texted Mike. "It's an Army of Frogs! Who knew?"

My purse started buzzing. I figured it was Jules or Jana commenting on Mike's outdoor shower picture, but it was a text from Lauren saying, "Call me now!!!!"

I did just that.

Ren said with a tremble in her voice, "Mom, someone broke into our house!"

Garage Sale Tip #13
Go back later for better bargains.

"Someone broke into our house? Are you okay?"

"Yes. I just got home from Jennifer's and saw that our front door handle was broken! Then I ran back to my car to call you. What should I do?"

"Lauren, you did the right thing. Now call the police and give them our address. Then go to Mrs. Garmin's and wait for them there. I'll be home as soon as I can."

I called Todd and explained the situation. "You'll need to keep Marie overnight, but please don't tell her about the break-in yet."

He said "Just a minute." I heard him ask Shelly if it was okay. There was a lot of vocal drama in the background, but after a few moments, he came back and said, "OK, we'll keep her." Why did he even have to ask Shelly? He's her father, and they aren't married.

Next, I called R.A, who also works for Tulsa Opinions, doing the video and sound for mock trials. I told him about the break-in and asked if he'd please come over and finish up for me. He said, "Of course, I'll be right there. Call me when you can and let me know if I need to go to your house." Again, my brother-in-law was a lifesaver.

I told the moderator my story and left. On my way home, I called Mrs. Garmin and asked if Ren could stay there, maybe even for the night.

She said, "Of course, dear. Whatever you need."

When I turned the corner onto our street, several police cars blocked the driveway. Red and blue lights reflected in Ren's car windows, making me shudder. I couldn't believe how disturbing that scene was. As I pulled up, I spotted Mike talking to another officer. Had he been dispatched to the house, or did he come on his own? He met me at my car door.

"Do you know what happened?" I asked nervously.

"The responding officers searched the house and didn't find anybody, but there are definite signs of a break-in."

Damn. So, someone was in my house for real. I said, "Can I go in and look?"

"Sure. I'll go with you," he said.

"Thank you." My hands shook as we walked to the porch. What in the world might I find? Were our pets ok? I felt sick.

Mike said, "This is really odd, but we found this cake sitting on your front porch. Does this mean anything?" Mike held it up.

Peeking through the clear plastic on top of the box, I read, *Sweets for the Sweetest Lady*. So that's what Kenny was doing at the bakery counter today. I rolled my eyes.

Mike said, "I've never heard of a burglar leaving a cake with a compliment."

"I'm pretty sure this has nothing do to with the break-in," I sighed. "I'll explain later."

He put the cake back down. My eyes flew to the broken handle as we entered the house. That alone gave me the willies. I stepped into the living room warily. Lamps were overturned, and books lay strewn on the floor. I put my shaky hands to my face. Someone had invaded our space. Edgar was in his cage looking bored as usual.

My voice croaked. "This is really creepy."

Mike shook his head. "I'm sure."

My thoughts immediately went to Harriet. I looked around the living room. Where was she? As if I'd said her name aloud, she barked. I followed the sound down the hallway and found her shut inside my bedroom. She jumped around anxiously so I cuddled the mass of white hair, wishing she could tell me who had put her in the room. Or what about Edgar? He can actually talk - why didn't he tell us?

Although there was no permanent damage to the house and nothing seemed to be missing, this break in angered me. Who had the right to enter my home? And why?

Another officer joined us and asked, "Ms. Kole, do you have any idea who may have done this?"

I didn't know of anyone unless it was Jay and Scott, but I was sure they didn't know where I lived. I shook my head slowly as I scanned my brain for other possible perpetrators.

I froze. "Mike, you don't think it has to do with the case, do you?" We both glanced up the stairs and simultaneously started up a step, but our combined width caused our shoulders to bang into the walls of the narrow stairwell. He gestured for me to go first.

Upon opening the door, we got our answer. Sure enough, the notes, the yearbook, and the class rosters were all gone. My whiteboard had been erased. Our entire command center was ruined. I quickly realized that I was on the right track in my suspicions and somebody knew it. But who even knew I was investigating?

I turned to Mike and frowned. "Now I wish I turned them in to the authorities."

Mike put his hand on my shoulder. "It's OK. You didn't know."

"I could have at least made copies." I closed my eyes. I couldn't believe it was all gone. So dumb. Then I had another horrible thought. "Do you think they'll come back?"

"Well, they got what they wanted, and also found out how much you know."

"Yeah, well now I know more. I know that somebody who was involved in Justin's murder all those years ago is still nearby and wants me to stop poking around!"

He nodded. "Right. You should be extremely cautious from now on. Do you want me to stay the night here, just in case?"

As upset as I was, the thought of having Mike spend the night was tempting in many ways. But I shook out my arms, stood taller and took a deep breath to loosen my nerves. I said with more confidence and a slight smile, "No, it's OK. I have my phone..." I picked up a set of drumsticks "and these...and I have Harriet." I added, "I'll stay upstairs and leave the door open, so I can hear if they come back. I'm a light sleeper. Ree is at her dad's, and Ren can stay at my neighbor's house. I'll be fine."

"Just remember I'm only a mile away and can be here in an instant if you need me."

"Thanks, Mike. I'm sure glad I called you to go buy my kayak for me. You've turned out to be pretty handy." I put my arms around him for a genuine hug. His wool uniform with a badge, pins, bulletproof vest, and gun belt wasn't at all comfortable to hug, but I immediately felt better anyway.

"Well," he cleared his throat and smiled. "We should finish the report. I'll drive by your house periodically while I'm on duty, and I'll keep my phone beside me when I'm home."

I was suddenly distracted from my worries because, in this light, his eyes looked green. I shook it off. "I should go see Ren."

We went downstairs and outdoors. The other officer who was writing notes stopped Mike. While walking next door, I looked back at him in his official uniform and thought about how much I liked this comforting new friend with chameleon eyes.

My tiny neighbor had just given Lauren a cup of decaf tea at her dining table when I entered. Mrs. Garmin's collection of bells surrounded the kitchen on little shelves, making her house a cozy, albeit stuffy place. I rushed to Ren. "Honey, are you okay?" I bent down and kissed her on the cheek.

"I was so scared when I saw the broken handle. I didn't know what to do." she said, holding her cup of tea with both hands. I was relieved to see she held it steady - no shaking.

"Oh Lauren, you did everything right. I'm very proud of you."

Ellen said, "Pity, can I get you some coffee or a cup of tea? That must have been very scary for you."

"Thank you, but I'm OK. They secured the doors, so everything should be fine."

Ren asked, "Did they take anything? Are the animals okay?"

"Yes. Everything seems fine. Only some overturned chairs and scattered books. There was no damage and nothing important is missing. Just a few things of mine from upstairs." I opted not to tell her what was taken. "But I want you to stay here tonight if you don't mind, and I'll call you first thing in the morning." I stroked Ren's wavy hair, hoping she was alright.

"Are you going home? What if they come back?"

"The police don't seem to think they will. I'm a very light sleeper and can call my friend Mike if I have to."

"Okay." She didn't look thrilled, then she said, "Mom...I need to tell you something that happened today. Coach Hamm said I can't swim in the big meet on Saturday." Her eyes welled up with tears.

"For heaven's sake, why not?" I couldn't think of any reason.

"He said my drug test came out positive! But that's impossible, Mom. You know I don't do drugs!" She sobbed.

I shook my head. "It must have been a mistake, Ren. Was it one of the random pee-in-the-cup tests?"

"Yes, and I swear I've never done anything like that. I was humiliated because he announced it in front of everyone!" she said through her tears. Her hands started to shake, and she put her teacup on the plastic flowered table cloth before it spilled.

"Hey, calm down sweetie." I hugged her. "I'll check it out. Better yet, why don't we just go take another drug test tomorrow and prove him wrong."

"Can we do that?" she said, as she sniffed into my shoulder.

"We will get it straightened out. Don't worry." I looked at Mrs. Garmin and she nodded, indicating she could handle things from here. I mouthed "Thank you" and gave Ren a kiss.

My fear from the break-in had changed to fury. What kind of jerk humiliates an innocent girl in front of her team? My heart pounded hard as I stormed next door. A policeman on my porch dusted the cake box for fingerprints and I walked past him and got myself a glass of ice water.

I was still fuming when Mike entered again. I explained the newest bit of information that had thrown me over the edge.

He said calmly, "I think that's a good plan to have her re-tested. I'm sure it was a mistake, and the coach will make it right. And about the notes, we saw them and know the details. It's not all lost."

I looked up at him. "Thanks, Mike. That makes me feel better. You should get back to work. I'll be fine."

The officer brought the cake inside and put it on the dining table, then all the officers left. I checked the semi-repaired door handle and found it to be pretty stable.

Then I called Marie's cell phone, told her we'd had a little break-in and all was OK. It would be better if she stayed with her dad until tomorrow afternoon.

I could hear the anxiety in her voice as she said, "I'm scared, Mom. Was it Mr. Jenkins?"

I considered this. Could he have been the intruder? I said, "Oh, honey. I don't think so, since Harriet was fine. We'll find the person who did it, though. It's going to be all right."

I let Harriet out and pondered the break-in and drug test results while eating a bowl of Life cereal. I brushed my teeth and put on pj's. To prove someone was home, I left the lights on in the living room and took my big girl upstairs with me. I kept the door open enough that I could hear if the perpetrator came back. Instead of pulling out the horribly uncomfortable sleeper sofa, I just stretched out on the couch with my natural blanket of Harriet beside me. I watched Jimmy Fallon to get my mind off the break-in. After his monologue, I turned off the light and fell asleep.

I had a nightmare involving those two idiots who refused to show me their IDs. The bad dream escalated as Scott squeezed my throat while Jay tried to take my purse. When I awoke, Harriet's paw was on my neck, hence the strangling reference, but I still heard a man's voice. Had I left the Tonight Show on? I looked at the TV, but the screen was black. No... that was a real voice. IN MY HOUSE!

"Wanna go for a walk?" The low voice came from downstairs. Oh, whew! It was only Edgar. That's why I should always turn the lights off at night or cover his cage. Otherwise, the goofy bird stays awake and talks to himself.

I moved Harriet's paw from my neck, sat up, and heard Edgar say, "Who was that?"

Funny, I'd never heard my bird utter that phrase before, and furthermore it wasn't in his usual old man voice. I gulped.

"I don't know," said another voice. Then in a stage whisper he said, "Maybe there is a boyfriend. We'd better go," I stood by the door, peeked down the stairs and saw the back of a denim jacket. That was definitely not my bird. My stomach dropped and I thought I might fall.

Edgar then said, "Want a drink of water?" with his usual drawl.

The man said, "There it was again."

Another voice said, "I think it was that there bird talkin'."

"But who actually said the words?"

"I said the bird said it, dumbshit."

"No, but who made the sounds?"

For a moment, I thought the second graders from years ago had come back to haunt me.

"Jay, are you stupit? It was the bird talkin'. Now let's go look fer that bitch who owes us our $50 and teach her a lesson. We didn't wait all this time fer nothin'."

I jumped as soon as I realized it was Scott and Jay. OMG! They must have followed me home and waited until the police left. I picked up my phone and dialed Mike.

He answered right away, "Are you OK?"

"Not so much," I whispered. "There are two other intruders in my house. Please come quickly. I'm upstairs."

"I'm on my way!" he said, "Stay on the line with me."

"OK, but I want to listen to what they're saying." Harriet finally woke up, heard the commotion downstairs, and perked up, ready to bark. I clamped my hand around her muzzle and whispered "Shhh. It's OK. Good girl."

One of them said. "Wonder why she left the lights on?"

"She ain't in the bedrooms. Must be upstairs," said the other.

I shut the door quickly and looked around the room in a panic. I turned on my cell phone flashlight to see and tried to think of how to defend myself. I quietly pushed the bass drum table by the door, so they'd have trouble getting in. I glanced at the other instruments, but none of them looked threatening. Then, I saw my perfect weapon.

Their feet clomped up the stairs and my heart raced. "They are coming upstairs," I whispered to Mike turned off the flashlight and threw the phone down on the couch. I held onto Harriet's collar, telling her to be quiet. The door pushed towards me a bit and then the drum started to move.

I recalled the scene in *Wait Until Dark*, where the blind Audrey Hepburn broke the lights so the killers would have trouble seeing. Well, I was now used to the dark but I knew these guys had just come from a brightly lit room, so hopefully, they would be temporarily blinded - unless, of course, they flipped the switch on, but I didn't plan to give them enough time to do that.

Just as Scott emerged through the door with Jay close behind, I let go of Harriet. She bounded over to them barking, maybe to protect me, but probably just to say hi. The massive hairy dog frightened Jay and he fell backward down the stairs a few steps. Then I reached into the aquarium and pulled out our huge iguana with both hands. Iggy had been sleeping and didn't like to be awakened, but I carried her carefully towards the door and tossed the heavy 4-foot iguana at Scott. I heard a loud scream – from Scott, not Iggy.

Then I grabbed a trumpet from the wall and started blatting loudly. Iggy's sharp claws scraped down Scott's forearms as she tried to hold on to his flailing arms. She landed on the floor unharmed and ran around the room while the two guys raced back down the stairs, not knowing what had hit them.

With my heart pounding so fast, I thought I'd have a heart attack, I watched them reach the front door. They ran smack dab into Mike, who stood aiming a gun at the frightened guys. They surrendered quickly, and Mike put them in handcuffs.

I let out a huge sigh of relief, turned on my light and put down the trumpet. Then I carefully covered Iggy with my O.U. throw and picked her up so I wouldn't get scratched myself, and put her gently back in her enormous aquarium. "Good girl!" I uncovered her, relieved to see she didn't have a mark on her.

I started down the stairs where the two men sat with their heads bent. I noticed drops of blood on the carpet and then caught Mike's eyes. He looked bewildered but relieved to see that I was safe. Once I had made my way past the culprits, I glared at them and said, "You idiots will never get your $50. You didn't follow the correct procedure." I smirked, then added, "And you might want to get those scratches looked at. You could get Salmonella." Scott had four long bloody slashes down each arm, making him look like the victim in a horror movie.

Scott scowled at me with a red face, but Jay remained pale and silent. Backup arrived, and an officer took the two away in his squad car, leaving me standing alone with Mike. We sat on the couch, and I explained the whole story of how I knew Scott and Jay. Mike quietly wrote down the information on a notepad. I guessed it was an official interview.

When I finished, he said, "Pity, you are the only person I've ever heard of to have two separate home invasions in one night. And I've been a cop for a long time!"

"What can I say? Maybe I wanted you to come back and see me." It was hard to believe I made a joke at this time, but I felt giddy that I had escaped a dangerous situation.

"You could have just called," he said with a sly grin. "But, what in the world made them come screaming down the stairs like that? And what's with the blood?" he asked in amazement.

"Oh, you remember the Bremen Town Musicians? Well, Edgar, Harriet, Iggy, and I played our own kind of music. I'll explain when I'm not so frazzled."

"Whatever you did, it worked," he said, nodding approvingly.

Thinking of what Ree had said earlier, I asked, "So one break-in is solved, but could someone interview Mac Jenkins to find out where he was during the first break-in?"

"Already on top of it. We called him as soon as I left your house. He wasn't at all happy we brought him in and claims to have an alibi. We'll check it out tomorrow."

"Oh, good," I sighed, "and you'll let me know?"

"Of course," he said. "Are you anticipating any more unwanted visitors tonight?"

"I sure hope not because I don't have any more tricks up my sleeves, and I'd actually like to get some sleep."

Before Mike left, he joked, "So what kind of issues do you have anyway?"

"Huh?" What was he talking about? He pointed to my top. I looked down. "Oh, yeah." I forgot I was wearing the pajamas with *More Issues Than Vogue* printed across the chest. My cheeks turn red. I said, "Hang around much longer and you'll find out."

Mike smiled and proceeded to barricade the front and back doors from the inside and then left through the garage. I'd be safe for the rest of the night – we could only hope.

I couldn't go to sleep with blood on the carpet, so I worked on that for a while. Everything else could wait until morning. It was 3:30 before I got into my own bed. Despite the hour, I still had trouble falling asleep.

I woke up too early at 7:30, worrying about what had happened the night before. No way I could fall back to sleep. The first break-in bothered me the most. Who had been in our house? It had to be someone who knew I was investigating Justin's death.

I made coffee to bring me out of my sleepy fog. I had to clear my head enough to make plans for the day. It was Friday of Fall Break. The house was a mess. I had no notes. Nothing remained from our investigation, and I had to take Lauren to the doctor. But I really wanted to do something fun with my girls.

I started picking up furniture that had been strewn around the rooms and used carpet spray to clean remaining spots of blood that were more visible in the daylight. I made an appointment to have Ren tested for drugs by her regular doctor, then called Mrs. Garmin to tell her I'd pick up Ren around nine o'clock.

Before leaving the house, I called Lin and Kim to fill them in on the previous night's craziness. As expected, they were shocked. R.A. was on speaker and told me I should have called him.

I said, "It all just happened so fast."

He said, "Well, I'm glad Mike was nearby to help out."

I was too.

I picked up Ren and thanked Mrs. Garmin for helping us. On the way to Dr. Smith's office, I saw a garage sale sign and automatically turned to follow the arrows.

"Mom, what are you doing?"

"Oh, I'm sorry, Ren. Liesel is still set on garage sale autopilot. But, in all fairness, it is Friday morning. We have time to hit some sales before the doctor's appointment, right?"

"No. My appointment is in 20 minutes."

"And it's only five minutes from here," I reasoned, as I parked at the first sale and jumped out of the car. I didn't see anything great, so I got back in and proceeded to search for any others we might see along the way.

Ren shook her head, looking at me as if I was crazy. "Mom, you have a problem."

"At least it's not gambling or drugs."

She grumbled. "Are you sure this is much better?"

Garage Sale Tip #14
Keep your eyes open or you'll miss something

I spotted another sign written on the side of a box two blocks away and followed some hard-to-read signs to the sale. The place was crawling with people, and I had to park three houses away. Not having checked Craigslist, I didn't know what it said, but the post must have been good to bring in so many people. "Wanna come?"

"No. Just hurry," Ren said impatiently.

I got out of the car quickly, not because she told me to, but because I couldn't wait to see what was in the boxes on the driveway. There were maybe 30 of them. As I got closer, I saw that each held different sports items - all brand new. I figured a sports store must have gone out of business.

Normally, I wouldn't get excited about anything sports-related, but I noticed two big boxes holding brand new University of Oklahoma items, and my eyes lit up. OU is my alma mater. I spotted an adorable cooler plastered with the crimson interlocking OU on its side. I rushed to pick it up, but another lady touched it first. She opened the lid and by golly, it played the fight song, "Boomer Sooner," out loud! I sang along quietly, "I'm Sooner born and Sooner bred and when I die, I'll be Sooner dead." When I saw the price was $5, I just had to have it! I had seen the same cooler online for $50!

In order to play it cool, I picked up a nice crimson and cream OU scarf and slung it over my arm. I asked the lady holding the cooler, "Did you go to OU?"

"No, my son is thinking about going to college there."

"I graduated from OU and played that song in the Pride of Oklahoma Band. I was a music major."

"Oh," she said, not catching the hint that I needed the cooler. I blurted out, "I would love that if you aren't going to get it." She tightened her grip on it. "Well, I think I might get it."

"Well, maybe your son would like this scarf just as much. It would surely keep him cozy warm," I said, realizing how stupid that sounded. I asked, "What other school is he considering attending?"

"Oklahoma State," she said. I could tell she was getting annoyed by me. If someone had bugged me like that, I would have said, 'Leave me alone,' but I just couldn't give up.

I immediately searched around for a box with OSU items. Lo and behold, I saw the same cooler with the Orange Cowboy on the side. I grabbed it and took the orange OSU cooler to her. "Do you think he would like this one?"

She shrugged and eyed me. "I don't know."

What a tease! I got an idea. "How about I buy this one for your son, if you just let me buy that one," I offered in a last-ditch effort.

"Let me think about it." She carried 'my' cooler around to look in other boxes. Now, I had to hold a stupid OSU cooler while I waited. How embarrassing to hold something in our rival's colors. I refused to even wear orange for fear someone might think I was an OSU fan.

I glanced in another box and found a gold mine - swim goggles. They were even the brand Ren used. I pulled my phone out of my pocket and called her, not wanting to lose sight of the woman. "Hey Ren, come here."

"Mom, we're going to be late."

"Just come here for a minute. They have swim stuff!"

"Gross. I don't want any used swim stuff."

"No. They're all new with the tags," I reassured her, "and at a great price, too."

"OK," she said slowly. Before long, she walked up. "Why are you carrying that? I didn't think you'd be caught dead with anything from OSU." She started looking at the goggles. "Wow, these are great," she said in earnest.

"I know! Pick out a few pairs for you, one for Jennifer and one for Ree."

"Why for Ree?" she looked up.

"She wants to swim next year, and I want to save money now."

"Seriously?"

"Yep, you'll have to help her out next year. Then, look at the box of swimsuits. I've got to go follow that lady."

She looked at the woman and nodded, figuring it out. "So…you want that cooler,"

"Yes. And she won't let me buy it." I lamented.

"Did you ask if it was the only OU cooler they had here?"

"No. I didn't even think of that." I walked to the owner and asked. "Do you happen to have another OU cooler?"

"Oh, yes. I have a few more." Jeez, all that for nothing. No matter. I was ecstatic, but controlled myself as she went to get it. I put the OSU cooler back down like it was a hot potato. When the woman brought the OU cooler to me, I thanked her and walked right up to my competition and said nicely, "I found another OU cooler, so I guess I won't be buying one for your son." The woman looked disappointed. She should have taken me up on my offer earlier.

We bought some of the incredibly cheap swim items and finally arrived at the doctor's office only four minutes late. After we checked in with the receptionist, we sat on a plaid couch in the waiting room. Although it wasn't an ideal place to talk about a murder, I decided I should fill Ren in on everything, figuring we would have a long wait.

I whispered, "You know the swimmer I told you about who died years ago?"

"Yes?" she said with an eyebrow raised.

"Well, I found a stack of old notes in that purple desk and..."

She interrupted, "Is that what you held behind your back?"

"Yes, but listen."

"So, it wasn't an early Christmas present?"

"No. But listen, the notes indicated his death wasn't an accident and that the boy probably was murdered!" I hurried on before she interrupted again. "I've been investigating, and I think someone involved in the crime broke into our house to get the evidence I'd collected." I winced, anticipating her response.

"What?" Ren, my 17-year-old voice of reason was both visibly and audibly upset.

"Shh," I pleaded. "I had help in my investigation. That's what we were doing upstairs Wednesday night. investigating. It's just that I've been asking around, and someone must want me to stop. I'm so sorry. I never thought anyone would break into our house."

"Are you sure that's the reason someone broke in?" she asked.

"Well, the only things missing were the notes, the class lists, and information written on a whiteboard. Oh, and they took the school yearbook. Shoot, I need to tell your school librarian that I'll pay for it." I sighed and frowned.

Ren's face softened, and she said, "It's OK, Mom. I'm sure you were trying to do the right thing." She must have seen that I was not my usual peppy self and felt sorry for me.

"Well, there's more," I admitted. "After the police left, I had two more intruders."

Ren's eyes widened and she spat, "Are you kidding?" The other waiting patients turned our way.

"I know," I whispered, "it was insane. Those horrible guys Lin and I met the other night at McNellie's came to Tulsa Opinions for a study last night, but they refused to show their IDs, so we had to turn them away. They were really mad, and I guess they followed me home and broke in after the police left."

Her eyes narrowed. "Mom, did they touch you?"

I shook my head proudly. "No, because they felt the wrath of a bird, a dog, an iguana, and a trumpet before they had a chance."

I proceeded to pantomime what happened with muted sound effects to go along with the story. By the time I finished, I'm pretty sure the other patients assumed I was at the doctor's office for a psychiatric evaluation.

"That is crazy!" she said in disbelief, "but I kinda wish I could have seen it."

The nurse appeared with her clipboard at the door and called "Lauren Peters?" We rose and followed her into the examining room.

Ren explained to Dr. Smith about her failed drug test and asked if she would give her another test since it had to be a mistake. The doctor agreed to analyze her blood, saying anything objectionable would still be in her system and that these screenings were far more sensitive and could pick up even a trace.

The nurse said it would be a few hours before they would have the results.

I said, "Let's go get your sister."

Ren ran up to her dad's door to get Marie. When she got in the car, Ree shook her head. "You got here just in the nick of time. Shelly got out the hairspray and was going to fix my hair." Thanks for saving me. So, tell me about the break-in."

I looked at Lauren, and we both nodded - time to fill in Blondie. I said, "Let's go to Braum's, and we'll tell you everything."

I drove us to our favorite ice cream store, and we ordered sundaes. Why not have ice cream at eleven a.m.?

Between bites of hot fudge and caramel, I explained everything to Ree. "Just to be extra cautious, I don't want you to stay at the house until we find out who broke in."

"But what about you, Mom? You shouldn't be there either," Ree said, concerned.

I considered this. "Probably not. I can stay with R.A. and Kim tonight. I'm going to Sand Springs with my friend, Mike, for Junquefest in the morning. I guess he can pick me up there since it's on the way." I made the plan out loud.

"But don't forget History Day," Ree said in horror.

I scoffed, "I won't."

Ree said, "I'm not so sure, Mom. I've seen how distracted you are at a good sale. You left me at one when I was only eight, and I had to borrow a phone and call you to come back and get me."

I cringed at the memory. "I'm much better now." I sure hoped I was. "I promise I'll be back in plenty of time to share your special day. But do you think Caitlyn's mother would let you spend the night and help set up your display tomorrow? I'll be there to take it down."

She said, "Yeah, I'm sure that's fine. Trish has to make sure everything is perfect. Our project is at her house anyway. But what about Harriet? She stay home alone. What if a burglar comes back?"

Ren said, "I'll take Harriet with me to Jennifer's house." She turned to Ree and pointed a spoonful of strawberry ice cream at her. "And I'll even take her to History Day for you tomorrow. It's your big day, and you can't be worried about everything."

"Thanks, Ren!" Marie smiled. "That would be great. I'm sure Trish will drive us, but she would never allow a dog in her Lexus."

I must have been really tired because seeing the girls being nice to each other just started the waterworks. When they stared at me, I said, "I'm OK, girls. I'm just worn out. No sleep."

Ree asked, "Did you really throw Iggy at those guys?"

I winced. "I sort of tossed her." I demonstrated how I did it and then explained, "I had no other choice because it was her or me, and she has much thicker skin than I do, literally. Believe me, she held her own. Iggy's a hero, you know."

Ree smiled and said, "I'll give her extra strawberries today." She shook her head at me. "Mom, you were a real live Kevin McCallister!"

I had to laugh at the *Home Alone* reference.

I started to feel a little better with something sweet hitting my lips and stomach, so I said, "Hey, let's forget about everything for a while and go play Putt-Putt. "What do you think?"

"Yeah!" they both said.

We hadn't played for ages. On the way, I had to retell the story I always told them when going to play miniature golf. The girls have heard the story oodles of times, but they let me tell it again anyway.

I reminisced aloud, "One summer when I was about your age, Ree, my Girl Scout troop went to Chandler Park to work on our emergency preparedness badge. Our leader, who happened to be your Grandma Kole, let us swim, then play miniature golf before working on the requirements for the badge.

My friend, Lena, stood right in front of me on the 3rd hole. She only had about 6 inches to putt, but took a huge swing back and hit me in the head with the club, yelling 'Fore!' - after she hit me.

I could see Ren cringing in the passenger seat and continued, "I stood there stunned. Although the club hit me really hard, I felt absolutely no pain. Suddenly blood gushed from a spot between my left eyebrow and my hairline. I was quickly soaked in red, kind of like Carrie at the prom."

"Gross," said Ree from the back seat.

I continued, "Lena took one look at me and lay on the grass banging her fists on the ground crying, 'I've killed her! I've killed her!' Concession workers brought ice for my head while Mom called for an ambulance. I was really embarrassed going to the hospital wearing a bikini, but when the pain kicked in, I knew needed medical help."

I turned a corner and pulled into the parking lot. "The ER doctor stitched me up and wrapped a bandage round and round my forehead. He told me to keep it on for five days! Thankfully, it was summer, so I didn't have to go to school looking like a mummy. I couldn't wash my hair, so it was a tangled disgusting dirty pink/brown color for days." Lauren shivered as she pictured it.

Ree said, "At least it wasn't green."

We laughed and I finished up. "That week, I looked like that injured fife player from the Revolutionary War, but I made the most of it by marching around the house playing songs from 1776 on my piccolo. I sure was a dork."

"Was?" said the girls in unison.

"Haha," I sang. "And now you know why I stand so far away from anyone holding a golf club."

We played a pretty pathetic round of miniature golf. None of us were very good at putting, but we laughed and had fun trying to get the balls under moving windmills, up tiny hills and around sharp corners. About the time we finished, the phone rang. It was the nurse calling back with the results.

"Mrs. Peters?" I didn't bother correcting the name and explaining that I took back my maiden name after the divorce. "Both of Lauren's drug tests are negative. If you would like to stop by and get a copy of the results, you'll need to be here before we close in 15 minutes."

I thanked her and hung up. "You're all clear, girl!" I gave Ren a high-five, "but we already knew that. We need to leave now to pick up the results." We left our clubs and tiny pencils at the register rushed out of the fun center, and got the lab results."

"Now, let's go show Coach Hamm," I said.

"It's too late. They had an early practice today," said Ren.

"OK, I'll talk to him tomorrow night before the meet."

"You're not going to do anything to embarrass me, are you?"

"I don't know? I might. But your coach can't tell lies about you."

"Well, I'm going to go with you just in case."

As we drove through our neighborhood, we passed Arrowstar Elementary. Dr. Love stood on the playground near a mom and her kids. I slowed the car down to see what was going on. He was writing something on what looked like a clipboard.

Ren said, "What is your principal doing there on his day off?"

Just then, he ripped off a paper and handed it to the woman. She took the paper, shook her head, and yanked her kids away. I said, "Oh my gosh, I think he's handing out tickets for being on the playground after school hours."

My girls said, "What?"

I was too stunned to say more and kept driving. I had to tell my buddies about this.

The girls walked into the house slowly, expecting to see a huge mess. But, with my unusually thorough cleaning, it actually looked better than it normally did. Ree ran upstairs to check on Iggy. I guess it could have been a bad decision, tossing her beloved iguana at the guys, but luckily all was good and she was just hungry, as usual. We fed our pets, and each of us packed a bag for the night. They noticed the cake and after reading it, Lauren asked, "Kenny?" I nodded and packed it in the car to take to Kim's house.

I called Lin to ask if she minded having two guests, Lauren and Harriet, stay the night. She said, "Oh, you betcha. Bring 'em over! Cuddles the Cat can just stay in my bedroom. Oh, and I made a hot dish, so we have plenty to eat. Pity, I still can't believe you had two break-ins in one night. Those jerks! You know I want all the details. Are you okay?"

"Not really. I'm so tired, but I'm going to stay at Kim's tonight where I'll get a good night's sleep. Ren can fill you in on the new drug test results when she gets there."

"She's not on drugs, is she?"

"Of course not. It's all a mistake. I'm going to confront Hamm about it before the meet tomorrow."

"Oh, I want to be there for that."

"See you tomorrow night, and thanks so much!"

I kissed Ren and told her to have a great evening. "I'll see you at History Day. And thanks for taking Harriet."

When I drove Ree up to Caitlyn's house, I asked, "Do you want me to go in?"

"No, I think Trish is still mad at you."

"Who isn't mad at me?" I grumbled.

"I'm not," she said, as she came around the car and gave me a hug – an unusual display for this 13-year-old.

"Thanks, Sweetie. I needed that more than you know. See you tomorrow at one o'clock sharp."

"OK," she said and made her way inside, carrying only her bag and pillow. I sat in the driveway for a moment thinking about how much I love my girls.

I thought about calling Kim as I headed across town, but I knew she was still working, so decided to just go straight to her library. She wouldn't care if I just dropped in to spend the night.

As I drove along I-44, I used my voice-to-text and composed a text to Jules, Becca, and Jana telling them about our deranged principal. As soon as I sent it, there were pings with their responses, but I sure couldn't read them while driving.

I noticed a few missed calls and voicemails and listened to the first on the car speaker.

It was from my friendly stalker: "Hi, Kitty. It's your guy, Kenny. I just wondered if you got my presents this week? You told me to stop sending flowers, so I thought I'd cheer you up in other ways. Are you free to go out this weekend? I miss you so much and want to see you again soon. I think about you all the time. Call me, please."

I felt sick. I should call and tell him to leave me alone completely.

Through my rearview mirror, I saw a red sports car swerving back and forth behind me. I made sure my hands were at 10 and 2 and took a deep breath, preparing to drive defensively. Should I slow down or speed up to avoid the wild driver? I chose to accelerate a little since nobody was directly in front of me on the highway.

The car sped up and started to pass me. I glanced over to see if the driver was drunk or texting, but the windows were too dark to see anyone. As it pulled ahead, I looked for the license tag numbers, but there was no plate at all. Then the red monster swerved into my lane and forced me off the road. It sped off and somehow, I managed to keep control of Liesel as I skidded onto the shoulder.

My heart pounded as I braked hard and came to a stop just before hitting the bridge piling. What a jerk!

Garage Sale Tip #15
Go to the first day of a sale to find the best stuff.

After the traumatic near-miss with the crazy driver, I wished I could stay by the side of the road to catch my breath, but it was a terribly busy spot on the highway. I backed up slowly on the shoulder and waited for traffic to clear then quickly accelerated but kept a slower pace while waiting for my heartbeat to slow too.

With several miles left on my drive, I pushed the voicemail button to hear the next message. It was from Mike.

"Hi, Kitty? I mean Pity...Oh, I still don't know what to call you.... Um, this is Mike. I'm calling with an update on your neighbor, Mac Jenkins. His alibi checked out. He couldn't have been the one inside your house last night. It might have been someone else involved in Justin's murder."

Well, that was good and bad news. I was glad it wasn't Mac, but who was it that was in my house?

His message continued, "Oh, and on your other two friends? It turns out they didn't want to show you their IDs at the focus group because both of their licenses were revoked for DUI. They each also had a warrant out for their arrest. Jay broke his restraining order from a previous girlfriend and Scott is wanted for an assault in Texas."

That explained everything - except how Jay got a girlfriend in the first place.

Mike went on, "I'll leave here at 7:30 in the morning and call you on my way. See you tomorrow. Oh, and get some sleep. You need to be alert for all the shopping."

Just hearing his calm voice relaxed me. I called him back and just got his voicemail, so I left a message telling him I was spending the night with my sister in Tulsa and that her house was on the way to Sand Springs. I would give him directions when he called in the morning.

As I drove up to Kim's library, it was bustling with people who were probably there to check out books for the weekend. As I entered, Kim's staff was busy at the front desk. I proceeded to look down the long rows of bookcases for my sister. I found her leaning over a man at a computer. The sign above the computer area read *Desktop computers are available for use by anyone with a library card*, along with directions and rules. The man seemed agitated, but Kim was even more upset. As I walked closer, she said with clenched teeth, "You cannot use our public computers to look up pornography, Mr. Griffin."

"That's not what I was doing," he scoffed, but clearly the site displayed on the screen was porn, as it said *Hot Dirty Moms*. Ick. She glanced at me and rolled her eyes. I pointed to her office. She could deal with him on her own. It wasn't long before she came back and collapsed in her chair.

"That is the third time he's logged on to those explicit sites from here. I had to ban him from the library for three months - again," she said shaking her head.

I shivered in disgust. "Why in the world would someone want to look at that stuff in a public place?"

She huffed, "Or anywhere? He must not have a computer at home. So how are you, Pity?"

"I'm OK but very tired. Can I spend the night with you tonight? Ree won't let me stay at our house until we know who broke in."

"Of course. Good plan. We want to hear all about it anyway."

I said, "I'll run to the thrift store next door and meet you at your house when you get off."

"Do it. You deserve some sale therapy."

I nodded because it was true. I don't eat when I'm stressed, but I do go to sales. If there is anything that will clear my head, wake me up, and make me feel better, it's the possibility of finding a treasure. Even if I find nothing, the hunt is always therapeutic.

"See you in a bit," I said.

Admittedly, garage sales are my obsession, but thrift stores have come through at times, despite the smell. A sign was posted on the door, "Take an extra 50% off clothes today." I don't have a problem buying used clothes at times and feel like I'm recycling perfectly good apparel. I do, however, wash them immediately when I get home. Today, I wasn't interested in clothes, despite the sale, and looked in the pet area to see if there was something I could add to the girls' project board. I found an adorable Super Dog cape that should fit Harriet.

In housewares, I held up a pink clock but put it back on the shelf and straightened a few items around it. A woman asked me, "Where do you keep your picture frames?"

I pointed and answered without hesitation, "Over on aisle three."

Another woman asked me, "Do you have a place to plug in this radio?"

"Yes, there's a power strip along the back wall." She walked in the direction where I had pointed. Ha! They thought I worked here.

I paid for the dog cape (surprisingly half price, too) and a small bell to give to Mrs. Garmin for her bell collection. The cashier asked, "Have you ever thought about working here? I saw you help the customers and you know the store as well as any employee. You would get a discount!"

Imagine that; a discount at a discount store on top of their discounts. I answered, "That's very tempting, but my plate is already full as a single mom with two jobs. Plus, I live in Broken Arrow, so it wouldn't be very convenient. Thank you, though."

As I sat in front of Kim and R.A.'s home in Brookside, I looked at the colorful wildflower garden in front of their porch. The butterflies were sure enjoying the purple coneflowers. Kim got Mom's green thumb, but I didn't. That's one reason I decorate my yard with so many items that don't grow.

There was movement behind the curtains, and KC peeked out the window. I've never been a real cat person, but I always liked KC. She was the first cat I've ever known to cuddle with me.

Kim arrived and I followed her inside their cozy home and collapsed on the couch while she checked the crockpot. I rested my head on the tall back. When KC jumped on my lap I said, "Hey there old girl." I stroked her back as I looked around the familiar 1960s living room decorated with antiques, quilts, and cool vintage clocks.

R.A. walked in and immediately sensed my need to decompress. He brought me a glass of red wine while Kim scooped up her famous chicken and noodles. Ahh, now that is the ultimate comfort food. Kim sat by me on the couch, and started knitting, as usual.

After eating, but before the wine had a chance to lull me to sleep, I told them the details of the two break-ins, of Lauren's drug test mess, and the news that Mac Jenkins may not be our man.

R.A. sipped his gin and tonic and listened with a concerned look. "I'll come over tomorrow and fix your door." I had my own wonderful fix-it man. How lucky was I?

I pointed to the cake and said, "Feel free to have some of the cake Kenny left on my doorstep."

R.A. curled his lip. "Do you think it's poisoned?"

"No," I scoffed. "It's Kenny; why would he poison me? He's obsessed."

R.A. shrugged. "Haven't you heard of the type who believes if he can't have you, nobody can? He seems pretty creepy to me."

"You are so dramatic, R.A. Here, I'll eat some." With my fork, I took a piece from the corner and popped it in my mouth. "So moist" Then I choked and keeled over, landing face-first on the couch.

I pulled myself up and found both of them shaking their heads at me. Kim asked, "What time is History Day tomorrow?"

"One o'clock. Ree will be thrilled that you are coming."

"Wouldn't miss it. We can go with you to the swim meet, too."

I smiled. "Great. The more the merrier."

"Yeah, I want to give that son of a bitch who won't let Lauren swim, a piece of my mind." R.A. tended to get riled up, but he was mostly just a big talker.

I sat back and listened to Kim as she described her recent drama of having a library across the street from an elementary school. Her library had become the free babysitting service for a whole hoard of wild kids, most of whom don't even open a book the whole time. It's a public building, so she can't kick them out unless they get really unruly. And I thought my job was stressful.

Although I felt bad for Kim, it was sort of nice to listen to her problems and not think about the murder.

I got a glass of milk and said, "I didn't get much sleep last night so I'm heading to bed. Thanks for letting me stay."

I gave them both hugs and crashed in their spare room.

By 7:30 a.m. I was showered, refreshed, and excited about going with Mike to Junquefest. He called to get directions to Kim's house, and his truck was in the driveway shortly thereafter.

R.A. said, "I'll probably see you two there."

Mike instantly said, "Why drive all the way there? Ride with us."

I gave wide eyes at R.A., shaking my head no, but without actually shaking my head. He didn't notice and said, "OK, thanks."

Kim made the same face at him. "What?" he asked innocently. I didn't want to say anything in front of Mike, so it was the three of us heading to Sand Springs on our "date." I frowned, envisioning Mike and R.A. hanging out the whole time, looking at tools and leaving me to hunt for treasures all by myself.

But it turned out just fine. Once we got to the giant warehouse holding Junquefest, R.A. went on his merry way to the tool area, and Mike and I stayed together to go check out nearly everything imaginable. I bought a square angel food cake pan for $2. I'd never seen one. All Kole family birthday cakes are angel food, and I could make a square one now.

Looking at the pan, he asked, "So, now will you tell me about your cake man?"

I told him all about my platonic two-date relationship with Kenny months ago and said, "I never encouraged him, but in his head, we're a couple. He's harmless, though."

"So, you don't think your admirer/stalker had anything to do with the break-in?"

"Oh, no." I shook my head, "I can't imagine him doing anything like that. He's so tame. As a matter of fact, I think he might still live with his mother."

"No, his sister," Mike said.

I turned to him. "He lives with his sister? How do you know?"

Mike shrugged. "Well, Lauren gave us his name, and I checked him out since he was at your house that night. And we had his fingerprints. He's squeaky clean, though. No prior arrests."

"See? Besides, he didn't even live in Broken Arrow in the 90s, so he would have no reason to take the stuff from our command central."

"OK, I believe you. In case you want to know, Kenny has never been married and has never worked a day in his life. Guess where he lives?" He didn't give me a chance to guess. "He lives in Arrow Ridge," Mike said with an eyebrow raised waiting for my response.

"Oh yeah?" I knew he was well off since he took me on a date in a limousine, but that's a fancy pants neighborhood. I asked, "He's really never had a job? His family must have more money than I thought?"

"Dunno."

"Speaking of cars," I said timidly, "a car ran me off the highway last night. I mean, it was acting all crazy, and I had to swerve off the road. But I was OK. Just shaken a little."

"Really? Did you get the license tag number?"

"No. There wasn't a tag at all."

Mike frowned, "What kind of car was it?

"Red."

"But what kind?"

"Red."

He thinned his lips wanting more.

I shrugged. "I don't know. I can't tell one car from another. Maybe a sports car? It had really dark windows."

"Do you think someone tried to harm you on purpose?"

"Nah. Probably just some drunk."

Mike shook his head and sighed. He picked up a movie reel marked $4. "This will look great on the wall of my media room."

I looked up at him thinking this man just kept getting better and better. "Media room?"

Uh...yeah...I like movies a little too much. When I have free time, I'm usually at a theater or watching old movies at home. My DVD collection is ridiculous."

I said, "You're kidding. Me too. If I had time and money, I'd go see every movie made."

"Well, maybe we could go to a show sometime," he suggested.

I thought about telling him about my brief stint as a stand-in, but that was better left for later when we had more time.

"Sure!" I got a brilliant idea, "Mike, you should come to my Oscar party! I have it every year. But you have to dress up and walk on the red carpet for pictures. We have contests, prizes, food, and we watch the Academy Awards Show. Wanna come?"

He nodded, smiling, "I could probably dress up. It's a date."

My heart did a little flip with the term but recovered with my usual gab. "Well, my gowns come from only the finest local thrift stores for this gala event."

He laughed. "Do you ever buy anything full price?"

"Rarely. Even at real stores, I find sales. I'm addicted to the shopper's thrill."

"Shopper's thrill? What's that?"

"Well, it's a wonderful sensation, kind of like a 'runner's high'."

"Oh, so you run?"

"Ha! Me? Run? Maybe if I'm trying to get to a sale first."

He shook his head and pointed to an old record player. "Do you like to dance?"

I was momentarily stumped. "Sure?"

"Well, there is another thing we could do." He took my right hand in his left and put his other arm behind my back and danced me over to the next table smoothly.

When R.A. approached, I wondered if he noticed me swooning against a shelf of records, but he just said, "Look! I've wanted one of these ever since I was a kid."

I peeled my eyes away from Mike and looked at the metal object with gears. I was happy for him, but not at all sure what the item was. A toy, maybe? Mike seemed to recognize it and the two discussed how it worked. They were busy, so I turned around to catch my breath from the sweet impromptu spin. When I glanced back at them, Mike gave me a cute wink.

My breath caught. "I think I kinda like him," I quietly sang to myself as I perused some books. I picked up one that surprised me, *Murder on the High Dive*. According to the inside cover, it was written in the 1950s. I flipped through the book and saw a crudely drawn picture of a competition pool with a man being pushed off the diving board. I wondered if the book's plot was anything like Justin's murder, so I opened the book to see if I could get any information. Of course, it was just a cheesy murder mystery, but I figured I needed it for a quarter anyway.

Mike walked up to me holding something behind his back. I raised my eyebrows. "Find something special?"

He grinned and handed me a bag. He said, "Just for you."

I pulled out a black t-shirt and read the white print.

I'm a yard sale addict on the road to recovery

Just kidding

I'm on the road to another yard sale

Mike wrinkled his nose at me, probably hoping I wasn't insulted.

I brightened and smiled at the funny saying. "You probably think I'm offended, but I love it! It may be my new Saturday morning uniform. Thank you!"

R.A. laughed. "Just don't wear it around Ren. She would be mortified."

True.

We found a few more goodies, but the only big thing we put in the truck bed was an enormous bagel chipper that R.A. had to have. I didn't even know he liked bagels.

I suggested R.A. sit in the front on the way back, so I could look through my new old book. As we headed back to Tulsa for an early lunch with Kim, something in the third chapter caught my eye. There was a picture of the diver looking in the stands at a girl who was spotlighted. It sure made me wish I hadn't lost the class roster and yearbook. I never really looked at the photos and needed to find out which girl was Patty Sue. I didn't even have the list of names anymore.

After a quick, yummy, greasy burger at Claude's Hamburgers, we left in three vehicles for Broken Arrow. Mike had to go to his sister's and then to work, so we agreed to talk later. The morning hadn't been much of a date, but it was sure fun.

Kim and R.A. parked next to me at the History Day venue. We made our way down each row of projects looking for the girls. There were elaborate display boards, some with ribbons and others without. After the judging, each group had to stand all afternoon to explain their projects to the public. The kids were eager to show their projects, so we stopped and listened to a few spiels. R.A congratulated some boys on their intricate piece of machinery.

After a few inventions piqued my interest, I wished I was rich and could give young entrepreneurs start-up money, like *Shark Tank*, but for kids.

We continued past a few more projects, and when we heard a lot of racket, I figured it must be our girls.

I was right. Blasting from their booth was "Who Let the Dogs Out?" I looked over and saw the girls demonstrating the scanner on Harriet for a young couple. When Harriet saw me, she wagged her tail so hard she practically knocked Caitlyn over. Ree looked up and beamed, "Mom, we got a purple ribbon!"

"Wow. Congratulations!" I walked up to pet Harriet, so she would settle down and do her job. I looked at the ribbon tacked just above the tiny plastic box holding the minuscule microchip, gave Ree a thumbs up, and smiled. We stood aside and waited for the girls to finish explaining the project to the couple. Ree handed them something, and when they moved on, we moved in.

Kim touched the hand-drawn diagram of a dog with a tiny chip between its shoulder blades. "Ree and Caitlyn, this is amazing."

"Thanks, Aunt Kim." Ree gave her a big hug.

R.A. asked to try out the scanner on Harriet, and Ree showed him how it worked. He inspected the handheld wand that displayed Harriet's long number. "Cool!".

Caitlyn said, "The judges said our project was clever and informative".

Ree added, "And everyone loves Harriet. They all want to know what breed she is, but we just say, 'She's just Harriet.'"

That's about as good an answer as one can give. After saving the lovable dog from the pound, we took her to the vet for a check-up. As to her breed, he was perplexed. He said she could be part Bearded Collie, Old English Sheepdog, or any number of large shaggy dogs, but he couldn't know for sure without a DNA test. I didn't have money for that, but maybe someday. Whatever she is, she's our baby, and we'll never find another like her. We only wish we could have seen her as a puppy; I'm sure she was an adorable ball of fur.

Mom and Dad arrived, and Ree gave them each a hug. The girls gave their whole demonstration, speaking up so Dad could hear.

A few minutes later, Todd and Shelly strode up. Shelly was dressed in a flashy short skirt, high heels, and big jewelry as usual. Who dolls up to go to History Day? Todd tipped his cowboy hat to my parents and R.A., but he ignored Kim and me. Typical.

The crowd had grown too large for the small hall space, so I motioned for Mom, Dad, Kim, and R.A. to come with me to a little seating area a few booths down. Mom and Dad sat down on the bench while we stood by a tall Ficus plant. Mom said, "Did you see what those girls are handing out?"

I said, "No. What?"

"A bag of chips to remind people to have their pets micro**chip**ped. Isn't that clever?"

So clever! I was proud of the girls and watched them do the routine for an interested Todd. Shelly, however? Well, she studied her fingernails instead of the presentation.

Out of the blue, Kim blurted, "Mom, Pity has a policeman!"

Mom and Dad said, "What?", not because they couldn't hear, but because they didn't understand how I 'had' a policeman.

"She means I met a guy who is a policeman." I made a face at Kim, feeling just like Ren did when Ree had said 'Lauren has a boyfriend!' I clarified, "He's just a friend and is very nice."

"I met him, and he's a good guy," nodded R.A.

My dad turned to me. "Well, I'm glad you have a friend who can keep you safe. Somebody needs to watch over you."

About that time, Ren walked up with Caitlyn's cute uncle, Andy. They each carried two bottles of water. "Hi!" she said as she gave hugs to her grandparents, Kim and R.A. Then she asked, "Grandma and Grandpa, do you know Andy? He's Caitlyn's uncle. These are my grandparents, my Aunt Kim and Uncle R.A." Ren looked up at the hot older guy with a huge grin.

Kim and Mom said, "Hi" as Dad and R.A shook Andy's hand.

I wasn't too excited to see Lauren with the older guy but remembered they had just gone to the snack bar to get bottled water. Calm down, Pity. It wasn't a date.

Ren continued, "Andy drove the girls here and bought their bags of chips because Trish wasn't feeling well this morning. We just got them some water, since they'll be talking so much," she said without taking a breath. I had never seen Lauren quite so giddy.

It was odd that Trish wasn't here. She was usually in the middle of the girls' booth, directing Caitlyn during her presentation. Maybe she thought she would get more attention by being "ill." At least I didn't have to deal with her drama today.

Todd and Shelly walked right past us without comment; all the better, because I didn't want to talk to them anyway. Shelly's perfume was so strong, I almost gagged. Mom said in her straightforward manner, "Well, she didn't spare the cologne today, did she?" I watched to see if Shelly had heard her, but she was making a big show of signing an autographed photo for a little girl. She had probably paid the child to ask for it. I'm probably bad to think that way, but my girls have told me too many stories about her.

When Harriet barked, I turned back toward Marie's display. A group of men and women wearing name tags stood by their exhibit. Harriet was clearly agitated. I was shocked to see Dr. Love standing in the group of judges. Great. At least that explained why Harriet was bothered – even dogs don't like him.

Ren leaned over. "Can you believe your principal is a judge?"

Kim said, "It's a good thing Ree has a different last name than you, or she wouldn't have gotten a ribbon at all with him as a judge."

"No joke," I said and watched the group move on to the next project, hoping the strange man didn't notice me.

When Harriet kept growling and pulling her leash, I walked over to the booth and greeted Caitlyn's Grandma Jean and Grandpa Brian before trying to settle Harriet down. She licked my hand, so I figured she wanted to go out.

"Well, what's all the clatter about, Harriet?" said Brian in his Irish accent. He started to pet her, but she backed away. Why did stupid Dr. Love get her all riled up?

"Come on, girl," I said as I took the leash. I turned to Caitlyn's grandparents, "Sorry about that. She probably needs a potty break. I'll take her." We walked away as Andy joined his parents. Harriet was fine and seemed glad to use the grass. I sat down with my big shaggy dog for a minute and hugged her. We've gone through a lot together over the years, and she was a great comfort when I got divorced. I could always depend on Harriet to make me feel better. I stroked her long hair, and she licked my face in thanks.

When we got back, Ree ran to me and said, "Since we got a purple ribbon, Grandpa Brian wants to take us to Oktoberfest to celebrate. Can I go and spend the night with Caitlyn? Please?"

Confused, I said, "Oktoberfest is this weekend?" How had I missed that?

Tulsa's Oktoberfest is one of the biggest German festivals in the U.S. It is such fun, with bands, dancing, food, and lots of beer. All ages love it. Ren usually works at the strudel booth with her German class, but since she was supposed to swim today, she didn't sign up to work. I had forgotten all about it. I would have to go check out my favorite festival before it was over. Maybe Mike could go with me over the weekend. I gave myself an internal wink.

"Of course, you can go. That's nice of him to take you. You'll have lots of fun. Look, if you don't need anything, we're going to go ahead and leave. What time should I be back to pack you up?"

"We need to leave by 3:30."

"OK, I'll be back in about an hour. Congratulations again, girls!" After giving them hugs, I walked back to the others. "R.A., do you want to come by and look at my lock?"

Dad said, "What's wrong with your lock?"

Oops, I didn't want to worry him, so I answered, "Oh, it's a long story. I'll tell you about it later," which I would once it was all straightened out. I added, "The front door just isn't working properly." Yeah, like it's not keeping creeps out of the house.

Mom said, "Well, we're going to go down to Oktoberfest this afternoon. It's not so crowded in the daytime. What time is Lauren's meet tonight?" she asked.

Crap. I didn't want them to know about that either. "Oh, she's not actually swimming tonight." I frantically tried to think of an excuse. "She has an earache." Again? I usually don't lie, but this week, I was in complete falsehood mode. "How about you come with me to the meet next Thursday, OK? Have fun doing the chicken dance!"

"Oh, we will," said Dad with a twinkle in his eye. He flapped his elbows twice.

They said goodbye to Ree and walked to Ren. Mom patted her on the back before leaving.

Lauren came to me and said sarcastically, "How is my earache, Mom?"

I shrugged and left with my sister.

Garage Sale Tip #16
Dress for comfort, not fashion, while shopping.

Back home, I took a shower and came out of my bedroom, brushing my hair while talking. "Do you two want to stay here while I go back to History Day to get Marie and Caitlyn? Drinks are in the fridge. Make yourselves at home."

I looked up and saw that Kim and R.A. were already watching TV with drinks in hand. They looked so comfortable you would think it was their house.

R.A. said, "Check out your new hardware."

"You already installed the locks?"

He stood and handed me the new keys and showed me the new doorknob. They seemed very secure. I breathed a sigh of relief. What would I do without R.A.?

One more History Day was in the books. We packed up the board, the CD player, the scanner, and the dog. First, I took the girls to the vet's office to return the machinery, then I drove them to Caitlyn's Grandpa's house. "Oh, Ree, come here a sec."

She came to my window.

"Here's a twenty, in case you need money at Oktoberfest."

She said, "You know Grandpa Brian won't let me pay."

"Well, you should at least offer."

"OK, Mom." She took the bill and stuffed it in her pocket.

"Don't forget to take your jacket. It'll get chilly tonight. See you in the morning, and have fun!"

Harriet and I chatted on the drive home. Well, I chatted and she panted. She sat up so tall in the passenger seat that she was the same height as me. At a stoplight, a lady driving the car next to me did a double-take, then laughed as she pointed out Harriet to the man next to her. It wasn't the first time Harriet had been mistaken for a woman with long white hair.

When I walked in my house, R.A. was sound asleep, his head nodding on his chest. Kim was almost finished knitting a sock, but I was able to rouse them by saying, 'Ready to confront Coach Hamm?"

R.A. sat up. "Do you have a plan?"

Kim said, "Since when does Pity have a plan?" She turned to me. "But you do have proof of her negative drug tests, right?"

"Yep. I have copies right here." I showed her the papers in my pocket. "Ren's going to meet us there. She wants to make sure I don't embarrass her."

Kim laughed, "Ha! As if you wouldn't embarrass her. Is Mike coming?"

"No, he has to work. Besides, we'll just be there for a minute, since Ren isn't on the roster to swim. Oh, and Lin will be there since Jennifer's swimming. With you guys, I have plenty of back-up."

We arrived at the pool plenty early. Kim and I put our jackets and purses down on the steps near the door since we didn't plan to stay. I spotted the Broken Arrow swimmers in their black and gold swimsuits. Most were either stretching or eating snacks from the table in the corner of the pool area. I felt a pang of sadness that Ren wasn't with them.

The opposing team, Jenks HS, was congregating on the other side of the pool wearing suits of maroon and white. A larger crowd than usual was expected tonight because of the big rivalry. I didn't see Lin or Ren, but I spotted Coach Hamm talking to the assistant coach near the starting blocks.

"There he is. It's showtime," I said as I marched toward him.

Kim and R.A. followed me around the far side of the 25-meter pool. When the assistant coach saw us approach with our determined faces, he stepped away.

I squared my shoulders and said, "Hello, Coach Hamm," I handed him the papers from the doctor's office. "I'm sure Lauren's positive drug test was a mistake. As you can see from these results, there were no drugs detected on two different tests administered at the doctor's office."

He scoffed, "This proves nothing. She took our drug test on Wednesday. When did you have this taken?"

"We had it done yesterday morning. The doctor's note explains that these tests are far more sensitive than the ones required at schools. Furthermore, the tests would have revealed anything in her system that was there on Wednesday. I don't know how you got the wrong results, but I believe you need to apologize to Ren in front of the whole team and let her swim at the earliest time.

He looked right into my eyes with a steely expression and said, "I believe you need to mind your own business."

Surprised by his response, I spat, "My daughter IS my business!" Just then, my ADD kicked in and I was distracted by Shelly who toddled in high heels very close to the pool's edge. She was fiddling with her fake fur coat and looked ridiculous in her mini skirt and high heels. Who wears a fur coat to a swim meet?

Coach Hamm mumbled something else to me that I didn't catch. I turned to him, "What did you say?"

In my peripheral vision, I saw Shelly lose her balance and fall towards the water. Her furry arms flapped as she tried to right herself, but down she went like an awkward ostrich, landing in the pool with an enormous splash. I expected to have quite a laugh watching her make her way to the side of the pool, sopping wet, but she didn't surface. The weight of her faux fur jacket must have pulled her further underwater. The only thing coming up was bubbles. Several people shouted, but nobody jumped in, not even Todd.

I left the coach and sprinted to the edge of the pool, looking in. She flailed under the water. Upon closer inspection, I could see her high heel was stuck in the grate on the bottom of the pool.

Nobody did anything, so I threw off my shoes and dove in. I swam across the pool and took a deep breath before diving to the bottom. I tried to free her heel from the metal frame, but she kept scratching me with her long fingernails.

I came up for air and was thankful to see Lauren jumping in to help. Most of the pool is fairly shallow, but of course, we had to be in the deepest part - 6 ½ feet. I dove to the bottom again and managed to unhook her shoe from her foot.

Once Shelly was freed, Ren started lifting her to the surface, thanks to her lifeguard training. I got to the top just before Shelly and watched her gasp for air. Either she didn't know how to swim, or her arms were so heavy, she couldn't. With great difficulty, Lauren and I pulled the waterlogged Shelly to the side of the pool where Todd and another man lifted her out of the water.

Except for being humiliated, she seemed to be fine. She was, however, a real mess. Mascara ran down her face, a fake eyelash was stuck to her cheek and her wet hair clung to her head. Of course, I didn't look much better, but at least I didn't have a short skirt sticking to me or a wet fake animal wrapped around my torso.

I was completely baffled. We were at a swim meet, so why didn't someone in a swimsuit jump in the water? One look at Todd and I knew why he didn't go in after her – his precious alligator boots.

Lauren got out and helped Shelly take off the heavy jacket. Todd wrapped a towel around his girlfriend. "Are you OK, dear?"

She barked, "Why didn't you jump in after me? Couldn't you see I was drowning?"

As they continued to fuss, I started to get out of the pool to go back to the rude coach, when over the loudspeaker I heard Kim's voice say, "Pity, he said to 'Stop poking around in things that don't concern you.'"

While treading water, I spotted Kim holding the microphone. I recognized that wide-eyed look. She was telling me to think about what she had just said.

But what did that mean? Stop poking around...? Then it dawned on me, and my eyes widened, too. I turned my gaze away from Kim and looked at Coach Hamm. I pulled myself out and onto the deck and sloshed over to him in my wet jeans and shirt, glad to see that most people were still paying attention to Shelly instead of me.

I burst out, "You know the truth about how Justin Jones died, don't you? That's why you kept Lauren from swimming. You don't want ME around, because you know I've been asking questions."

"I don't know what you are talking about," he growled but avoided eye contact.

"Oh, I think you know exactly what I'm talking about. As a matter of fact, you know it was a murder and I think you were involved," I bluffed.

The coach shifted his gaze and stared at me silently, then he with wild eyes and said, "You have no proof of anything."

I felt confident that I was on the right track and continued, "The police are very interested and they will soon find out all about you."

He ran over to a duffle bag and grabbed the starter pistol. Then he pointed the gun directly at me. I knew it was filled with blanks, but I was startled just the same.

In a flash, R.A. snuck up behind the coach and knocked the gun out of his hand. With the movement, the gun discharged. Everyone in the pool area froze at the unexpected burst of sound that echoed throughout the natatorium.

Then, as if in slow motion, Coach Hamm silently fell forward hitting the water with a big splash. The crowd was stunned silent, but when a cloud of blood started forming around his floating body, the entire pool area echoed with screams and gasps. Had the gun been loaded with real bullets?

I ran to the starting block of his lane, jumped in, and swam to the partially submerged body. From out of nowhere, Lin joined me in the water and helped drag the coach to the side. Having been a swimmer and lifeguard in high school, she knew exactly what to do.

R.A. and Chris pulled the coach out of the water and onto the deck. They lay his head on a life jacket as I climbed out of the pool, this time using the ladder. Breathing heavily, I leaned over the wet man and saw the blood oozing from his left shoulder. I looked at Kim who stood frozen with the microphone still in her hand and I dialed an imaginary phone in my hand.

Kim's voice boomed over the loudspeakers. "Someone please call 9-1-1 and ask for an ambulance." She thought for a second then added, "and the police."

Although I knew he was in pain, I asked the Coach, "Did you murder Justin Jones?"

He said nothing, so I repeated the question louder. "Coach Hamm, did you murder Justin Jones? We know it wasn't an accident and believe you had something to do with it." Funny thing is, I would never have suspected him if he hadn't said I was poking around. I just went with my gut.

His eyes widened, but he remained silent.

I continued, "You realize you just threatened to shoot me in front of two hundred people. That seems like a pretty good admission of guilt. Now you've lost a lot of blood and you could die." I knew that was a bit dramatic, but figured it was worth a try to get him to talk.

When he opened his mouth, I leaned forward to hear him. "I liked Justin," he whispered with tears in his eyes.

I continued, "And did you like Patty Sue?"

He croaked out, "What? Who?" as if I was speaking French.

I decided to forgo that line of questioning. "Well, if you liked Justin, you owe it to his memory, to tell the truth. I doubt you'll get away with anything now, so just tell me what you did."

He finally said in a mere whisper "It wasn't just me."

Oh, now we're getting somewhere. I asked, "It wasn't just you?"

"I didn't plan it," he said, gasping.

"Someone else was involved?"

"Yes."

"Who else was in on it with you?"

"It was..." he said in pained breaths. "It was... Mr. Murphy. He paid me to do it."

I thought he must be delirious from the pain and talking nonsense. Why would an English teacher want to kill Justin? I asked, "The teacher, Mr. Murphy?"

He grimaced as he nodded his head. "I didn't want to, but he..." he took a deep breath, "he knew I had gambling debts that he would pay off. And if I didn't do it, he'd get me fired..." He went limp before finishing his sentence.

"If you didn't do what?" I considered shaking him awake, but the EMTs showed up and pushed me away to look at his wound.

Kim handed towels to Lin and me. I wrapped myself up and gave my sister a hug. R.A. leaned over me and said, "Well, girl, you found out who did it."

"I know. Sort of." I shook my head, then remembered what R.A. had done. I looked at him. "And you saved my life, R.A." I reached out and hugged him.

"It was just a reaction. I sure didn't know the gun was loaded." He shook his head. "Do you know this Mr. Murphy?"

I shrugged. "I think he's the teacher in the room where the desk lived." I tilted my head, thinking aloud. "If the notes were from the killer, then either Coach Hamm or Mr. Murphy wrote them. But he…" I pointed to the prostrate man "didn't even seem to know who Patty Sue was, so Mr. Murphy had an affair with a student? I'm so confused and cold."

R.A. said, "And you could be in shock. You should sit down."

Kim guided me to the place where we had left our purses and jackets. I sat on the concrete bench and shivered from the drama of having a gun pointed at me, witnessing a man being shot, and from jumping in the pool twice.

Lin joined us with her hair still dripping. She said, "I called Mike and asked him to get over here as soon as he could. He should be here anytime."

Some officers had already arrived. I watched them ask the swim officials questions, then inspect the bloody spot where the coach had lain. Someone took photos of the gun on the bottom of the pool, then one of the policemen fished it out with a net.

I shuddered when the EMTs took Coach Hamm away on a stretcher. People couldn't die from being shot in the shoulder, could they? After the ambulance had gone, someone announced the meet was canceled and would be rescheduled. Everyone should go home. Obviously, nobody could swim in a pool with bloody water. Well, except Lin and me, I guess.

Most of the spectators stared at me as they filed out. One woman said, "Did you see Lauren's mom save that woman and that coach?" Other comments included, "Why were there real bullets in the gun?"

and "Wasn't that the lady from the Big Jack's Cadillac commercials?" A familiar little kid's voice asked "Why did that man try to shoot Mrs. Kole?" I looked up to see which of my students it was, but he/she was already lost in the crowd.

The officers were talking to a few swimmers and parents, and I knew they would be heading my way soon.

Mrs. Bates walked by and gave me a sweet wave, and Todd walked past us looking miserable. Can't blame him, since Shelly was still bitching at him. Thankfully, nobody spoke to me directly. I sure wasn't in the mood to talk to anyone except my group.

Ren left her friends and walked up with a towel draped around her shoulders. Lin scooted over, so she could sit by me. With tears in her eyes, she said, "The team is so confused about what just happened, Mom."

I put my arm around my damp daughter and said quietly, "Honey, it looks like your coach was somehow involved in the murder of Justin Jones back in 1997."

She flinched at the news and looked as though she would cry. I hugged her tighter, feeling awful that my child had to hear that her coach wasn't who she thought he was. I said, "Don't tell the other kids yet, except maybe Jennifer."

She nodded, then put her wet head on my wet shoulder. In a muffled voice, she said, "I'm so glad you're alright, Mom."

I nodded. "It was a close call. Hey, Ren, do you know a Mr. Murphy from school?"

She said, "I don't think so."

I was relieved that she didn't know a man who could have once been involved with a student and worse yet, a murder.

An attractive young policewoman and an older male officer with a scrunched face walked towards us just as Mike entered. He talked with them, then stepped to the side as the detectives introduced themselves to our group. I gave Mike a little wave, but his brow just furrowed. Who could blame him? I was far too much of a mess to be his friend.

When the detectives asked us to explain what happened, I let out the breath I'd been holding and began, "I guess I should start from the very beginning." I told the officers about the notes and continued to the break-in. The woman took copious notes as the grouchy cop scowled.

He said, "Did you turn in your evidence to the police?"

I shook my head. "No, I didn't. I thought they could have been just a writing assignment. About the time I realized they were real, they were stolen."

The detective looked wary at my statement, and I felt like a dope. I went on and explained the details of this evening. "So, in conclusion, Coach Hamm confessed to being involved in the murder in front of all of us." I took a deep breath, glad to be finished with the story.

The woman looked at her notes and asked, "Do you know this Mr. Murphy?"

"No. All I know is that he taught in room 202 at the high school and retired from teaching years ago. Oh, and he still subs at Broken Arrow High sometimes."

She smiled. "Thank you for the information, Ms. Kole. I'm sure the evening was traumatic for you. We'll need you to stay in town, as we may call you in for further questioning."

The grumpy man added, "And please leave the detective work to the professionals from now on."

I nodded, having heard that before. As they turned to interview R.A., I said, "Wait. Why did the starter pistol have real bullets in it?"

The grumpy man said, "It wasn't a starter pistol. It was a Glock 19 registered to the victim, Mr. Hamm."

Wow. Why had he brought a real gun to a swim meet? My mind whirred with scary thoughts. Ren looked just as horrified as I felt.

Mike put a warm hand on my shoulder and whispered, "I thought you were going to stay out of trouble." I could tell he wasn't mad, just concerned.

I nodded and frowned. "So... I guess you heard most of the story?"

R.A. was finished with his statement, so I grabbed his hand and pulled him to us. "Mike, did you hear that my sweet brother-in-law saved my life?"

He nodded. "I heard. Pity told me you're her fixer, but you took your job to a new level tonight."

I added, "And if Kim hadn't warned me, no telling what would have happened." I reached out and squeezed my sister's hand.

Kim said, "But did you hear that Pity saved her ex-husband's girlfriend's life?"

Mike cocked his head at me. "No, I didn't hear that one." He listened intently as R.A. described, with pantomimes, Shelly's underwater aerobics act, and the rescue by me and Ren.

Mike shook his head, then nodded. "Oh! I saw a soggy woman stomp by with a man in cowboy boots. I thought I recognized him. That lady was quite a sight."

I said, "She always is. She's just not usually so wet."

"Well as long as you are alright, I should get back to work."

I smiled. "Thanks for coming, Mike. I'm so glad you got to see me with disgusting hair again." I rolled my eyes at that thought.

He laughed and waved. I was glad he didn't hate me.

I checked my phone to make sure Marie hadn't tried to reach me and saw a missed call and voicemail from Texas. I punched the play button. After hearing the first words, I called to Mike, who hadn't made it to the door yet, "Hold on. Everyone, come here." When my whole gang was assembled, I started the recording again, playing it aloud on speaker for Mike, Kim, R.A., Ren, and Lin.

"Hi, Ms. Kole, this is Steven Bates. I was looking through the yearbook and found Patty Sue's picture. Her name was Patricia Murphy. I should have remembered that because her father was our English teacher. Well, I hope this helps. Call if you need anything else." The recording ended.

Kim squinted and said, "So wait a minute. Mr. Murphy, the teacher, was writing the notes to his daughter in his class?"

I nodded slowly as that sunk in. "That's weird."

Lin said, "Now I want to read the clues again."

Ren said, "Mom."

I said, "I don't get it. Why did he write those notes to his…"

Ren tried again louder, "Mom!"

I turned to see Ren's face had turned white. She said, "Mom, I know who Patricia Murphy is."

All five of us said in unison, "Who?"

She said with a shaky voice, "I remember seeing her name in the yearbook. Patricia Murphy is Trish!"

"Patty Sue is Trish?" I scoffed in disbelief, then a shiver went through me as the realization hit. "Patty Sue is Trish?"

Everyone looked surprised, except Mike who asked, "Who's Trish?"

I stared into space as if in a trance and answered slowly, "Trish is Caitlyn's mom." I swallowed hard. "Which means…Mr. Murphy is her father." It was hard to speak with a lump forming in my throat but I croaked out the terrifying words, "The murderer is Grandpa Brian, and Ree is with him right now at Oktoberfest!"

Garage Sale Tip #17
Take along friends who shop at your pace

I jumped up and tried to put on my jacket, but it wouldn't slide over my damp sleeves. Mike took hold of my arm and said firmly, but gently, "Slow down, Pity. Let's figure out what we need to do before rushing into things."

"But my baby is with a monster. I've got to get her!" I pulled my arm away from him.

Kim said, "Wait, Pity. Breathe." She helped me put my jacket on, then held my arms still. "It's going to be alright, but Mike's right. We have to have a plan."

R.A., thinking aloud said, "Oh…that's probably why Harriet growled at Caitlyn's grandpa at History Day." He looked at me. "He must be the one who broke into your house." The others nodded their heads slowly.

"Right…that's why I have to go there now!" I said louder than I intended.

Lin agreed with the others, "Yeah, but if we go barging down there…no telling what he could do."

Ren said, "But, how can Grandpa Brian be a killer? He's so nice." She looked as if she could cry.

I hugged my girl. "I don't know, but if we're right, I have to go protect Ree."

Mike soothed, "OK, Pity, you're right and we'll go. But listen. He doesn't know that we know he's involved, right? She's probably perfectly safe right now. We have time to make a plan. I'll call into the department and make this an official investigation."

Kim said, "Let's go to your house and get you some dry clothes or you'll freeze walking around Oktoberfest. We can work out a plan quickly there. You ride with me, and R.A. can drive your car to your house." She looked at R.A.

He said, "Sure. Where are the keys?"

I handed them to him, realizing my friends were right. I had to collect myself and think. We walked quickly to the parking lot. I turned to Ren and said calmly, "Would you go to Jennifer's house, sweetie? I can't bear to have you involved any more than you already are. We will get your sister. I promise." I gave her a big hug.

With tears welling up in her eyes, she pleaded, "OK, bring her home safely – and please be careful." She left with Jennifer who had been standing a few feet away. Lin followed the girls to her house to dry off and get them settled in.

The rest of us drove to my house. I changed clothes and dried my hair as fast as I could. Kim got me a glass of water, but I was too upset to drink and paced the room.

Lin joined us and said, "What's the plan?".

I said with conviction, "I don't know. But first, I'm calling Marie to make sure she's OK."

Everyone nodded. Kim said, "Yes. And see if you can find out where they are so we'll have something to go on."

Mike said, "Good idea. But don't startle her or say anything that might upset her."

I nodded, picked up my phone and nervously called my youngest daughter's cell phone, putting it on speaker so the others could hear. I held my breath as it rang. When she picked up, we could hear the recognizable oom-pah-pah of a polka band in the background even before she spoke. She said cheerfully, "Hi Mom!"

I sighed in relief to hear my cheerful girl. "Hi, sweetie." My voice cracked a little. I swallowed and asked, "Are you having fun?"

"Yes!" she shouted into the phone, "We already ate bratwurst and had German soda. Now we're listening to a silly band that tells dumb jokes. Grandpa Brian bought us chicken hats, and Caitlyn keeps clucking like a dork." We could hear Caitlyn clucking as both girls giggled through the phone's speaker.

"Oh, good. I just wanted to check on you. What time do you think you'll be home?"

"I don't know. There is a weenie dog race we're going to watch in about an hour. And Grandpa Brian wants to watch the beer keg race after that. It's really cold here. Glad I brought a jacket."

"See? Your mother knows a few things. Have fun, honey, and call me if you need anything at all." My mouth had gone dry. I was surprised I could even get the words out.

"Okay, bye!" and the phone and all its background noise went silent. I was thrilled to know she was fine, but I felt so anxious, my stomach hurt.

Mike said, "That sounded good and we have a little time."

Lin shrugged her shoulders. "Couldn't we just wait 'til he brings Ree home, and then send the police to go get him at his house?"

I shook my head. "I'm worried that someone from the swim meet will run into them and tell them about what happened. Then he might snap. I could never live with myself if he hurt Ree. I need her back now."

Kim suggested, "Why not just send the police there to get him?"

Mike answered, "I've already called my buddy on duty in the Tulsa PD, so they are alerted to the situation and will be there. Since there is no clear danger to the girls or others, I hate to have them scare him. Our first priority is to get Marie away from Brian safely without him knowing anything about it. Then the police can close in."

I added, "And we can't forget poor Caitlyn. She can't be caught up in this any more than Marie." Despite my worry or maybe because of it, I concocted a plan that just might work. I explained my idea to the group, and they said it was better than anything they had thought of, so we worked out the details. Then, in two vehicles, we headed to Tulsa.

Oktoberfest is held on the west side of the Arkansas River every year. I teared up when I remembered the last time my girls and I spent a day there together.

My nerves intensified as we neared the festival. Just seeing the crowds of people laughing as they made their way across the walking bridge to Oktoberfest tormented me. Why were they acting so normal when my daughter could be in danger?

I looked around for a place to park, expecting to walk a mile to the entrance, but Mike flashed his badge and told the traffic cop it was official business. We got to park both cars right by the vendor area, saving us a good thirty minutes.

It was already eight o'clock, and I exited the truck quickly. It was colder than expected, but I was dry and had prepared myself with a jacket in addition to the gear I needed for our mission. Everyone had their individual assignments, and we were ready for action.

We approached the entrance and paid the admission, then dodged the throngs of festival-goers who sang and held beer pitchers. The sounds of music and laughter coupled with the smells of German food should have been fun and enticing, but not tonight.

The five of us scouted out the scene. There were about ten large tents in the center with booths and rides surrounding them. Of course, the beer booths were the most popular, with lines stretching into the walkway. We had to cut through several long lines of thirsty people to make our way through the festival.

I said, "OK. We'll leave you to go your posts. Good luck Kim, R. A. and Lin."

We split up and moved in different directions: R.A. to the tent where his friend, Jesse, worked on sound equipment, Kim to the west side of the festival, and Lin to the far east side near the river to meet up with her beer distributor friend. I sure hoped the plans worked.

With Mike walking next to me I shouted, "What if they see us?"

I hoped he could hear me beyond the tubas and hollering from a yodeling contest.

He yelled back, "We'll just have to keep a low profile and hope we spot them first."

Bright, colorful lights shone on the whole park, so it was easy to see everything. But with all the people wearing jackets in the cool fall air it was hard to recognize anyone. I scoured the area looking for Ree.

I said, "Now remember, the girls are both wearing chicken hats." I became baffled as I saw a boy with a big chicken head on his hat and just after, a girl wore a whole chicken body and silly legs hanging down by her ears. Looking over the crowd, I saw feathered hats in brown, yellow, and white. And I thought their chicken hats would be easy to spot.

I reminded Mike, "Ree is pretty tall and Caitlyn is short. And Brian is your height with red hair.'

"OK. I'm looking," he said with a focus I appreciated.

I grabbed his wrist and asked, "Do you think I should get ready now?"

"Hmm. Why don't you wait until we spot them?" He turned to inspect me. "Maybe put your hood up, so they won't notice you."

I pulled the hood of my sweatshirt over my head and kept walking slowly, searching for the girls.

"What about you?" I asked. "You're so tall that you stand out, and the girls might recognize you."

He scoffed, "Believe me, they weren't paying any attention to me when we met. It was all about the pizza."

"Oh, yeah. That's the way they roll. I'm glad you are disguised with a coat to cover up your uniform. That might have gotten some attention."

When we got to the end of the first row of vendors, we entered the largest tent where people stood on tables dancing to the loud German music.

"Is that them?" asked Mike pointing across the large tent. I saw Marie and Caitlyn, arms hooked dancing around in a circle. Brian stood, drinking a beer and watching a woman dance nearby.

"Yes, that's them!"

I started to head that way and Mike caught my arm yet again. "Hey, don't forget the plan."

What? I looked at him and took a deep breath. Sure enough, I had forgotten my job. While he kept an eye on the trio, I called Kim and told her which tent we were in. Then I put my hair in a ponytail, got the wig out of my bag, and placed it on my head.

Just as I was about to move into action, I heard a most familiar voice, "Pity, why are you wearing that wig?"

I looked up and saw my parents walking toward me. Mom was in an embroidered dirndl and Dad was wearing his old leather lederhosen. OMG. You have to be kidding. I would have thought they were cute or maybe embarrassing at any other time, but this was not the time for either.

"Um, Mom and Dad. I really need you to listen."

Mom shouted, "What? It's so loud in here, I can't hear a word you are saying!" I ducked down and motioned for them to follow me outside where it wasn't so noisy.

Dad shouted, as we left the tent, "Did you see Marie in her silly hat? She sure is having a good time."

Once in the clear, I said, "Mom, Dad, I love you, but there is an emergency and I need you to leave the park right now. It's a matter of life and death." I know that was a cliché and maybe too dramatic, but I didn't care. They needed to leave.

"We were just going to watch the wiener dog race," said Dad furrowing his brow. His little German feathered hat moved down on his forehead, causing him to look even sillier.

"Was that your policeman friend in there?" Mom looked very interested for a change.

"Yes, it's Mike. I'm sorry, guys, but I'm not kidding. You can come back tomorrow, but you really need to go home now." I clasped my hands in front of me, begging them to leave. Tears streamed down my face. "I promise I'll explain everything tomorrow. I really need you to do this for me."

At that, they looked at each other and realized I meant it. Mom said with a worried expression, "OK," and kissed me on the cheek.

Dad squeezed my hand and said, "Be careful, darling." The two walked towards the exit slowly, but surely.

I wiped my eyes and went back into the tent. Mike motioned to me that the three had just gone outside in the other direction. We spotted them and were able to follow, hunkering down as we walked. I called Kim to make sure she was behind us and gave her an update, not mentioning Mom and Dad's appearance (not the fact that they were here or how they were dressed.)

Avoiding all the nutty people made it very difficult to keep up with the three, but I could still see the top of Brian's head bobbing as he walked 30 feet ahead of us.

A voice boomed over the loudspeakers announcing the wiener dog race was about to begin. When Brian, Caitlyn, and Ree stopped, we found a prime location across the small track from them. I hid behind Mike as I traded my hoodie for another jacket and put on my final touches. The announcer stood at the starting line and spoke into a microphone: "Get your pooches ready to run."

I studied the scene so I could plan my timing. About ten owners came to the starting line with varying sizes and colors of dachshunds, but all with unmistakable short legs and long bodies. The racecourse looked to be about 40 feet long. All the dogs had to do was run to the other end where a giant poster of a dachshund puppy hung over the finish line.

When all the dogs were assembled, the announcer shouted with a German accent that he didn't seem to have earlier, "It's time for zee Dachshund Dash!" A horn sounded, and the wiener dogs were off and running. Well, some ran, some walked, one sat down, and another turned around and ran back to its owner.

The dogs were so cute, but I couldn't get distracted. I had to step into action.

I put my sunglasses on and yelled in my best impersonation of Trish, "Catie Lynn! I'm over here!" I waved as I called. "Come here, baby! I want to see you."

The girls glanced at me in surprise, and Marie let out a sigh and rolled her eyes. That's when I realized phase one of my plan had worked. She actually thought I was Trish. Caitlyn waved, then told her grandpa something, and the girls ran around the crowd to get to my side. When they were close enough to realize I wasn't Trish, Ree exclaimed, "MOM?"

Brian looked at me and squinted, probably trying to figure out what had just happened. I looked at the girls and, without giving Ree a hug, I said, "Quick. It's an emergency. Go with Aunt Kim now!"

Kim grabbed the girls' arms and pulled them to the side. She quickly whisked them away through the crowd.

I heard Caitlyn say "What about my grandpa?" as Kim pulled the girls toward the exit.

When Brian saw them leave, he came barreling across the track through the racing dogs. He nearly stepped on one pup that was lying down, apparently taking a well-deserved rest. I took off my sunglasses and wig so that I could see just as Mike stepped forward to stop Brian from chasing the girls. Seeing the oversized man ready to grab him, Brian made a last-minute turn to move out of Mike's reach. He ran straight for me. Before I knew it, he had me by the arm. Mike got slowed down by a group of women trying to take pictures in the middle of the walkway.

The older man pulled me in the direction of the river. Even though my jacket, I could feel his cold fingers digging into my skin. He dragged me roughly through the crowds of people and said, "You just had to get involved. I should have run you off the bridge instead of the road."

What was he talking about? Then I remembered the red car. "That was...you?" I stammered. I looked back in desperation. Mike was gaining on us and I silently pleaded/prayed that he could save me. Suddenly Brian stopped and shifted his hold on me so that his arm was around my waist. He reached in his pocket for something, and in an instant, a cold metallic object was pressed against my neck. Oh my gosh, it was a knife.

Mike stopped in his tracks when he saw the knife. Brian whispered with an eerily disturbing Irish accent, "Now I wish I had rung that stupid dog's neck, or better yet, pulled your sweet daughter,

Lauren, inside your house that night and taken care of her. Maybe then you would have learned to keep to yourself."

That did it. Nobody threatened my daughter! With surprising agility and force, I pushed Brian's hand away from my throat, twisted around, and kneed him hard in the leg. I had aimed for his crotch but missed. My bony knee jabbing his thigh surprised him enough that he dropped the knife. I turned away from him to run, but he reached out and grabbed my sleeve and pulled me with him again. He forced me alongside him another ten feet, but Mike was again in pursuit.

Luckily, being a natural klutz, I tripped over a tent spike and fell face down in the grass, unlocking his grip from my arm. Brian must have realized Mike's proximity and finally gave up on me. He took off running alone.

Mike stopped to see if I was OK. I said, "I'm fine. Just get him!" He chased after Brian while I fumbled for my phone and called the police who were standing by. I described the location and urged them to hurry.

I looked up and saw R.A. looming high above me. He had climbed a speaker pole, erected near a tent, to be our lookout man and keep tabs on everything in case Brian ran. He was perched on a tiny step 20 feet up in the air, clinging to the side of the pole with one arm, and holding a microphone with the other. He announced through the speakers, loud enough for everyone outside the tents to hear; "Stop that man with the green jacket and red hair!" He pointed to Brian. The Dachshund Dash was over, so people turned and looked to see who needed to be caught.

You would think the man in his mid-60s would tire easily, but he was in amazing shape. A teenage boy tried to grab him, but Brian shook him off. Although another couple of guys joined the chase, Mike was still the closest and gained on him just as they approached a dead end, the river.

I followed behind, limping a little, and prayed that Brian wouldn't attempt a swim across the Arkansas. Just as we hoped, he turned North and headed right to the area where Lin was ready to take action.

He made it ten more yards and Bingo! The plan was set in motion - literally. A row of beer barrels rolled down a chute towards Brian. He was forced to jump over some of the enormous kegs and managed to dodge others. They clattered as they hit each other and bounced along with a metallic echo. Finally, as we hoped, Brian couldn't avoid all of the barrels, and one of them knocked his legs out from under him. He fell with a thud and tried to get up, but another couple of kegs hit him, rendering him temporarily out of commission.

Ironically, the band in the nearest tent started playing "Roll Out the Barrel."

Mike ran to Brian. He pulled handcuffs out of his back pocket and subdued the culprit. The timing was perfect as three on-duty policemen, two on foot and one on horseback, arrived to arrest Brian Murphy for the murder of Justin Jones.

Garage Sale Tip #18
Look closely - things aren't always as they seem.

I stood, arms folded in fury, as the officers lifted Brian Murphy to his feet. He glared at me with the nastiest expression I had ever seen. Where was that jovial sweet Grandpa Brian we knew and loved? This guy was truly a monster, plain and simple.

The crowd parted as the officers led Brian away. I heard one man say, "I think that's Mr. Murphy. He was my high school English teacher." Just another reminder that former students are around us at all times. Once a teacher, always a teacher.

It was hard to believe I was cold earlier, for I was so hot that all I wanted to do was take my jacket off to cool down. Must have been because of all the running and excitement. Exhausted, I sat down on one of the cold, metal beer barrels, put my head in my hands, and finally took a deep breath. I exhaled slowly, relieved that the girls were safe with my sister and the nightmare was over.

R.A. rushed up and asked, "Are you OK, Pity?" I stood and gave him a hug for the second time that night.

"Yes. I'm just glad we got the girls. Thank you so much for your help." I sat back down, too tired to stand, and turned to him, "Weren't you scared to be up so high?"

"Nah. You know I used to be a lineman and climbed telephone poles three times that high. And if I recall, you did something similar not too long ago."

"Oh, that's right." I had forgotten about his love of heights and my crazy, death-defying feat last spring. Mike walked up and sat by me on the big barrel.

"You did it!" he said, placing his arm around my shoulders. "You got the girls away from that creep."

Suddenly, the barrel seemed much more comfortable, sharing it with Mike. I turned to him, "And you caught him. Thank you so much. We couldn't have done this without you." I rested my head on his shoulder.

We sat silently for a minute, catching our breath before he said, "Come on, let's go see your daughter." He stood and held out his hand to me.

He helped me up, and I said, "Yes, let's do that." I didn't let go of his hand as we walked beside R.A.

Lin caught up with us shaking her head. "I hope that son of a biscuit is put where he belongs."

"Me too," I said, as we hurried to the parking lot. "Lin, you couldn't have timed the release of the barrels any better. And did you ask the band to play 'Roll Out the Barrel'?"

"No, but it sure was funny. Uffda!"

When we reached Kim's car, Ree ran up and gave me a tearful hug. "I was so worried about you, Mom."

I squeezed her tight, not wanting to let go. I whispered, "My baby is safe," as I buried my face in her hair, breathing in her familiar shampoo scent.

She pulled away. "What was that all about?"

Caitlyn stood behind Ree, and I wondered how to explain what had happened without mentioning her grandfather. I opted to wait until I had talked to her mother.

"It's very complicated, Marie. It has something to do with the story I told you over ice cream at Braum's yesterday." Was that really only yesterday? Jeez! Today seemed like it lasted a week. Of course, I had gone to Junquefest, History Day, and the unbelievable swim meet all before coming here. No wonder I was beat.

I said, "It's been a very long day for all of us. I will tell you all about it soon, but you two must be exhausted."

"Yeah, I'm tired, but I'm supposed to spend the night at Caitlyn's house. Who's going to take us?"

Kim looked at me and said quickly in a bright voice, "Hey, kiddos, why don't you both stay at my house tonight?" She added, "I'm working on a new quilt and need some expert color advice."

I sighed with the perfect solution. Kim always came through for me.

I told them, "I'll call Caitlyn's mom and get everything straightened out, then come get you both in the morning." I turned to Caitlyn. "Honey, is that alright with you?"

She stood, crossing her arms with her bottom lip trembling. When she finally spoke, she sounded nothing like my number one fan. She croaked, "I don't know what's going on. Where's Grandpa and why did you pretend to be my mother?"

I felt a pang of guilt and a whole lot of sympathy for her. I took the confused girl in my arms and held her, stroking her hair. "It's going to be alright, Caitlyn. I have to work through a few things before I can explain it to you. Your grandfather is fine, but I need to talk to your mother before I can tell you any more about this evening. Okay?" With my hands on her shoulders, I held her out at arm's length.

She slowly shrugged the tiniest bit, which I took as an OK.

"You girls go have fun and get a good night's sleep. I'll call you in the morning." I gave Kim a hug and whispered, "Thank you so much."

She whispered back, "Of course. What are sisters for?"

I nodded, but she did way more for me than I ever did for her.

Before breaking the embrace, she said, "Call me tonight."

As the four of them walked to the car, R.A. said, "Did you get enough to eat or shall we stop at Taco Bueno?"

I couldn't hear the girls' response but knew they were in good hands with those two.

Standing beside Mike's truck I sighed. "Well, I guess I should tell Trish about this, but I have no idea how." I stepped up onto the running board.

Mike said, "I'll call Officer Jacobs and ask him to meet us at her house. He was in on the original investigation and is on duty tonight. Hopefully, she doesn't know anything yet, and we can explain everything on an official level."

Lin said, "So if Trish was the one in the notes, she knows what he did, right?"

"I assume so, but I have to tell her where Caitlyn is. I still can't believe Trish is the girl in the notes."

Mike called Jacobs and explained the whole situation and asked him not to go to her door until we arrived in about 20 minutes.

We all entered the truck. I called Lauren. and told her all was OK and that Ree was safe and staying at Kim and R.A.'s

She said in a rush "Oh, good! I've been on pins and needles, waiting. So, your plan worked?"

"Believe it or not, it did. We're going to head over to Trish's house now and fill her in."

Mike started the truck and turned on the heater.

Ren said, "Um. Trish isn't at her house."

I was confused. "How would you know Trish isn't at her house?" I put my phone on speaker, so Mike and Lin could hear too.

"Jennifer and I ran home to get the *Pretty in Pink* DVD, but Trish's car was in our driveway. She jumped out and asked me where her daughter was. I told her Caitlyn was with her grandpa and Marie.

She freaked out and said something like, 'She wasn't supposed to be with him tonight. He told me she would be at your house'."

"Then she demanded to know where they had gone. I didn't want to tell her, but she screamed, 'Where are they?' so loud, I was afraid the neighbors would complain. So, I said, Oktoberfest. She gave a terrified look and drove off in a panic."

I said, "Oh, my! What time was that?"

"Maybe 30 minutes ago? She was acting crazy – even for her. I wanted to warn you, but I didn't want to interrupt your plan."

"It's OK, Ren. I wouldn't have answered the phone then anyway. I'll try to sort this out and will call you back. Thanks, sweetie. I'll fill you in on everything later. I promise."

I hung up and said, "I guess we'll try to find Trish here."

"Mike asked, do you have her phone number?"

I had refused to put her number in my phone, so I wouldn't have to see the vile woman's name in my contact list. Now, I wished I had.

Lin said, "You probably don't want to ask Caitlyn for it now."

"No. Not in the state she's in."

Mike turned the engine off and called the Sergeant, asking him to meet us at Oktoberfest rather than at Trish's house. We started our hunt all over again, but now for the unbearable woman.

This time, walking through the fall air, I was chilled to the bone. I wore both jackets but with the cooling sweat from my workout and without the adrenaline rush, I was tired, hungry, and very cold.

The noise hadn't died down any. As a matter of fact, it had pumped up a level with the crazier adult crowd arriving. We dodged people wearing German attire as we made our way past the tents. I felt bad for thinking my folks looked silly because compared to some of these characters, Mom and Dad looked almost normal.

Lin asked, "Should we split up?"

Mike shrugged. "I wouldn't do much good alone, since I've never seen Trish."

She nodded. "Oh, yeah, well then why don't you two go that way?" She pointed straight ahead. "And I'll go this way and call if I see her. Good luck." She headed off to the right.

Although we went a different direction from the last hunt, Mike and I started out together, again looking for a tall redhead.

Mike said, "Are you doing OK, Pity?"

"Yes, I'm not as frantic this time, but I'm sure ready for this day to be over. Oh, I forgot to tell you that Brian admitted he was the one in my house, and guess what?"

"What?" Mike turned to me.

"He's the one who ran me off the road last night."

His lips tightened. "Two more counts against that bastard! Glad we got him."

"Yeah," I said solemnly.

We looked inside a packed and noisy tent, but we didn't see Trish. Oktoberfest is always the most crowded on Saturday evenings, so we were trying to find the proverbial needle in the haystack.

A lady asked me something in German, but I didn't understand, so I shrugged and said, "Ich spreche nur ein bisschen Deutsch," and kept walking.

Mike asked "What did you say?" as we walked outside again.

I answered, "I said, 'I only speak a little German.'"

When we passed a bratwurst stand, my mouth watered with the delicious smell. I was really hungry, but we didn't have time to waste.

We entered another tent and there was a familiar blonde woman standing on a table with two guys doing the chicken dance. I smiled as I watched the crowd admiring Becca's exuberance. She caught sight of me and jumped off the table leaving the guys alone. They looked embarrassed to be left dancing together and jumped down, too.

Becca screamed above the noise, "Pity! Is this your policeman?" Her enormous blinking beer mug earrings clanked as she grabbed his arms and looked him up and down, checking him out. Nothing subtle about this girl.

"Mike, this is Becca, my friend from school. She has no filter, so watch out."

He smiled. "Pleased to meet you." I'm sure he really was pleased to meet her – after all, she's Becca.

"Well, you got yourself a looker, Pity. You didn't tell me you were coming tonight."

"We're on official business – a police case that I'm helping with. I can't tell you now, but I'll fill you and the girls in on Monday. I promise."

"OK, then. I'll let you two do your…" She winked then said, "police work."

I shook my head and said, "See you on Monday, Becca!"

Mike smirked at me, "You sure know some interesting people."

"If I wasn't so tired and wasn't on a mission, I'd want to stay there for a while. She's so much fun."

On our way past another tent, I tripped over a table leg. You would think I'd learn to watch where I was going after tripping earlier. I righted myself before Mike noticed, or so I hoped. As soon as we walked through the large opening, I saw Trish. She stood on a bench amid polka dancers, I assumed to look for her daughter. As we pushed through the crowd, I called. "Trish!"

She didn't hear me, so this time I yelled, "Patricia Murphy!"

She looked right at me, jumped down and ran to us. She grabbed my hands with cold bony fingers that strangely reminded me of her father's grip. She pleaded, "Where is Catie Linn?"

"Caitlyn is safe. She's with Marie at my sister's house here in Tulsa. We have to talk to you, though," I said firmly, but with kindness.

She closed her eyes, leaned her head back, taking a deep breath and blowing it out slowly. "Oh. Thank God, she's safe."

"Come here and sit down, Trish. I have something to tell you." I coaxed her outside to get away from the din and pointed to the same table where I'd tripped.

I sat next to Mike and directly across from Trish. "This is my friend, Mike Potter. He's a sergeant with the Broken Arrow police department." I took a breath. "I recently learned about Justin Jones' death and came across information proving that he was murdered. I believe you may know something about this?" I winced, expecting her to react with her typical fury, but she just hung her head, listening.

Mike said gently, "Trish, a detective will be here shortly to ask you some official questions about the murder of Justin Jones."

She covered her face with her hands and said softly, "I knew this would happen someday. It has ruined my life, and I'm ready for this ordeal to be over."

Then she looked at me with tears staining her face. "How did you find out about it, and where is my father?"

I studied Trish from a new perspective. She had a different air about her as if she was actually human for once.

Mike's phone rang, and he stepped away to take the call.

I answered, "First of all, your dad is in the Tulsa jail."

She closed her eyes, but I couldn't tell if she was relieved or upset.

I continued, "I got involved because, of all things, I went to a garage sale and purchased a school desk. In the back of the desk, I found some notes."

She stared blankly and nodded her head as I spoke. "We managed to figure out the notes had something to do with Justin's death. I became an amateur sleuth and asked around, finding more information. A few days later, someone broke into my house and stole every bit of research and evidence. That's when I realized I was onto something. I guess Coach Hamm figured out I was poking around because he named your father as the one who paid him to murder Justin."

I didn't feel this was the time to tell her the coach almost shot me, but her eyes widened as she listened even without adding that bombshell.

"With the girls in possible danger, we immediately rushed down here and got them away from your dad. Then Tulsa police arrested him." When Trish switched from a nod to shaking her head, I said, "I'm so sorry."

She licked her lips. "Believe me, I'm not worried about him. I'm glad he's locked up. Maybe this nightmare is finally over."

Mike walked up with a uniformed officer and introduced him to us as Sergeant Jacobs. The detective said he had read the report on Coach Hamm's arrest and contacted the Tulsa police to get information about Brian Murphy. Mike filled him in on some details before the official questioning of Trish began. While they got ready to talk, I called Lin to tell her where we were, almost forgetting she was still out looking for Trish.

Jacobs produced a clipboard and pen. I sat motionless as Trish told her story.

"I was 17 and completely in love with Justin. He was the sweetest, most handsome boy in school. But my father had big ideas for me. I was to be the next big lawyer in town." She shook her head. "He didn't want me dating anyone, especially Justin. According to my dad, I was too good for him." She shrugged slowly. "I guess Justin smarted off in his classes a bit too much, which didn't go over well with my father. Despite his urges for me to break up with Justin, we got carried away, and I ended up getting pregnant."

So far, the story was exactly as I had thought.

She pushed some hair from her face. "My father was always so strict and protective that I didn't know how to break the news to him.

When I started feeling sick, Dad started writing notes to me in his class. I just stuck them in the back of my desk. I never thought about anyone finding them at the time, and forgot all about them until you mentioned them."

I asked, "And you went by Patty Sue back then?"

"Yes, most of my friends and family called me that."

Lin arrived and joined the four of us at the white resin table. The dew was heavy and little beads of water began to form on the table. I kept my hands in my lap as I focused on Trish.

Detective Jacobs had been writing constantly and asked in a professional tone, "And what happened when your father found out you were expecting

"Well, as you guessed, I ended up telling my parents that I was pregnant. Dad was furious, but not so much with me as he was with Justin. He told me under no circumstances could I tell him about the pregnancy."

"And did you?" he asked while writing his notes.

"No. I wanted so bad to tell Justin, but you don't know my father. He was...*is* so controlling. If he doesn't get his way, he makes you pay. I was terrified he would make me abort the baby, but I never dreamed he would do anything to Justin."

Listening to what she had said so far, it was hard for me to believe this was the same Trish I'd known. Her snippy, haughty manner was gone. She was transformed into an innocent 17-year-old girl.

I said, "One of the notes suggested your father tried to bribe Justin?"

"Yes, he said he offered him money to break up with me, but Justin refused. That's when Dad told me I had to break up with him. He said if I did, everything would be OK. I assumed that meant that I could keep the baby. I went to Justin's house as my father instructed and told him that I couldn't see him anymore. Although he didn't know about the baby, he begged me to stay. He said he loved me and wanted to get married. He didn't understand why I was breaking up with him. It broke my heart to walk away. That's when I vowed to secretly tell Justin about the baby later, once it was too late for an abortion."

A group of noisy beer drinkers walked by, interrupting Trish's story. I had been so enthralled; I had tuned everything out and even forgot where we were.

The detective asked, "Would you rather go to the police station to finish the questioning?"

"No," she sighed, "Let's just get it over with now".

Lin said, "I'll go get us all something hot to drink." I nodded and mouthed 'thanks' to her as she left.

"OK," he continued, "so you broke up with Justin. Then what happened?"

"Dad told me Justin didn't really want to marry me and that he would always be a nuisance. He even told me he'd seen Justin with another girl, which I have never believed. Then he said he had a plan to get rid of Justin completely. Of course, I pleaded with him that there had to be another way."

I spoke up. "I still don't understand why your father felt the need to kill Justin?"

She pounded the table with her hand, causing a little splash. "He's a monster, that's why. He threatened me and said if I didn't go along with his plan, or if I told anyone about it, he'd disown me and the baby and tell everyone I was a no-good whore. He said it was all for my own good, and he loved me so much, so this was the only way."

Mike was taken aback. "So, he threatened you and told you he loved you in the same sentence?"

"I know. I was so naïve and mentally abused by my father that I believed him. Of course, as time went by, I realized I could have had it all. I could have run off with Justin and the baby and made a life for us, even without my father's support. I've regretted not doing that every day all these years."

The detective asked, "So what happened after Justin died?"

"I was a mess – practically suicidal. But one day I snuck away and went to see his mother. I told her I was so sorry that he'd died. When I got home from her house, my father's next plan was set in motion. That very day, my mother drove me to my aunt's house in Dallas. I stayed there until the baby was born. and then…my dad and mom raised my baby as their own."

Wow. That was a plot twist I didn't expect. Then the realization hit and I blurted out, "Wait a minute! Does that mean that your baby is…Andy?"

Garage Sale Tip #19
Check social media sites for other local bargains.

Lin arrived and stood beside me holding a cardboard carrier with five hot drinks. She must have been there in time to catch the revelation because she was too stunned to speak.

"Yes. Everybody thinks Andy is my little brother. I started college in the fall and had to pretend I'd never had a child. My father said I would be able to live my life without ever having to worry about my 'mistake,' as he put it."

I shook my head as the incredible story sunk in. I thanked Lin and helped her hand out the hot chocolate. We all sipped in silence.

I turned to Trish. "I still can't believe Caitlyn's Uncle Andy is your son!" I took another drink. "Does he know?"

She shook her head. "Oh, no. He believes Mom and Dad are his parents. But he's really my sweet, sweet boy. It's been awful having to pretend he was my younger brother all these years. I see so much of Justin in him and often think how he would have adored Andy. And Justin's parents should have gotten to know their grandson, but I could never do anything about it."

My eyes welled up at the thought of sweet Mrs. Jones and her angel food cake. For 24 years she never knew she had a grandson.

The detective asked, "And your mother was in on this the whole time?"

"Well, not really. She thought I got pregnant by some boy who didn't want to be a father. She certainly had no idea my father had anything to do with Justin's death. Over the course of time, I found out that my parents weren't able to have a second child and this was the perfect way to get the son they had always wanted. Andy just fell in their laps. My mom was actually a great mother to him - better than I would have been at that age." Trish started to cry.

I put my hand on hers, feeling the pain.

Mike asked, "Why didn't you ever come forward?"

"You don't know how much I wanted to tell the truth." She sobbed. "My father has kept his thumb on me since 1997, always holding Justin's death over my head. Somehow he made me believe it was all my fault." She sighed, "He's been involved in every major decision I've made; which college to attend, where to live. He even chose my husband for me."

She started breathing harder, and then she spoke with force, "My life has been a type of prison. I'm just so glad it's over, even if it means I go to prison for real. It will be a relief to get away from him."

Mike nodded. I could tell he believed her story. We all did. Nobody could act that well. When Trish held her cup of steaming cocoa, she seemed to relax a little.

I lifted my cup and took a drink. My stomach started to growl. It made sense. I hadn't eaten anything since an early lunch and it was almost 10 o'clock. I said, "I can't imagine what you went through all these years. But why were you so worried about Caitlyn tonight? Ren said you were frantic."

She shivered. "My father told me a few days ago somebody was poking around about Justin's death. He said if he found out that I had told anyone anything, he would make Caitlyn disappear."

I sucked in my cocoa and choked. Mike hit my back until I cleared my lungs enough to repeat the word, "Disappear?"

"Yes." She closed her eyes and took a breath before continuing. "I promised him I hadn't said a word to anybody, but I was still afraid to let Caitlyn leave my side. Then, this week I started to feel ill. Dad came over to check on me daily. This morning, I felt so sick that I had to miss her big day. My dad asked Andy to take the girls to History Day and he told me they would go to your house after the event."

Trish put her cup on the table. "Tonight, when I went in the kitchen, I found a bottle of pills behind the toaster and got suspicious." She looked in her purse and pulled out a small prescription bottle and handed it to the detective. "I think he was putting something in my food the past few days to keep me out of the way. I figured if he could do that, what could he do to my baby?"

My mouth dropped open at the thought.

"Yes. I was frantic. I forced myself to drive to your house to make sure the girls were okay. When Lauren told me they had gone with him to Oktoberfest, I really freaked out."

Lin frowned. "You think he would really hurt his own granddaughter?"

Trish let go, "Yes. He's an animal! He's threatened to hurt her ever since she was born. He knew she was all I had. That's why I've been so protective of Caitlyn all her life. I was afraid he would find a way to take her from me like he had Andy. Or worse yet, injure her."

She put her cup on the table so hard some of it splashed out. "When I realized he had drugged me, I knew he had it in him to kill again."

I'd been holding my breath for far too long and let it out in a whoosh. "That is one awful story." I started shivering again with the thought that Ree had been in real danger.

Trish put her arms on the cold, wet, table. She laid her head down on them, and sobbed, "I'm glad the bastard is finally in jail."

I patted her hand, finding it hard to believe I now felt real compassion for the woman who had been a thorn in my side for years.

Once Trish had composed herself somewhat, Detective Jacobs got her contact information. He told her there was no need to arrest her at this time, but she shouldn't leave town. He did inform her that depending on the laws and statute of limitations, she could be held accountable for covering up a crime all these years.

When Mike walked Sergeant Jacobs to his patrol car, Trish let out a sigh and spoke with a shaky voice. "Well, at least I wasn't arrested tonight."

Lin asked, "Does your husband know anything about this?"

"Oh, heavens no. I'll lose him over this, I'm just sure." She held her hand to her chest.

I suggested, "Oh, Trish, you don't know that, but you'll need to tell him right away. And I think it's best that the girls go ahead and stay at my sister's tonight. We didn't tell them anything, but with all they've been through, I hate to upset them even more tonight."

She sniffed and nodded. "You're right. I need to go home and tell the judge everything tonight. Caitlyn can't be there for that."

I asked, "Want me to ride with you or drive you home?"

She stood up and squared her shoulders in her more typical posture. "No, I'll use the drive time to prepare my speech. Thank you, Kitty. I appreciate everything you have done for Caitlyn and for bringing all of this to light."

I walked around the table and put my arm on her shoulder. "It's time to start fresh, girl."

She gave a faint smile and headed toward the parking lot. Mike stopped and spoke to her on his way back.

Lin shook her head and said, "That was unbelievable."

"Yes. It sure proves that things aren't always as they seem."

Mike appeared and said, "Wow. That was some story."

I looked him in the eye. "Do you think she'll be charged and put in jail?"

He lifted his shoulders. "I don't know but I do know what the three of us need."

We both spoke at once, "What?"

"Bratwurst and beer."

I closed my eyes and said, "Yes! I'm famished."

Lin clapped her hands together and said, "Me, too!"

The beer and brat sure did the trick. It's amazing how much a full tummy can lift your mood.

On the drive home, Lin called Jennifer to tell the girls we had found Trish, while I called Kim and explained what happened.

She said, "Wow, so Andy is ..."

"Shhh," I interrupted her before she finished the sentence. "Can Caitlyn hear you?"

"I think they are both asleep, but you better do the talking. I'll fill R.A. in after."

"Yes, Caitlyn's uncle is actually her half-brother. Crazy, huh?"

She whispered, "Amazing. And can you believe that our Patty Sue was someone you knew all along? It's just bizarre."

I hadn't thought of how odd that was until just then. "I know. I'll call in the morning, but not too early. I'm beat."

When I finally walked in the front door of my house, I skipped my nightly milk, fell on the bed, and was out like a light. I don't think I moved until the next morning at nine.

I stretched my arms over my head and felt the ache of newly-used muscles. In fact, I ached all over. Oh yeah, I did swim a lot last night, plus I ran, was manhandled, and I fell down twice. No wonder I was sore. But, despite all that, I felt good. Everyone was safe and the mystery was solved. All I needed to do now was take a shower and get my babies back home. I called Kim about getting Marie and Caitlin.

"Actually, R.A. and I thought we'd go to the pumpkin patch in Bixby. We'll drop off the girls on the way."

"That would be great!" I said, relieved not to have to drive back to Tulsa again. "Thanks so much for everything, Kim."

"Like there weren't times when you watched our boys? Sisters do what needs to be done."

That was true. I loved spending time with Eli and Alex, but it had been years since I was needed for her older boys.

I said, "Speaking of Bixby, remind me to tell you about my visit there the other day."

"OK? Sounds interesting. See ya in a bit."

I called Lauren and told her I needed my big girl to come home when she could.

I called my parents last. Not an easy one to make. They both got on the phone, which drives me crazy because Mom has to repeat most of what I say to Dad, and neither of them listens to me because they are too busy talking to each other. But I managed to explain last night's scenario to them. I emphasized the fact that Marie had been in danger. They were, of course, shocked by my story, and I think they forgave me for sending them home so abruptly.

I thanked them for understanding and, on the spot, I invited them for today's Sunday dinner today at five. I would explain it all in more detail then.

Mom said, "We would love to come. What can we bring?"

"You know what I need? Your amazing chocolate cake if that's possible."

"Of course."

"By the way, you both looked adorable in your German attire."

Mom said, "Oh, that was your dad's idea. But Pity, I think you should stick with your own hair color. Red is not very becoming on you." I laughed and agreed. Dad piped in, "Are you going to let us meet your policeman?" Hmmm. My policeman. Dad's question reminded me that I still hadn't asked Mike much about his life. Then I came up with the best way to get all the scoop. Dad's nickname is 'the perfect host.' He asks just the right questions of every new guest to make them feel at home. If I invited Mike to dinner, Dad would get him to divulge more than I ever could. I said, "Great idea, Pops. I'll invite him, too. Love you guys – see you this afternoon."

I took a package of pork tenderloins from the freezer, mixed up my marinade, and poured it over the meat. Then I fed Iggy and Edgar and decided to lie on the couch next to Harriet while I thought about everything that had transpired over the last week. The mystery was pretty well wrapped up, but I worried about Caitlyn and how she would take everything.

I sat up and called Trish to see how she was doing. The judge answered, and I warily asked for Trish, worrying he had kicked her out last night. But lo and behold, he called her to the phone. I said with concern, "Hi, Trish. It's Kitty. How are you?"

She sounded more chipper than I expected, "I'm actually doing well."

I sort of whispered, "Did you tell him everything?"

"Yes, I did - everything. Jasper is so wonderful."

So, that was her husband's name. I'd only heard him referred to as *The Judge* before. She continued, "He was very upset at first, but then as I explained further, he said we would work through it as a family. He also said he never did trust my father."

Nervously, I asked, "Since he's a judge, does he think you will be prosecuted for withholding evidence?"

She said, "He told me we'll definitely need good lawyers, but no matter what happens he will support me."

I smiled. "Oh, I'm so glad to hear that. You deserve some good luck," I said in earnest.

"I'm not sure about that, but thank you. Jasper even went with me last night to tell my mother everything. She was so distraught, we brought her home with us. I think she'll be okay with time."

"Oh my, the poor thing. Listen, Trish, I'll drop Caitlyn off at your house within the hour. Since she doesn't know anything, I'm sure she's very confused."

"Oh, thank you. I will find a way to explain it to her, but can you tell me how you got the girls away from my dad?"

I went ahead and told her my extraction plan and detailed the dramatic chase and arrest.

"Oh, my! You were creative and pretty gutsy to confront him. I'm so sorry for all he put you through. But now you know what I've lived with most of my life."

I nodded in agreement even though she couldn't see me.

She continued, "After I tell Caitlyn everything, I'll have a heart-to-heart with Andy. That will be another tough conversation."

"I don't envy you, but don't be too hard on yourself," I said.

"OK. Thanks again, Kitty."

About ten minutes later, the front door opened. It was Kim, R.A., and the kids. I gave both girls a hug and said to Caitlyn, "Let's get you home to your mom." I asked Kim if she would ride with me over to Caitlyn's. I told Ree, "I'll be right back. Stay with R.A. and don't move."

"Harriet wants me here anyway." She cuddled her furry friend.

When we arrived at Caitlyn's house, Trish came outside and took her daughter in a big hug. She waved to me and thanked us again. Wow-what a difference this has made to her personality – incredible.

On the way home, I lightened the mood and told Kim my Bixby parade story. She laughed and said, "How embarrassing...but most shocking is that you didn't go to the sale afterward."

"I was laughing so hard I just couldn't. How were the girls?"

"Oh, they were fun. They helped me design the quilt and wanted to know how to do it."

"Well, better them than me. Quilting is as foreign to me as rocket science. I don't know how you and Mom figure it all out."

"Pity, you would probably love it."

Back at home, Lauren had already arrived. I walked R.A. and Kim to the door. "Again, I can't thank you enough for all your help."

R.A. said, "We're starting to enjoy your crazy schemes."

As they walked down the front steps, Kim said, "You won't believe what Pity did in Bixby...."

I shut the door and called my girls over to me. Giving them a big collective hug, I said, "You are a sight for sore eyes. I am sorry either of you had to be involved in all of that."

"I still don't know what happened last night," said Ree.

"Make yourselves comfy, because this story is a doozy.

We sat on the couch, and I told them everything that happened the night before, starting with the swim meet. I answered their questions as they came up. The girls were as shocked as I was to discover that Andy was Caitlyn's brother and they were horrified to learn Grandpa Brian could have killed someone.

"I know," I agreed, "I'm really bummed to find out he wasn't the person we thought he was. On the bright side, I found out that Trish isn't nearly as bad as she seems. She's actually a pretty nice person - she's just been under enormous strain for 23 years. So, things should be better for Caitlyn now."

Ree said, "Good." She twirled her hair in her fingers. "I wonder if that's why she didn't want Caitlyn to swim – because of the way that boy died?"

I nodded my head. "I'll bet you are right. Hey, Ree, I'm just curious, do you know what kind of car Grandpa Brian drives?"

"He has two cars; a 2015 black Mercedes CLS Class sedan and a classic red 1968 Ford Mustang in mint condition."

I stared at my child in disbelief. "How do you know that?"

She shrugged. "Unlike you, I pay attention."

I shook my head. Well, now at least I could tell Mike what kind of car Brian drove when he ran me off the road. Maybe I should start paying attention, too.

"Oh, I invited Grandma and Grandpa over for dinner this afternoon." I hoped to lighten the mood.

Ree said, "Goodie!" then turned to Ren. "They were so funny in their German outfits at Oktoberfest last night!"

"Did Grandpa wear his lederhosen?"

We both nodded. I said, "You don't mind if I invite my new friend, Mike, over, do you?"

Ren said, "Well he deserves a dinner after helping with all that."

I agreed wholeheartedly. "Oh yeah, he does. Go pick up your rooms and finish any homework while I invite him." I called Mike.

"5 would be perfect since I work at 7. Can I bring anything?"

"No, just you and don't forget your handcuffs. I mean, you sure got some good use out of them last night." I looked up to see Ren walk by carrying a trash can. She made a disgusted face at me, and I frantically shook my head at her.

He laughed, "OK, I'll see you at five then."

We hung up, and I turned to Ren and explained, "It wasn't anything weird, Lauren. I meant when he handcuffed Brian."

"What?" She pulled her earbuds out and lifted her eyebrows.

"Oh, nothing," I said, relieved that she was just disgusted by the trash and not about my handcuff comment.

I spent an hour writing a real article about Justin Jones for the swim team newsletter, careful to word it as a tribute. By doing so, I felt vindicated for at least some of my lies this week, but mainly I was glad others would learn about the talented boy.

Ren went to the store for me while Ree got the backyard ready for our outdoor dinner and I made a batch of our famous Okie Spice Girl Dip. Just as I put it in the fridge to chill, the doorbell rang.

I opened the door and found Lin standing there with her hands on her hips. "So, what great garage sale find do I just have to see? I've been dying to find out, but we kept diving in pools and running around Oktoberfest so you haven't told me what you got."

"I know. Sorry 'bout that. They're in the garage. My folks are coming for dinner, and I invited Mike, too," I said with a sheepish smile.

"Oooh, you are ready to have him meet your parents? Wow...do I detect a romance?"

I shrugged. "But you'll be proud to know I just made Okie Spice Storm dip."

"Mmm, can I have some?" she asked, heading for the fridge.

"Of course, but we have to wait for Ren to come back from the store with the chips." I pulled her into the garage and squeezed past my car. I bent down to grab hold of the box from under the shelf and showed her the tile molds."

She looked over my shoulder and said, "Oh, fer cool! There are so many shapes and sizes. I just can't wait."

"Well, you have to wait. I'm booked today."

"Can I make some pavers for my house, too?" she asked.

"Of course! Knock yourself out!" I stood straight up, forgetting about the wooden ladder hanging from the garage ceiling directly overhead and everything went black.

My eyes opened slowly, revealing Lin's upside-down face and Ree fanning me with a piece of cardboard. I looked to my left and saw a tire, Liesel's tire. Why was I lying on the garage floor?

"Mom, are you OK?"

"What happened?" I asked with a croaky voice.

Lin said, "Look at me and tell me your name. I want to check your pupils."

I looked at her, realizing she was holding my head in her lap. I said, "Kitty Elizabeth Kole, oftentimes known as Pity."

Lin shook her head, "Whew. Pity, it was so funny; You had just said "Knock yourself out," then you stood up and knocked yourself out on that ladder." She pointed straight up.

"I did?"

Ree said, "Yeah, Mom. You scared us. We were going to call 9-1-1, but Lin knew the trick to wake you up."

I sat up, wincing with pain and wondering what the trick was. Maybe smelling salts? I felt the top of my head where a lump had formed. "Ouch."

Ree said, "At least there wasn't blood like in your miniature golf story. But will you be okay?"

"Oh, yeah. I'm sure I'm fine. Just don't let me fall asleep anytime soon." I stood up and felt OK, but I held the counter as I walked into the kitchen. I looked over the food. Most everything was done, so I turned and said, "Hey, we have some time now. Didn't I hear there was a garage sale up the street?"

Lin and Ree looked at each other and smiled, "Yeah, but you're not going to go, are you?" asked Lin.

"Why not? I have plenty of time before people get here, and I don't feel dizzy or nauseous. Stop staring at me. I'm fine." I filled a baggie with ice and held it to my head as I grabbed my wallet. Ree started towards her room, shaking her head as she went.

Lin and I walked slowly around the corner of my block to the house holding the sale. It belonged to the mother of one of my former students. I frequently run into her at other sales. When I saw her, I said, "Have you sold a lot?"

"Yeah. I wondered if you would stop by."

I picked up a cute wooden box. "Look, Lin. I used to have one sort of like this. I can send it to Kay for Christmas."

Seeing nothing else of interest, I paid for the box and went back home with Lin to get ready for dinner. Ren's car was back in the driveway.

We walked into the house, and Lin said, "Hope she remembered the…" Lin grabbed a bag and held it up like a prize, "…chips!"

I got the dip, and we sat down at the kitchen counter and dug in, giggling like teens. She closed her eyes and said, "It is so good!"

"I know, our Okie Spice Storm is like crack. We should really try to market it. It's so addictive."

Lin ate a few more chips, checked my head, then said, "I've gotta go, but have a good time at dinner."

After the door closed, my girls joined me in the kitchen.

Ren said, "Heard you got a goose egg. You don't have a concussion, do you?" She gently studied my head and sighed, "So what did you buy at the sale?"

I pointed to the box on the counter and crunched on a chip.

She opened the wooden box. "Mom, there are notes inside the box. Is it another mystery?"

I gasped. "Oh no… I didn't even look inside it." I started to imagine the worst and shook my head. Not more murder clues, please. My head started to throb.

Ree looked over Ren's shoulder and read silently. I watched their expressions change from startled to worried as they read. Then they started laughing at the same time.

"What is it?" I asked, and they handed me a note. It read:

I saw what you did.

It could happen to you.

It happened one night.

And then there were none.

The Sixth Sense.

Oh my gosh! It was just a list of movie titles. It wasn't another murder at all. I relaxed.

Ree said with a giggle, "Mom, that's your handwriting."

I looked at the list more closely. Jeez. It was true. Before I had started making lists on my phone, I wrote them the old school way – on paper. This was actually my list of movies.

Ren giggled, "And you bought your own box back. Now that is hilarious."

I tried to hide my embarrassment by saying, "Very funny. Enough of that. Go take your showers and forget about this nonsense."

I chuckled to myself as I got ready for our guests. I guess it was only a matter of time before I bought back something I had sold at my garage sale.

Garage Sale Tip #20
Always buy from children selling food

I put the meat on the grill, set the table, and then took some much-needed ibuprofen.

Mike showed up first in full uniform, of course. He brought a bottle of chilled Chardonnay and flowers, which I thought was sweet. Ree put the flowers in a vase, and Lauren offered him a drink.

I said, "I can't believe you want to hang around me after all I put you through last night."

"How else can I find out what you are up to? I don't always want to find out on the police radio. Oh, by the way, do you know a Dr. Love that works at your school?"

I rolled my eyes. "Yes. Unfortunately. He's my awful principal. Why?"

He nodded. "Oh. I had just gotten into work yesterday when calls came in that someone was handing out tickets to children for being on school property."

I slapped my hand across my mouth. "Really?"

"Apparently, the children and their parents were very upset. I went to Arrowstar and confronted the man."

My eyes grew wide. "And?"

"Well, first of all, he's a real piece of work. He stood with his arms folded and told me it was to protect the school grounds."

I nodded.

"I told him, that according to the city, using the school playground on weekends and holidays is permitted unless a sign is clearly posted."

"And?"

Well, he sputtered and said, he would erect signs and fence off the area right away.

I shook my head. "So, you couldn't lock him up and throw away the key?"

He laughed. "No, but the city did fine him for writing illegal tickets."

I chuckled at that, thinking I had even more to tell Jules, Becca, and Jana tomorrow. "Now you know who I get to put up with every day."

I led Mike to the backyard where he breathed in deeply and said, "Something smells great."

The door opened and Mom and Dad walked out with both girls.

"There's my baby," said Mom. She walked up and kissed me on the cheek, and Dad followed suit.

"Mom, Dad, this is Mike Potter." I pointed to Mike, then back to my parents, "and these are my folks, the ones who put up with me for 45 years, Jim and Betty Kole,"

"Hello, Mr. and Mrs. Kole." He shook hands with them both, scoring brownie points by calling them Mr. and Mrs. rather than using their first names.

As predicted, Ree brightened. She said, "Your last name is Potter? Too bad your first name isn't Harry."

He smiled at Ree. "Actually, my brother's name is Harry. Nobody lets him forget it, either. At least he has blonde hair and no glasses."

She nodded. "That's funny."

Reveling in the excitement of my little party, I said, "Didn't the weather turn out perfect for eating outside? After the cold yesterday, I can hardly believe it is 75 today."

Dad piped up, "Well, as Oklahoma's favorite son, Will Rogers, said, 'If you don't like the weather in Oklahoma, wait a minute and it will change.'" So true.

He turned to Mike and said, "So, what do you think of Pity's unusual outdoor decorations?" They looked across the yard.

"It's certainly creative, and I kind of like it." Mike nodded. "She gave me the full tour a few days ago."

Dad said, "You know, I like it too. I just don't get the blue sink." He shook his head.

"Blue sink?" Mike looked puzzled.

"Oh, you didn't see it? Come over here. I'll show you."

The two walked over, and Dad showed him my blue sink semi-hidden by a tree. Mike watched as the water ran continuously through the faucet with a pump R.A. had rigged up. It's my favorite feature. I couldn't believe I forgot to show Mike.

Dad scratched his head. "It just doesn't make sense to have a sink in your yard."

Ren, who had been placing silverware on the table, shook her head. "Grandpa is funny. He thinks shower doors and bowling pins are fine, but the sink is weird?"

I smiled and called, "Hey, why don't you guys pick some apples as long as you're out there?" Shouting didn't do my head any good, so I decided to keep calm going forward.

As they walked, Dad explained, "Pity's neighbor gave her this apple tree when Lauren was born and this other one when Marie came along. You can see how both are strong, just like my granddaughters."

I smiled as I turned the large pieces of meat over on the grill.

Mom moved in beside me and said, "He seems like a nice boy, Pity."

That was funny because "the boy" was almost 50.

"And he's handsome, too. Maybe it's because of that uniform."

I followed her gaze and studied Mike standing with my dad. He did look pretty nice.

The men returned with a few apples in each hand, and I put them in a basket.

Ree appeared holding a bag. She announced, "My basketball team is selling lollipops for only one dollar. We can get new uniforms if we sell enough of them. Anyone want one? She pulled the round pops out of the bag one at a time and read the flavors.

"We have bubblegum, lime, banana, peppermint, pina colada, root beer, cherry, and lots more!"

Mike spoke first "May I look in the bag?"

"Sure," she said, handing it to him.

Mom said "I want a fruit flavor – maybe the banana. Jim, do you want a root beer?"

Dad said, "You read my mind." He pulled out two dollars and handed them to Ree.

Mike handed a banana and root beer to Mom and told Ree, "I'll take these three." He held up three colorful pops and handed a five-dollar bill to Ree. "I'll buy you and your sister one with the change."

Ree said, "Thanks as she took the money and the bag, digging through to find just the right one.

Ren piped up, "Give me the bubblegum."

I added, "I'll wait to see what's left and buy some tomorrow. Then I said, "Men, have a seat. Ladies, follow me. Dinner's about ready."

Mom and the girls followed me inside and I said, "Hey, Ree, would you take my new singing cooler outside?"

She put her candy bag on the hearth and said, "Singing cooler?"

I watched her struggle to lift the cooler full of canned drinks but Ren jumped in to help. Not long after they got outside with the heavy cooler, I heard the familiar song, then laughter as the group checked out my new OU bargain.

I took the chips and Okie Spice Girl dip out to the table. While they snacked and Mom put a salad together, I ran to my room and changed clothes.

I stepped outside and said, "Check out the t-shirt Mike gave me." Mike laughed.

Once everyone had a chance to read the silly saying about being a yard sale addict, Mom said, "Well, you sure do know my daughter."

Ren held her hands together and begged, "Please don't wear that around me in public."

I waggled my head and said, "We'll see."

When everything was ready, we sat down and passed the food.

Harriet sat on the floor by Dad's chair because she's smart and she knew he would share his food by dropping tidbits for her.

Then, as I had hoped, Dad started his interrogation, "So, Mike did you grow up in Broken Arrow?"

"No, I'm originally from Denver. My parents still live there, as does my brother."

Mom passed the green beans and asked, "What brought you to Oklahoma?"

He hesitated before speaking. "I was married briefly. My wife was from Tulsa, so we moved here to be close to her family. Then my sister moved to Broken Arrow for work, and I just stayed." Mike took his first bite of the pork tenderloin. "This meat is amazing."

So, he had been married before. I imagined him with a wife that looked like a model and frowned. When Ren kicked me under the table, I realized Mike had complimented me and said, "Thanks."

Harriet jumped up and laid her head on the table to look at the food – obviously, Dad wasn't fulfilling her snack needs. I ushered the dog to the door and put her inside, reprimanding her on the way.

Ree speared a piece of meat on her fork and asked Mike, "Do you have any kids?" She took a bite and chewed as she waited for his answer. In contrast, I stopped chewing in anticipation of his reply.

"No, I wasn't even married a year, and…" he paused, biting his lip, "we didn't really have time to think about starting a family." Wow, that was a brief marriage.

"So, how long have you been here?" asked my dad.

"About five years."

"Hello, Kitty?" A male voice interrupted from the side of the house.

Simultaneously, all six heads whipped around to find a thin man with plastered down brown hair, wearing khakis and a sweater tied around his shoulders. He peered at me with a smug look on his face.

What the…? My mouth went dry, but I managed to say, "Kenny?" I shook my head at the man who casually leaned against the rock siding of my house with his arms folded. He wore the same shirt he had worn on both our dates six months ago. This baffled me yet again.

I was confused and embarrassed. My lovely evening had just taken an unexpected turn. "What are you doing here, Kenny?" I put my napkin on the table.

"Well, I had a delivery for you, and nobody answered the door. When I heard talking, I came around to find you." His face practically glowed with happiness.

Not knowing what else to do, I said, "Uh… Mom, Dad, Mike, girls, this is Kenny. He's a… friend?"

Leaning his head to the side, he spoke as if I was joking. "Oh, now, Kitty, you know we're more than friends." He winked.

My eyes widened in horror as my parents' mouths dropped open and Mike raised his eyebrows. Then the corners of his mouth curled in amusement.

Kenny leaned down and picked up an amazing carved pumpkin filled with small boxes. "Here, sweetheart, I brought a little gift for you and your girls." He strode up to the table with unbelievable confidence and held the pumpkin out for all to see.

That did it. I said firmly, "Kenny, follow me…now." I stood up, walked around the table, and waited for him.

Kenny handed the pumpkin to Ree, bowed to the table, and said, "It was so very nice to meet you at long last." He turned and followed me back around the house.

When we got to the driveway, I spouted, "Sweetheart? Seriously? What made you say that? We've only had two dates, and they were months ago."

Ignoring my comment, he gushed, "Oh, Kitty, I'm so glad to see you again. I've been dreaming of what you must look like after all these months. Your hair is so nice. Is that a new color?" He said that so sweetly, it reminded me of an actor in a bad soap opera, and I almost laughed.

Instead, I looked straight into his beady brown eyes, "Did you see the guy in the police uniform?"

"Yes, dear."

I closed my eyes in frustration and took a deep breath. "Kenny, I'm dating him now. I am not interested in you in that way and never have been." There. It was out. I said it. He had to leave me alone now.

Unshaken, Kenny lifted his eyebrows and nodded. "So, I have competition. If you have a new male friend, it just means I have to work harder to convince you that I'm perfect for you."

Mike stepped from the side of the house and asked, "Is everything OK?"

"Yes. He's leaving and won't come back anytime soon, right?"

"OK, OK." Kenny held up his perfectly manicured hands in concession and nodded, "I'll let you have some time to miss me and see the light. Absence makes the heart grow fonder. You'll see," he said with a lilt in his voice.

He sauntered to his sports car, lifted the door, and climbed in, giving a wave that looked like it should be accompanied with a 'ta-ta.' After lowering the vertical door, he slowly drove down the street.

Mike stood dumbstruck, "Your stalker drives a Lamborghini?"

I shrugged. "I told you I don't know cars. I still can't believe he just showed up like that. I'm so sorry." I was so embarrassed but turned to face Mike. "You do know I'm not interested in him at all?"

"Yes, but I might be. I've always wanted a car like that."

I punched his arm, then grabbed his wool uniform shirt and pulled him close to me. Staring straight into his blue-green eyes and said, "I'd rather have a hard-working, gun-toting, Brian-chasing man than ten fancy sports cars."

"Oh, yeah?" Mike leaned in further and gave me a warm kiss. "Pity Kole, you are something else."

Although my body and soul wanted to kiss him again, I used restraint. I let go of his shirt, still reeling from his sweet kiss, and said reluctantly, "We'd better get back."

I took his hand and led him around the house to join the others. We dropped hands before turning the corner.

Ren said, "Well, that was interesting, Mom. Did you get rid of Kenny once and for all?"

"I'm afraid not. Now he thinks he has competition and considers it a challenge to win me back as if I was ever his!"

Mom said, "He seems a little stiff for you, dear."

Nice to know even Mom could see it. I said, "You ain't kidding."

Ree stared at the pumpkin filled with little boxes of expensive candy and wiggled her eyebrows. I said, "After dinner, you can take what you want."

We discussed Kenny ad nauseam, then finished our meal on a variety of topics. It was a lovely visit. At one point, I caught Mike staring at me. My stomach fluttered when he gave me a wink. We topped off the evening with Mom's amazing chocolate cake.

"Mom, that was delicious. How about we move this party inside? It's getting chilly out here," I suggested.

Mike stood, looked at his watch, and said "I need to get to work. It was very nice to meet all of you." He shook Dad's hand and turned to me. "Thank you, Pity, for the delicious dinner. But now I don't believe you cook from a box."

Ree said, "Oh, she usually does." She started to lead the group inside the house. As soon as she got through the door, she said, "Oh my gosh!" and started laughing. Dad went next, and there was a guffaw. When Ren walked in, there was additional laughter, which continued as Mom entered. What would cause such a commotion? Mike and I carried our plates inside to see what the fuss was all about.

There, in the middle of the living room, sat Harriet, looking more like a white porcupine than a dog – Yes, our sweet adorable shaggy girl had apparently gotten into the bag of remaining lollipops. She had managed to unwrap and eat the majority of the candy, leaving gooey white sticks poking out from her shaggy hair all over her body. Little pieces of blue, red, and yellow candy stuck to her in various places, making a very sticky mess. She just sat there smiling with her mouth open, looking adorable and happy from her unexpected treat. I should have scolded her, but I just couldn't bring myself to do it since she was so darned happy.

Ren took pictures of Harriet with her cell phone.

Once I caught my breath from laughing, I sighed. "Looks like you get another bath tonight – the second one this week."

Holding up the candy bag, Ree said, "She pretty much slobbered on the rest – we may have to pay for all of it." She frowned.

"It's OK, honey, we'll make it right. I just hope she doesn't get sick from all the sugar."

Mike shook his head and said, "Never a dull moment at your house, huh?"

Ree said, "Speaking of which, Mom knocked herself out in the garage today."

I had forgotten about that, but instantly put my hand on my head to see if the goose egg was still there. It was, but not as big.

Mom walked over to me and asked, "Are you OK?"

"I'm fine. The swelling has already gone down."

Ree said, "Wanna know how Lin revived her?"

Everyone looked at her, curious to hear - including me.

"We talked to her, shook her, and put a cold rag on her forehead but she was out cold. We were just about to call 9-1-1, but then Lin told her about the garage sale up the street, and her eyes popped open immediately."

I scoffed in disbelief. "That's not true." But then I wondered how I would have known about the sale if she hadn't told me. I felt my face turn red.

"Oh yes, it is true," she said, crossing her heart. "It was pretty amazing."

Mom felt my head, "You'll be alright, dear, but be careful."

Dad said, "I'll move that ladder before I leave tonight."

After Mike said goodbye to everyone, I walked him to his truck. I leaned against his door and said, "Thanks so much for all of your help this past week. I feel sorry for you getting involved in my hijinks."

"I've never met such a busy girl with garage sales, teaching, backyard decorating, second job, and amateur detective work."

Hearing all that, I sounded like a kook. I really should focus on my girls and teaching, but couldn't seem to help getting involved in everything.

Mike gave me a serious look and said, "Pity Kole, would you mind if I gave you a real kiss?"

I replied a little too quickly, "I think I'd like that, Mike Potter"

He leaned over, and his lips met mine. It was a nice, lengthy, real kiss, and one I wanted to repeat soon.

He gave me a warm hug and said, "I'll call you tomorrow after school if that's all right."

"That would be lovely," I said without hesitation and watched him get in his truck and drive away. I was left standing there all tingly, a feeling I hadn't felt in far too long. "Hmm." I breathed in the brisk autumn air and skipped up to the door.

Mom was putting the dishes in the dishwasher and said "Your father and the girls are moving that deadly garage ladder."

"Good. Here, let me help you."

"I like your new friend. He seems very nice."

Before we got the chance to discuss Mike further, the girls entered with my dad. He said, "You should be safe now."

The folks stayed another hour listening to me retell the entire murder story clue by clue, which I had inadvertently memorized.

Dad said, "That sounds dangerous, Pity. I sure hope you don't make a habit of this detective work."

Mom said, "I thought you learned your lesson last time."

I said, "I know. I sure don't plan to get involved in any more murder investigations."

As mom cut another slice of cake for me to take for lunch the next day, I told her about the icing recipe I'd gotten from Mrs. Jones. "Mom, you would really like Linda. I think I'll invite her to Thursday's swim meet, so I can introduce you."

"That would be nice. But first she needs to meet her grandson."

"I know. I've been thinking about that a lot. I'll call Trish later and see how everything is going."

Dad put his hands on Mom's shoulders. "Well, we'd better leave before we turn into pumpkins." They collected their jackets and we kissed them goodbye.

After they left, the girls joined me on the couch, and I said, "Well, I'm pretty sure we all know the most memorable things that happened this week," I said very seriously.

They both looked solemn and nodded, thinking of all the upsetting events. I brightened and said, "It was Ren winning the 100-meter breaststroke and Ree getting another purple ribbon at History Day!" I hollered loud enough to surprise myself.

"You guys celebrate with your lollipop or treats from Kenny's pumpkin while I give Harriet a bath before she gets the whole house sticky." Just as I made it to the hallway, the doorbell rang.

I turned and looked at the girls – they shrugged. Mom probably forgot her purse or something. I opened the door and was surprised to see Trish and Caitlyn.

"Hi," I said in a surprised voice as I opened the door wider to welcome them in.

The woman who used to rub me raw walked in like a new person. She looked relaxed with a pleasant expression. "We won't stay long. I just wanted to stop by and thank you again for everything."

Caitlyn gave me a big bear hug, then ran over to Marie squealing, "Did you hear? Andy is really my brother!"

"Yeah, I heard. That is so cool!" Ree said with a smile.

The redhead beamed, and the two girls disappeared into Ree's room as I offered Trish a seat.

I turned to Ren, but before I said anything, she said with a nod, "I'll go wash Harriet."

"Oh, thank you so much, honey."

Facing Trish, I said, "It must have gone pretty well?"

"Better than I dreamed. Andy was so mature about the whole situation once it sunk in. And as you can see, Caitlyn is going to be fine. Of course, the devastating part was telling everyone about my father's actions. It will take them some time to process it all, but they are holding up better than I expected."

She continued, "We're still hoping I won't have to do prison time. Can you imagine me in a cell?" She made a horrid face. "But my family was so kind and said they would be supportive no matter what. I think they sensed a change in me. Actually, I sense a change in me – a type of freedom."

"Oh, Trish, I'm so happy for you."

"If it wasn't for you, Kitty, I might have been in that hellish personal prison forever."

"Nothing noble on my part – I just found notes in the desk and got obsessed with finding out the story. I'm just sorry it ended up involving you."

"Well, we just wanted to stop by to thank you and to apologize for being so hateful to you all these years. You didn't deserve that. I just couldn't seem to stop. Maybe counseling can help me work through my multitude of problems."

I replied, "It's OK, Trish. I don't know how I would act if I was in your shoes all those years."

She added with a smile, "I'm also thankful for Ree's friendship with Caitlyn. She needs her now more than ever."

"Um, Trish? I know this is really early to talk about, but during my investigation I met Justin's mother. I'm not sure if you heard, but her husband died recently and she's pretty sad. I'm sure she would love to get to know her grandson. If the police haven't told her, I could break the news if you like, so she has time to get used to the idea of having a grown grandson. Maybe I could even introduce them to each other unless you want to do it?"

"Oh, that would be wonderful. She'll never forgive me for keeping the truth from the authorities and her family. I wouldn't blame her," she said quietly.

"Well, maybe she'll forgive you in time," I said.

"And her daughters will be furious. I'm so ashamed." Trish hung her head.

"Let me see what happens when I talk to her, OK? Maybe it will be better than you think."

"All right. Thank you." She stood, "Well, we'd better get moving. School starts early and you and your girls need to get ready, too." Trish called, "Caitlyn, we need to go."

I had not expected their visit, but it sure made me feel better to know all was OK.

After they left, I gave Ree a hug and said, "I wasn't sure if Caitlyn would be ready, but she's going back to school tomorrow. I think she needs to have a normal day." I looked at my sweet girl. "And you can help her by bragging about your big win at History Day."

"Oh, we already have that planned."

I got a glass of milk and found both girls standing in the doorway of the kitchen, smirking.

"What?"

Ren said, 'We wanted to tell you that we like Mike."

"Oh, is that right?" I lifted an eyebrow.

Ree nodded. "Yeah, Mom. And what about you? Do you like him?"

"I think I do like him," I said with a smile as I walked over and kissed the cheek of my green-eyed angel. I ducked down to look in the baby blues of my sweet Ree and gave her a kiss. Then, I kneeled down to part the wet hair of my shaggy girl and kissed my brown-eyed Harriet on the top of her wet head. "But I LOVE my girls."

I headed off to bed and to a night of many dreams: Dreams of great garage sales, dreams of Andy, Trish, and Linda Jones going to a swim meet to watch Caitlyn swim, dreams of making ugly patio pavers with Lin, dreams of getting a new principal, dreams of more unwanted gifts from Kenny, dreams of many more kisses with Mike, and even dreams of solving another murder...

All of which came true. Well, except one.

About the Author

Martha Kemm Landes is a former music teacher who wrote numerous musicals and hundreds of songs for her students while teaching music in Oklahoma. She is most known for writing the Oklahoma State Children's Song, <u>Oklahoma My Native Land</u>.

Martha retired early and lives with her screenwriter husband and three adopted dogs just outside of Albuquerque, New Mexico. They enjoy spending time at their cabin in the nearby Jemez Mountains, which they also rent out on VRBO.

Besides writing mystery novels, Martha quilts, gardens, and volunteers by delivering Meals On Wheels. Like Pity, she enjoys finding bargains and can be seen most weekends scouting local garage and yard sales looking for that unusual or much-needed item.

Martha loves to be outdoors and finds the weather perfect in New Mexico for hiking, gardening, and hosting weekly movies at their large backyard movie theater.

Scan for a quick link to the website

Made in the USA
Monee, IL
08 September 2022